Prai...
ALEXANDRIA BELLEFLEUR

"Alexandria Bellefleur powers this fake dating masterpiece with boatloads of heart and the result is perhaps her most divine tale yet."

—BuzzFeed on *The Fiancée Farce*

"*The Fiancée Farce* is rom-com at its absolute finest. A down-on-her-luck heroine who invents a fake girlfriend? A fake girlfriend who turns up looking for a marriage of convenience to land her inheritance? Set the whole thing in a cozy bookstore? Alexandria Bellefleur delivers funny, sexy, romance reader catnip. No notes."

—Sarah MacLean, *New York Times* bestselling author

"Bellefleur doesn't shy away from letting her heroines yearn for one another, which is a delight. . . . The genuine investment Margot's friends had in her happiness made the happy ending all the sweeter."

—*USA Today* (four stars) on *Count Your Lucky Stars*

"With perfectly woven vulnerability and playfulness, *Written in the Stars* is a riotous and heartfelt read. I was hooked from the very first page!"

—Christina Lauren, *New York Times* bestselling author

Truly, Madly, Deeply

Also by Alexandria Bellefleur

Written in the Stars series
Written in the Stars
Hang the Moon
Count Your Lucky Stars

Standalones
The Fiancée Farce

Truly, Madly, Deeply

A Novel

ALEXANDRIA BELLEFLEUR

AVON

An Imprint of HarperCollinsPublishers

TRULY, MADLY, DEEPLY. Copyright © 2024 by Alexandria Bellefleur. All rights reserved. Printed in the United States of America. No part of this book may be used or reproduced in any manner whatsoever without written permission except in the case of brief quotations embodied in critical articles and reviews. For information, address HarperCollins Publishers, 195 Broadway, New York, NY 10007.

HarperCollins books may be purchased for educational, business, or sales promotional use. For information, please email the Special Markets Department at SPsales@harpercollins.com.

FIRST EDITION

Designed by Diahann Sturge-Campbell
Stack of books © Jakub Caja/The Noun Project
Winking emoji; emoticon face blowing a kiss © Yael Weiss/Stock.Adobe.com
Chef emoji © Sughra/Stock.Adobe.com

Library of Congress Cataloging-in-Publication Data has been applied for.

ISBN 978-0-06-325853-2

24 25 26 27 28 LBC 5 4 3 2 1

To the romance authors, veterans of this industry and debuts alike—thank you for writing the kind of love worth believing in and giving readers (including me) hope

Truly, Madly, Deeply

Chapter One

Six years ago, almost to the day, Truly first spotted Justin Gallagher in all his dreamy, sun-kissed, green-eyed glory and thought, *I'm gonna marry that guy.* Now, bare from the waist down, wearing nothing but a red muscle tee, her fiancé looked the furthest thing from dreamy she could imagine.

He looked like Winnie-the-Pooh.

If Pooh Bear were a lying, cheating bastard.

With one hand shielding her eyes from the tableau of bare skin she had zero desire to see, Truly braced for the inevitable crush of sadness to steal over her. Any second now, she was going to feel something other than this . . . distant mortification that she'd wasted six precious years on a dumbass who, when caught with his dick in another girl's mouth, said, *this isn't what it looks like.*

Any second now . . . *any* second . . .

"True, *hon*, whatever you're thinking, it's not that. Jessica's a vocal performance major. I was just helping her practice. You gotta believe me."

Her hand dropped and with it, her jaw, her mouth hanging open. That had to be, without a doubt, the worst, most half-baked excuse she'd ever had the displeasure of hearing. "With your dick out, Justin? Really? It's not a fucking microphone."

Maybe it was her withering glare that did it, but he gulped and cupped his package protectively. "We were just—we were working on her breath control. Tell her, Jess."

Breath control. Christ.

She wasn't sure what offended her more—that he had cheated, or that he honest to God thought she was stupid enough to believe that the pretty blonde frantically throwing her clothes on had been getting up close and personal with his dick in the name of *music.*

"I am so sorry." The girl—Jessica?—stole a furtive glance at Truly as she breezed past on her way out of Justin's front door. "This fuckwad told me he was single."

Fuckwad, indeed.

As soon as the front door slammed shut, Justin held up both hands, palms facing out, fingers spread, placating. "Honey, listen—"

"Don't." Truly snatched the throw blanket she'd crocheted him two Christmases ago off the back of the couch and hurled it at his head. Dicks looked weird on a good day; she really didn't want to keep seeing his out of the corner of her eye. "Do us both a favor and cover yourself."

He clutched the blanket around his shoulders like a cape. "It's nothing you haven't seen before."

"And it's nothing I have any desire to see ever again."

"Don't be like that," he whined. "You don't get to be mad at me. We're on a break, remember?"

A break she'd agreed to take against her better judgment, because Justin had sworn up and down that his desire to press pause had nothing to do with wanting to see other people.

"Because you told me you couldn't handle any distractions while you're on tour. Because you told me you were, and I quote, *investing in our future*. That when you *hit it big with the band*, it would all be worth it."

Privately, she'd believed it to be a classic case of cold feet. That with a little time apart, he'd realize, unequivocally, just how good he had it.

Had she known he wanted to sow some wild oats before even hitting the road, she never would've agreed to spend any time apart.

"Fine. You want the truth?" He stood, blanket falling and with it, any semblance of his dignity. "Have you ever stopped to think that maybe the fact that my girlfriend proposed to *me* might've been a little emasculating? Huh? You ever think about that?"

She didn't have the time nor inclination to unpack how sexist that was. "So, you're, what? Saying this is *my* fault? You're sleeping around to reestablish your masculinity? Prove to yourself you can still pull?"

"Now that sounds like a trap." Justin set his hands on his bare hips. "And speaking of traps, yeah, all right, that's how you made me feel. Trapped. Smothered. I needed space to get my head on straight. Sue me."

Her breath hitched, lungs constricting. "You *are* saying this is my fault."

Unbelievable.

"I'm saying that we shouldn't be throwing glass houses here."

"Stones," she said, faintly horrified. "It's *stones*, Justin."

"Well, yeah." He scoffed. "If you throw glass houses, someone's stones are bound to get hurt." He cupped his balls unabashedly. "Namely, mine."

She raked her fingers through her hair, messing up the curls she'd spent an hour and a quarter of a can of hair spray artfully constructing, earning herself an awful burn on her thumb from her curling iron in the process. "I can't believe this."

"You do look kind of pale." He patted the couch cushion nearest him. "Do you want to sit down?"

His living room smelled faintly of sex, all musk and sweat, and it made her stomach roll. "I don't have time for this."

In forty minutes she was due across town, guest starring on the fifth most popular podcast on Spotify. *Unhinged* offered listeners a blend of advice and lifestyle content, often irreverent but always real. Booking the podcast was a *pinch me* moment if there ever was one, only this dream opportunity now felt more like a nightmare because Truly? Truly wasn't just promoting her next book; as a self-professed romantic, and because she was *such* an expert, she had agreed to give relationship advice to *Unhinged*'s four million listeners.

She'd laugh at the irony if it didn't make her want to cry.

"True, don't be like that." He followed her into the kitchen. "You know how much I hate it when you're passive-aggressive and shit."

She studied her keychain, trying to figure out the best way to get his key off it. "Honestly, Justin, what exactly is the proper response to walking in on your fiancé cheating on you? Would you rather I be aggressive-aggressive? Hm? *Hm?*"

"I resent that accusation."

Accusation? She scoffed, fighting with her metal O-ring keychain, trying to pry it apart with grip strength and sheer force of will. "I literally walked in on you with your dick in another girl's mouth. Where I come from, we call that cheating."

"Except we are on a break." He spoke slowly, as if she were the one struggling to grasp the gravity of this whole fucked-up situation. "And even if we weren't, it's, like, ethical non-monogamy."

She stared at him. "Are you shitting me?"

"I'm just saying." Justin shrugged. "You should look it up. *Ethical non-monogamy.*"

"You think I should look it up? I think you should go fuck yourself."

He sighed. "Don't be like that."

"Like what? Like someone with standards? Self-respect?"

"Come on," he said. "We can fix this."

In theory, sure. Couples had persevered through much worse and plenty had come out the other side stronger than ever.

Except those couples all had one thing in common.

They all wanted to fix it.

And Truly?

Truly didn't.

Had anyone asked her this morning if she loved Justin, she'd have sworn she did. It was unequivocal. The sky was blue, the grass was green, and she, Truly Livingston, was going to spend the rest of her life with Justin Gallagher.

But now? She'd rather eat a bowl of her own hair than let Justin touch her. Maybe the slide from adoration to mounting frustration to outright vexation had been gradual, but the realization that she didn't care enough to try anymore was like flipping a switch.

Finally, Justin's key came free from her keychain. It must've only weighed a few ounces, but slapping it down on the counter felt like shedding pounds of dead weight. "Have a nice life, Justin."

She turned on her heel and made a beeline for the door, shoving her feet inside her sneakers, not caring that the tongues were tucked awkwardly inside.

Justin caught up to her in the hall. The dish towel clutched against his crotch afforded him a shred of modesty. He held up her old key.

"Who's gonna feed my betta fish?"

"SECOND CIRCLE OF Hell, this is Lulu speaking."

"Aw, shucks. I figured they'd have promoted you by now."

Sharp, staticky laughter burst from the speakers as Truly's best friend laughed. "I'm kinda partial to this circle. Lust and all that jazz."

Great. Now she was going to be humming showtunes for the rest of the day. Mom and Dad would be so proud.

"If I tell you something, will you promise not to, like, have a conniption?" Truly pulled into the Starbucks drive-through behind a silver Tesla.

"Who the fuck your age even says *conniption*? Lord, people my age don't say that. I don't even think my mother's used that word. My grandma, maybe, but she's older than graveyard dirt."

"Lulu."

"True-True."

Fuck it. "I broke up with Justin."

A beat of silence passed, long enough that she dug her phone out of her cupholder to make sure her Bluetooth connection hadn't dropped. "Lu?"

"Sorry, I'm here. I'm just trying to find the right words to express my heartfelt sympathy because I know you were, like, in love with that sentient jar of mayo, but *fuck*, babe. I kind of want to bust out a bottle of Bollinger Brut and have a party." Lulu huffed. "And this? This is why I wasn't saying anything. You interrupted my thought gathering and now I've put my foot in my mouth. Don't hate me."

"A sentient jar of mayo?" Damn. As far as insults went, that was impressive. "Permission to use that in a book?"

"Granted," Lulu said. "Better put me in your acknowledgments, though."

"As if you aren't already in all of them in perpetuity."

Lulu hummed, pleased. "So, you're not mad at me for likening your ex to the most loathsome condiment on the planet?"

"As if I wasn't well aware you didn't approve." She eased off the brake as the car in front of her moved up to order. "You haven't exactly been subtle."

"I've tried! You've gotta admit, I've toned down the snark by, like, fifty percent in the last two years."

"You have, and I appreciate you trying to make nice. Or I did." Now she couldn't give less of a damn. "So no, I'm not mad at you. Justin, on the other hand . . ."

"What did the fucker do this time? It must've been something awful if it finally forced you to see the light. Do I need to rearrange his face? If you're good for bail money, I'm down. I've been itching to take a swing at that wannabe rockstar for ages."

Eight years of knowing Lulu and Truly could still only reliably tell if she was joking a good seventy-five percent of the time. "If you promise not to resort to violence, I'll tell you what happened as soon as I'm done ordering my coffee."

"Cross my heart."

She pulled up to the drive-through and ordered her usual, plus an extra shot of espresso for good measure.

"Okay, you remember how Justin practically begged me to drop by and feed his fish while he's on tour? And how I didn't want his fish to die just because he didn't have anyone else who could do it, so I said yes?"

"Do I remember being pissed to high heaven that he had the audacity to ask you for a favor a mere week after telling you he wanted to take a break? Sounds familiar. Go on."

"He must've gotten his dates screwed up because I let myself into his apartment today and was greeted by the lovely sight of Justin getting his dick sucked by a pretty, leggy blonde with really fantastic tits."

As a lifelong card-carrying member of the Itty-Bitty Titty Committee, she wasn't going to lie and say it didn't sting that Justin had chosen a girl to cheat with who was her aesthetic opposite in almost every way.

"His mother should've swallowed, I swear." Lulu paused. "Are you okay?"

Sorely undercaffeinated and a little emotionally bruised, but when she did a quick self-diagnostic, it was her ego that had taken the hit, not her heart. "I'm fine."

"*Truly.*"

"I mean it. Just a sec." She pulled up to the next window and handed her card to the cashier before accepting her receipt and coffee. "Okay, fine. I'm pissed, but more about how it went down and less that we're over. He had the nerve to tell me that my proposing to him made him feel emasculated."

"God, I hate that son of a bitch."

"Don't get me wrong, I'm livid. But mostly? I'm . . . *God*, I'm so over it." Sick and tired of Justin's waffling, waiting for him to grow up, being put through the emotional wringer, putting effort into a relationship and being met with the bare minimum. "I'm honestly more concerned with what the hell I'm supposed to post on Instagram."

A pitfall of having two hundred thousand followers who'd witnessed your relationship milestones and very public engagement announcement meant being unable to let that relationship go quietly into the good night. She couldn't just stop posting about Justin. Not without an explanation.

Lulu made a soft, sympathetic sound. "Fuck Instagram. You can worry about that later. Look, I'm not trying to tell you that you don't know what you're feeling, but do you think it's possible you're in shock? Like, maybe you haven't fully processed?"

She made a right onto Denny Way. "I don't think so?"

Lulu sighed. "Okay, let me call Benny and see if he minds if I close early. You go home, get comfy, get that weird-ass potato peel book club movie you love queued up on Netflix, and I'll head over to yours with a bottle or three as soon as I get off. We can get wine drunk and you can tell Mama Lulu all about how *over it* you really are. Sound good?"

"It's *The Guernsey Literary and Potato Peel Pie Society* and you know it." She smiled. "And yeah, that sounds great except you've got Mai's recital tonight at seven, remember?"

"Shit . . . do you want me to call Dan?"

Truly recoiled in horror, accidentally tapping her brake. Lulu's ex? God no. "I wouldn't dream of asking you to miss out on your weekend with Mai. I'm not heartless."

Lulu grumbled. "You weren't asking, I was offering. But hey, if you're good with a PG night, I could bring the kids over later and we could, I don't know, have a sleepover and binge *Paw Patrol*. I probably shouldn't drink too much, but you could, like, take a shot every time Mayor Humdinger comes up with an evil plan. With enough episodes, I can guarantee you'll black out."

As much as Truly adored her godchildren, the fact that she, a childless twenty-seven-year-old, knew who Mayor Humdinger was verged on tragic.

"No offense, but I have zero desire to turn a children's show into a drinking game." *Again.* Been there, done that, spent the night praying to the porcelain goddess. "Rain check? Don't feel bad—I've got that podcast I told you about and I'm almost at the studio. Plus, I've got brunch with my parents tomorrow and despite it happening over a year ago, Dad still hasn't stopped teasing me about the last time I showed up hungover."

"I must've heard you wrong, because it sounded like you said you were going to work, but I know that can't be right since you just found out your fiancé's been dicking around on you."

"Yeah, and?" She wasn't hemorrhaging or concussed or experiencing a family emergency; she had no reason to cancel a professional engagement less than an hour in advance.

"Cancel! Go home!"

"And do what? Wallow? No thank you."

Lulu sighed. "Next weekend? I'm taking you out on the town so we can find you some pretty little piece of ass because the best way to get over someone is to get your back blown out by someone new."

"It's a date." She had zero intention of rebounding with anyone, but she wasn't about to argue with Lulu when she was on a schedule. "Give the kids a hug from Auntie Truly, okay?"

"Of course. And good luck with your podcast. Break a leg or whatever? I don't know. Try to have a good time."

"Thanks, Lu." Truly ended the call.

A good time was probably a reach, but at least there was no way this day could get any worse.

Chapter Two

"Truly St. James, in the flesh." Caitlin McCrory—tattooed, pink-haired goddess, and host of *Unhinged*—smiled from the open doorway of Studio 615. "Huge fan. I can't tell you how many friends I've bullied into reading your books. *A Duchess in Disguise*?" Caitlin kissed her fingertips. "Life-changing."

A blush crept into her cheeks. "I'm so happy you loved it. And sorry I'm late. The elevator's out of order."

"God no, you're right on time." Caitlin swept out a hand, gesturing Truly through the door. She wandered over to the gleaming silver bar cart wedged between an impressive stack of vinyl records and a desk covered in an array of computer equipment, leaving Truly unmoored in the middle of the room. "Can I get you something to drink? Coffee? Hot tea? A martini, maybe? I know it's only after three, but it's after five o'clock somewhere, right?"

She rattled the ice in her latte. "I'm good, thanks."

Coffee, in retrospect, was not her brightest idea. The jitters were beginning to set in, and the abundance of caffeine circulating through her bloodstream wasn't helping. Podcasts—any promo that required she speak—made her nervous on a good day. And this? Was a no good, terrible, very bad day.

Caitlin snagged a bottle of smartwater off the bar cart. "Have a seat. Make yourself at home. Just watch for the mic cords so you don't trip."

Truly took a seat on the plush-looking neon-yellow velvet sectional that was nestled against the cobalt accent wall, three fluffy-looking Barbie-pink microphones positioned nearby.

"I know this is far from your first rodeo, but do you have any questions while I finish setting up and we wait for—speak of the devil." Caitlin set her hands on her leather-pant-clad hips. "You're late, asswipe."

She didn't know what the guy standing in the doorway had done to Caitlin to earn a greeting that abrasive, but *fuck* was he gorgeous. All mole-splattered skin and brown doe-eyes framed with black lashes so thick that at first glance she'd have sworn he was wearing eyeliner. Actually, no, *brown* wasn't right. Her eyes were brown, but his were the color of the tiger's-eye wedged in her front pocket, the one she'd handpicked out of a big crate of polished stones on a fifth-grade field trip to Greenwater. The same stone she brought with her to every event for good luck. Dark penny shot through with tawny and gold. Chestnut hair fell in swooping waves across his forehead and grazed the collar of the lavender sweater-vest he wore over a plain white tee that hugged his biceps.

"Hi." Tiny creases formed at the corners of his eyes when he smiled and offered her his hand. "It's nice to meet you. I'm Colin."

His hand dwarfed hers, his long, thick-knuckled fingers folding around her palm as soon as she reached out, accepting the handshake. Chipped remnants of purple polish adorned three of his nails, and the oddest assortment of rings decorated his fingers.

Her breath hitched, brain buzzing, head full of static.

"I'm nice to meet." *Fuck.* "I mean, likewise. Truly. Is my name. And it is also nice to meet you."

Colin laughed. Not a mean laugh, but one that sounded like he genuinely found her funny. "My sister's done nothing but talk my ear off about you agreeing to record this episode. She's a huge fan."

"Yeah, yeah, I already fangirled in an appropriate manner. Now, I'm sure Truly has important things to do and we shouldn't keep her any longer than necessary. Why doesn't everyone sit?"

Oh yeah, important things like going home to her empty apartment, ordering copious amounts of takeout, and figuring out what the hell she was doing with her future now that it had a Justin-shaped hole in it.

"Any questions before we get started?"

Her publicist had briefed her, and she'd gone back and forth with Caitlin via IG DMs to fill in any blanks, but she liked her *i*'s dotted and *t*'s crossed. "We're giving relationship advice to your listeners? Viewers?" She wasn't sure what to call them since, while technically *Unhinged* was a podcast, episodes were also re-corded and uploaded to YouTube and Instagram. "Kind of like *Loveline*?"

"Exactly, only minus the medical advice and not live, obvi-ously." Caitlin sat, long legs sprawling across the chaise side of the sectional. "Basically, I was thinking it would be cool to give advice from two different perspectives—that of a romantic and that of a realist."

Three guesses who Truly was and the first two didn't count.

Romantic advice. She could do that. She just needed to chan-nel the Truly of this morning before she walked in on Justin. Or the Truly of two weeks ago before she'd agreed to Justin's bullshit desire to go on a break. Or the Truly of four years ago whose first book had just come out, the Truly who remembered what it felt like to have butterflies.

"Awesome," she said, trying inconspicuously to make sure she wasn't visibly sweating through her pale blue seersucker blouse. All clear, praise extra-strength deodorant.

"And you, Colin? Any questions?"

"Nah. All good." He grabbed a bottle of water off the bar cart before joining Truly on the couch. He was taller than her—not that that was saying much, since even the occasional sixth grader surpassed her in height. But he wasn't too tall, not like Justin, whose mouth she'd had to stand on tiptoe to reach—and why on Earth was she thinking about how nice it would be not to have to crane her neck if she and Colin kissed?

Lulu was right. She should've canceled. Clearly, she was going through *something*. Losing her mind because even if Lulu thought it was the best way to get over someone, Truly didn't believe in rebounds. She was a relationship girl, a one-partner—man, woman, gender didn't matter to her—girl. She didn't know how to separate sex and feelings, so until she was ready to date? Ménage à moi, it was.

Caitlin fiddled with the shock mount of the mic in front of her. "Of course, Colin's the realist to your romantic." *Of course.* "I'll be here, facilitating the conversation. Giving my two cents—"

"Giving us shit," Colin said, grinning, a little wrinkle forming along the bridge of his cute nose. Yes, *cute.* Ever so slightly upturned, giving him a puckish quality totally at odds with his broad shoulders and thick thighs that strained the denim of his dark wash jeans.

Caitlin threw a pen at him. He ducked and the BIC hit the wall behind him with a soft *tink*. "Giving *you* shit. I'd never dream of deriding Truly."

"Are you a relationship therapist? Couples' counselor?" She racked her brain for what sort of job a relationship realist might have. "Life coach?"

"Colin's a divorce attorney."

Talk about throwing a glass of cold water on her libido.

"Family law, technically," he said. "But I do handle divorces."

Relationships ended. *Hello.* People got divorced. Hell, Lulu was divorced and good riddance to her ex because Dan was a prick and Lulu deserved *so* much better. Truly loved love as much as the next person, but no one deserved to spend their life tethered to someone who wasn't right for them, wasn't good *to* them.

Still. Divorce was one of those realities of life she preferred not to think about unless it was staring her in the face. Like death and taxes and Pap smears. Someone had to be a mortician, a CPA, a gynecologist. She respected that. But being a divorce lawyer sounded like *such* a dirty job. Depressing, watching people who had once vowed to love each other forever suddenly bicker over 401ks and alimony. Their whole lives, ones they had built together, reduced to assets.

Being a romance writer was more than her job—it was who she was. What did Colin's job say about him? What little kid dreamed of being a divorce lawyer?

"And that makes you qualified to give relationship advice?" She cringed. "Sorry. That was rude. I only meant—"

"It's fine." Colin's smile was warm and a little lopsided, the corners of his eyes creasing. If he was offended, it didn't show. "To be honest, I'm probably *not* qualified to be giving anyone advice.

But my sister seems to think I am. And I'm incapable of saying no to her, so here I am."

Caitlin rolled her eyes. "He's being modest. Colin's a champ at spotting a red flag."

Fair enough. Anyone who spent that much time watching the dissolution of marriages had to have a decent working knowledge of what spelled doom for a relationship.

"If you don't have any other questions, quick run of show—I'll introduce you both and we'll dive right in. If you lose your train of thought or want to start a sentence over, just take a breath, and I can edit it out in post. Sound good?"

Truly nodded and so did Colin.

"Okay, here we go. In three . . . two . . . one . . ." Caitlin smiled at the camera. "Welcome back, my little heathens, to a new episode of *Unhinged*. I'm your host and the devil on your shoulder, Caitlin McCrory. You all are in for a treat because today I have not one, but *two* guests joining me for a special episode all about"—she dropped her voice—"*relationships*. Anything goes today, guys, gals, and nonbinary pals. Which, if you know me, is saying something." Caitlin's smirk widened, totally in her element. "I opened my inbox last week, for all of you lovely listeners to submit your most burning questions about love and sex—though, for the dude who wrote in seeking help for some *literal* burning, I'm going to advise you contact your primary care physician. On that note, a reminder that neither myself nor my esteemed guests are medical professionals. *But*"—she paused, tossing Colin a grin—"we do have a legal expert in the house today. Please welcome our first guest, the dipshit who stole my first Barbie, my brother, Colin McCrory."

He flipped her off with a grin. "I can't believe you're still bringing that up twenty years later. Get over it."

Caitlin rolled her eyes. "Colin, the heartless bastard that he is, has a decade of experience working as a family lawyer here in the Emerald City and as I was telling our second guest, he can spot a red flag a mile away. And speaking of our second guest, I'm ecstatic to introduce none other than the internationally bestselling author of over a dozen historical romances, Truly St. James."

Blood rushed to Truly's cheeks, her blush deepening as Caitlin cheered, Colin clapping beside her. Truly smiled at the camera and waved.

"Her books have been translated into over ten languages and featured by outlets such as the *Washington Post*, NPR, the *New York Daily News*, BuzzFeed, and *Cosmo*. *Entertainment Weekly* named Truly 'one of historical romance's brightest stars' and called her most recent release 'a triumph.' When Truly isn't writing, she can be found haunting her local coffee shop here in Seattle and—okay, I have a question for you, Truly. Feel free to tell me to fuck off, but is that *really* your name? *Truly?*"

"It is." She cleared her throat as quietly as possible, hating how her nerves turned her voice thready. "My parents, they're big into theater. My dad's the artistic director of the Emerald City Repertory Theatre and my mom is a retired stage actress. Emerald City Rep was putting on a rendition of *Chitty Chitty Bang Bang,* my dad was the show's orchestral conductor, and my mom was cast as one of the leads, Truly Scrumptious. That's how they met. Hence, the name. This August, they will have been married thirty-three years."

"Truly, all I can say is, thank God your parents didn't meet on *Funny Girl,* because Fanny St. James doesn't exactly scream sexy historical romance novelist."

"I don't know." Colin looked thoughtful. "In the UK, fanny *does* mean—uh . . ."

Caitlin leaned her hand on her chin, grin devious. "Go on, Colin. Say *pussy* on air. Make my day."

The tips of his ears pinked and Truly had no business finding it as adorable as she did. "Aren't we supposed to be giving relationship advice or something?" Colin asked.

"As a matter of fact, yes. Yes, we are." Caitlin flipped to her next notecard. "So, we've got a realist"—she pointed at Colin—"we've got a romantic"—she gestured to Truly, Vanna White–style—"and we've got listeners in desperate need of relationship advice. And these two are going to give it to you straight." Caitlin paused, lips quirking. "Or you know, *not*, because this podcast is many things, but straight isn't one of them. But before we get down to it, I want to know—Colin, do you self-identify as a realist? And if so, how do you define that in your own words?"

His brow furrowed and his lips parted and . . . wasn't that a sight? His bubblegum-pink tongue sweeping out against his plush bottom lip, *wetting* it. "I would say I am, yes. I prefer to accept and deal with situations and people as they are, not what they could be."

"You heard it here, folks, my brother the realist." Caitlin turned to Truly. "Truly, same question. Do you self-identify as a hopeless romantic and how do you define that?"

"I wouldn't say I'm *hopeless*." She tucked her hair behind her ears and smiled at the camera. "But yeah, I'm a romantic. I've never met two people more perfect for each other than my parents. Even after thirty-three years, they're just as madly in love with each other as they were the day they met. I've never even seen them fight before. That's how perfect they are for each other."

"Are you serious?" Caitlin sounded shocked. "Never?"

"No. Never. They've served as a sort of . . . blueprint for me for what a relationship should look like. And I guess that's what makes me a romantic. I believe in happily ever afters because I've seen one in real life."

It was a variation on what she said anytime someone asked her, *why romance?* Because she'd witnessed a forever love, a love that could go the distance—persevering through a cancer diagnosis (Dad), a dementia diagnosis in a parent (Mom's mom) that led to home health care, the subsequent death of all four of Truly's grandparents, even a random IRS audit.

Lesser couples would have folded after just one of those bumps in the road. But Dad still bought Mom flowers every Sunday and they still slow danced—poorly—to music only they could hear.

That's why she wrote the books she did—to remind readers that love was real and it was out there and to never give up hope.

Not even upon discovering your fiancé was a lying, cheating douchenozzle.

"God, that's dreamy." Caitlin smiled. "I love that. All right, now that you all know a little more about Truly and Colin, without further ado, let's get to it." Caitlin tossed that notecard over her shoulder, moving on to the next. *"Dear Caitlin & Co., I've been with my boyfriend for almost seven months. He's a great guy, we share a lot of common interests, he makes me laugh, and my family really likes him, which is important to me. There's just one problem—not once has he ever gone down on me."*

Never? *Yeesh.* Poor thing.

Caitlin continued, *"I tried to talk to him about it and he didn't have much to say, only that 'it's not his thing.' It's not like I don't occasionally get off when I'm with him, but I won't lie and say that it doesn't suck that I'm, well, willing to suck and he won't reciprocate. Any advice?* Signed, *Sick and Tired of Being an Uptown Girl."* Caitlin sighed deeply and slumped back against the couch. "Oh, Uptown Girl. My deepest condolences that your boy won't go downtown for you. Truly? Colin? Either of you want to start us off and give our girl some advice?"

Colin looked at her, brows raised, the left corner of his mouth quirking higher than the right, and there was no way she was imagining the way his voice went slightly husky as he murmured, "Ladies first?"

It wasn't her fault that she was suddenly picturing Colin Mc-Crory repeating those words as he made a home for his head between her thighs.

"What a gentleman." Truly flashed a smile and looked away, feigning interest in the mic in front of her. Anything except for his stupidly pink mouth.

"No one should feel pressured to do anything—sexually or otherwise—that they don't feel comfortable with. Consent is paramount. Full stop. There are plenty of reasons why someone might not feel comfortable with performing certain sexual acts. It could be trauma, it could be a lack of experience manifesting as an insecurity. Or maybe your boyfriend doesn't know how to get you off orally and he's afraid of looking stupid, so he'd rather not try. Or maybe it's just patriarchal socialization courtesy of the internet and bad porn so he thinks his cock is, like, God's gift to womankind or something and believes you should be satisfied with intercourse alone. Who's to say? I don't know and you don't know, either, clearly, or else you wouldn't have written in, because all he's told you is that it's *not his thing*. He could be lazy or selfish or traumatized and you don't know because he's not communicating, which might not be the issue you wrote in about, but I do believe it's a big one."

She paused, catching her breath. She had a bad tendency to speak too fast when she was nervous and today was no exception.

"A lot of women, *people*, are afraid of hurting their partner's feelings so they'd rather stay silent than rock the boat and risk rejection, but that's not going to serve either of you. Unexpressed anger or even just frustration is going to breed resentment. I think Uptown Girl needs to consider, one, whether the lack of reciprocity is a deal-breaker for her and, two, whether she can handle her boyfriend's lack of an explanation. And then she needs to tell him."

"You heard it here first, *communication*. All the cool kids are doing it. Truly, thank you so much. Colin, what words of wisdom do you have to impart upon our poor Uptown Girl?"

"Short answer?" Colin said. "Honestly, I don't see you and your boyfriend working out long term, Uptown Girl. Long answer? It sounds to me like sexual compatibility isn't the only issue you two are up against. Sounds like he might be conflict averse and not exactly the most communicative considering his lackluster if not defensive response to the question of why he isn't willing to, er, orally reciprocate, which isn't *our* business, but certainly is yours. *Not his thing* could mean just about anything, but without further explanation? It sounds like a cop-out to me. I'm also slightly concerned at the phrasing"—Colin cleared his throat, the tips of his ears turning pink—"*occasionally get off with him*. Not sure if I'm paraphrasing there or—"

"No." Caitlin shook her head. "That is unfortunately verbatim."

"Yeah." Colin cringed. "That phrase isn't inspiring a lot of confidence in me. Personally." He held up his hands. "I'm not saying sex needs to be a *tit-for-tat* sort of deal—don't fucking make a joke, Caitie—it's more complex than that, or I guess it should be, but there is something to be said for all parties being on the same page regarding satisfaction and I'm getting the sense that's not happening here. Does he care about your pleasure at all or is it incidental to him? In my opinion, your partner should worship at the altar of your body and if they don't, they're probably not the partner for you."

Color her impressed. Colin McCrory wasn't entirely hopeless.

"Truly, Colin, I want to extend my sincerest thanks for handling that with such aplomb." Caitlin's gaze flitted to the notecard in her hands. "Fair warning, this next question is a bit of a doozy and quite possibly divisive. *Dear Caitlin & Co., My partner and I have been together for just over three years. I'm happy and I thought she was happy until recently, she sat me down and said she wants to take a break. We're both supposed to be starting grad school in the fall, but now she says she's thinking about deferring for the semester and backpacking in Spain with a group of friends. She told me she needs to prioritize herself and that she doesn't have the energy to devote to our relationship right now, but I don't understand why she can't go on this trip and put her needs first without us having to press pause on our relationship.*"

It was eerie how this stranger had ripped a page right out of Truly's diary. Eerie enough that she had to tamp down the urge to shift uneasily.

"*I asked her if she wants to break up and she was adamant she doesn't,*" Caitlin continued. "*I'm feeling uneasy about this whole thing, but I really don't want to lose her. Help!* Signed, *Dazed and Confused*. Colin? Since Truly went first on our last question, do you want to start us off?"

"Sure." He crossed one leg over the other, left ankle resting across his right knee, dark denim tightening across his thighs, *straining*. "Change can be really frightening, and I can see why the idea of taking a break might make you feel uncertain. To be perfectly honest, the stats aren't in your favor. Roughly eighty percent of married couples who separate end up divorcing. Grim, I know, but that being said, I don't think what your partner is suggesting is necessarily a bad thing."

"Way to give us whiplash," Caitlin said.

It was like she'd read Truly's mind.

"Hold on. They aren't married, so those stats I mentioned? Not entirely relevant to their situation. Dazed and Confused mentioned grad school, so I'm assuming they're both young? Early to mid-twenties? Recent studies show that roughly sixty percent of couples who get married between twenty and twenty-five divorce. Not that they said they were discussing marriage, but it sounds like Dazed and Confused's partner realizes she has some growing to do and, if she takes this time now, and if they're able to make it work, big *if* granted, perhaps she'll wind up being a better partner in the long run."

"A better partner to someone else." The words escaped before Truly had even realized she'd opened her mouth.

Both Colin and Caitlin stared at her.

Heat flooded her cheeks. "Sorry. I didn't mean to—"

"No, by all means." Colin smiled. "That's what this is about, right? Different perspectives? I'd love to hear what you have to say."

Even before she'd been burned by Justin, even before he'd suggested taking a break, she'd never been sold on the concept. Sure, she'd clung to the hope of having a stronger, happier relationship, but a tiny, niggling voice in the back of her head had whispered something wasn't right.

Maybe at first blush it didn't seem like what a dyed-in-the-wool romantic would say, but she could hardly in good conscience advise someone to ignore their gut the way she had.

Truly perfected her posture, leaning in toward the mic. "Let's be generous and go with Colin's interpretation of Dazed and Confused's partner's motivations and say she realizes she needs to grow. What's stopping her from doing that with Dazed and Confused? Why does her growth necessitate distance from her partner and their life together—be it physical or emotional? No offense, but the entire concept of taking a break is bullshit to me. It's nothing more than inviting in unnecessary uncertainty. Are you allowed to call them? Are you still exclusive? What if you have—"

"I think those are all things Dazed and Confused and their partner should discuss so that their time apart can be constructive."

"I wasn't finished." She tugged on the hem of her skirt, hands shaking. "As I was saying—is your partner really looking to grow, or is it just an excuse to hook up with someone new? There's nothing romantic about not being someone's first priority. Don't you want to be the first thing they think about in the morning and the last thing they think about at night? Don't you want to be with someone who can't stand the idea of being apart from you? Shouldn't you be their confidant and their rock and their—their port in a storm? Shouldn't they be yours? Are they always going to ask for space in a crisis? What kind of relationship do you have if you're the first thing on the chopping block every time the going gets hard? What sort of faith does that instill, huh? What if you're the one going through a crisis? What if you need them? What about for better or for worse? What if you get sick? Are they going to run for the hills every time the going gets tough?"

Everything she'd said was some variation of what Lulu had

told her two weeks ago, advice she wished—because of course, hindsight was twenty-twenty—she'd listened to. If she could spare someone else the heartache? She was all for speaking the truth.

Colin stared. "Hm."

She stared back. "What's *hm* supposed to mean?"

"I feel like you're making a lot of assumptions here."

"The writing's on the wall. A break is nothing more than delaying the inevitable."

"That's a little reductive, don't you think?"

"I don't, actually. Seeing as I said it."

"Are you familiar with attachment styles?"

What? "Sure." Vaguely. *Ish.*

Colin steepled his fingers and nodded slowly, chipped purple polish glinting in the bright glow of the ring light. "Interesting."

Her tongue poked against the side of her cheek. "What exactly is so interesting about that?"

He shrugged, shoulders rising slowly and falling leisurely, irritatingly nonchalant and stupidly graceful. "I'm no psychologist, but based on what *I* know of attachment styles, it sounds like the concerns you've outlined are that of an anxious attachment. Low self-esteem, fear of rejection or abandonment, clinginess . . ."

Crimson tinged the edges of her vision. "Clingy—" She scoffed. "I didn't come here to—to . . ."

A telltale burning took up residence behind her lids, her throat suddenly tight.

Shit.

The reality of catching Justin cheating, the fact that her longest relationship, the one that was supposed to be forever, was over . . . it was finally hitting her. That was it. It had to be. Otherwise she was just a weirdo who cried when pissed and how pathetic was that? She didn't shed a single tear upon catching Justin in the act and yet this . . . this *stranger* had managed to get under her skin? No. No, it was a latent reaction.

Colin's mouth twitched like he was trying not to smile. "You didn't come here to . . . what, exactly?"

Her hands curled into fists, nails biting into the skin of her palms. She would not flip him off. She *wouldn't*.

She took a deep breath and unclenched her jaw. "I didn't come here to be psychoanalyzed by some guy whose only expertise lies in *un*happily ever afters."

He chuckled and shook his head. "Okay, now that's *definitely* reductive."

Screw this. She had better things to do than sit here and let some guy, some lawyer, call her reductive and clingy and tell her she feared abandonment as if he knew a single goddamn thing about her life. Even if she didn't have better things to do, anything would be preferable to sitting here another second.

Truly stood. "Caitlin, thank you so much for thinking of me for your podcast. Really."

Caitlin's brows slanted low, the jut of her bottom lip suggesting concern rather than anger. "Maybe if we take five and cool off we can—"

Truly shook her head, already inching in the direction of the door. The day had gone from bad to abysmal and she wasn't keen on sticking around for it to get worse. "Sorry for wasting your time, but no." She threw a scowl over her shoulder in Colin's general direction. "I don't think so."

Chapter Three

"Hate is an awfully strong word, Pumpkin Butt."

"Why do you think I used it?"

Mom smiled patiently over her mimosa.

"*Ugh.*" Truly let her head flop back dramatically. "Fine. I don't *hate* him. I strongly dislike him. Better?"

"Getting there," Mom said. "It wouldn't hurt to know why exactly you strongly dislike this boy."

"He's a man, Mom. A *man*."

Colin McCrory was *not* a boy. He had creases at the corners of his eyes, laugh lines, and chest hair, enough that it peeked out from beneath the V-neck of his stupid purple sweater-vest that she did *not* find attractive.

"He's a pompous asshole," she said, settling on a slightly more rational reason than her brain's weird hyper-fixation on Colin freaking McCrory's body hair. "He's a lawyer. A *divorce* lawyer. Isn't that reason enough?"

Mom pursed her lips. "Truly."

Okay, fine. Maybe she was being a little ridiculous.

Yes, Colin was a pompous ass. Yes, he'd pushed her buttons—most of them the wrong ones, but some of them oh so right—

and yes, he'd poked at no fewer than a dozen of her insecurities, professional, personal, and everything in between, but more than anything, more than she was willing to admit upon pain of death? Colin McCrory had made her feel small. He had made her feel small and stupid. He had hurt her feelings, and *that*? That was a damnable offense.

"He's a jerk, Mom. I guess you had to have been there."

"I guess so. But I *am* sorry this boy—excuse me, *man*—upset you. That wasn't very nice of him."

"No," she said, picking at a loose thread on her pleated skirt. "It really wasn't."

"Do mine ears deceive me or am I hearing laymen speak in the Sondheim room?" Dad's voice came booming down the hall. He paused in the doorway of the sunroom, a spritz in one hand and a tray in the other. "Tut, tut. You know the rule, Truly Scrumptious Livingston—"

"Not my middle name," she grumbled.

Dad managed to look astounded. "Diane, dear, what is this nonsense I hear?"

"*Impossible!*" Mom gasped, playing along, pressing the back of her hand against her forehead and swooning against the arm of the sofa. "Oh, Stanley, it can't be! *The Poor Thing* must be mistaken."

"You both *know* it's Stella." After Stella Adler, famed actress and acting teacher. There was a signed picture of her hanging in the upstairs hall, for Christ's sake.

Dad ignored her. "Diane, did you hear something?"

Mom cupped one hand around her ear. "*Perhaps . . .*"

"You can't be serious."

Mom tutted. "Must've just been the *Rain on the Roof.*"

Truly buried her face in her hands, muffling a groan.

One rule was enforced in the Livingston household, and one rule only. Every room on the lower level of the house—save for the foyer and halls—was named after a composer of musical theater. There was the Sondheim sunroom, the Andrew Lloyd Webber living room, the Irving Berlin half bath, and last, but not least, the Gershwin garage, where Truly's father spent the bulk of his free time tinkering around on his precious vintage cars, clothed in custom-made coveralls splattered with grease, humming showtunes.

If you wanted to carry on a conversation within the confines of one of these spaces? You'd better know a song or twelve. Titles and lyrics were fair game; Truly relied heavily on the former, refusing to sing.

If history had taught her anything, it was easier to just give in. "I said, it's Stella. *Remember?*"

"Ah, Stella!" Dad took a step over the threshold and thus began his inclusion in the awful, *awful* tradition. "*Glad T' See Ya*, Truly m'dear."

Truly took the Aperol Spritz from him. "Sometimes when I'm around you two I feel like I'm *Losing My Mind*."

"Well, sure you are." Dad slid the bridge of his thick black-framed glasses up his nose and grinned. "*Home is the Place* you can be yourself, after all."

Truly choked, sputtering out an indignant laugh. Prosecco dripped off her chin, one drop soaking into the wool of her skirt. "Did you just call me crazy?" Um . . . "*Overture?*"

She tended to abuse those when playing Mom and Dad's silly little showtunes game; overtures, preludes, and finales were free spaces as far as she was concerned.

Dad snorted. "Truly—"

"For *Once in Your Life*, give the girl a break. This is brunch, not one of your guest lectures."

Dad heaved a hearty sigh. "I can see I've been ganged up on." He brandished the tray balanced on his right hand. "These might not be *The Worst Pies in London*, but I did manage to whip up a quick brunch torte and of course your favorite, Truly."

"Nonna Luzzatto's bouche de dame?"

"The one and only, *All For You*, Buttercup." Dad set the white cake adorned with almonds down on the coffee table and razzle-dazzled his fingers. "Ta-da!"

The scent of sugared almonds hit her nose, nutty and sweet, and her mouth watered.

She snatched a plate off the table and thrust it at Dad. "*I Love You Et Cetera.* Cut me a slice, please."

Dad took the plate from her with a warm smile. "Catch me up. What were you *Lovely Ladies* discussing while I was playing bartender? Any good *Gossip*? Share, share."

"*Men*," Mom supplied, digging her fork into her breakfast torte. "We were discussing men."

"*Men?*" He sounded intrigued. "Oh, do tell, Buttercup. Was Justin *The Reason Why* you stomped in here today in such a mood?"

"I wasn't in a mood, and no, we weren't talking about Justin. But now that we are, I might as well let you know that Justin and I are no longer together. I'm, um . . . back to looking for my *Happily Ever After.*"

"Oh, sweetie." Mom rubbed Truly's arm. "What happened?"

"I caught him with a girl, pants down. Off, actually."

Mom gasped. "You *Poor Thing.*"

"In flagrante delicto." Dad tutted and shook his head. "Good riddance. From the moment I met him, I knew that boy was *Unworthy of Your Love*, Pumpkin."

"*Stan*," Mom chided.

Dad held up his hands. "You didn't like him, either."

"Our thoughts on Justin aside, six years is a long time to be with someone. The last thing Truly needs to hear right now is *I told you so*."

"I'm okay. Seriously. You can put the kid gloves away."

"See, Diane? Our *Broadway Baby* is made of sturdier stuff."

Mom pursed her lips. "I just want you to know that it's okay if you aren't okay."

"Thanks. But I just really, *really* want to move on."

"That's the spirit," Dad said. "Never fear, *A Hero Is Coming*. Or heroine. You know your mother and I just want you to be happy."

"Thank you. Now, no offense, can we talk about literally anything else? What's new with you?"

Mom drained her mimosa. "*Interesting Questions*. Let's see . . . I was named vice chair of the Laurelhurst Community Horticulture Society. Which is something."

"Mom!" She set her fork down so she could squeeze Mom's arm. "That's more than something. That's amazing. Uh . . ." Sondheim, Sondheim . . . "I'm *So Happy* for you."

"*Thank You So Much*." Mom reached out, squeezing Truly back. "As for your father—"

"Truly, your mother and I have decided to take some time apart."

She held her breath, waiting for the punch line, for the Sondheim that never came.

They had one rule, one rule only. The circumstances had never mattered; not once had there been an exception. Not when Truly had had friends over, not when she'd had strep and couldn't speak and had to rely on her phone's text-to-voice reader. She'd *still* been expected to communicate in stupid showtunes.

Her fork clattered against her plate. "That's not funny."

"Truly—"

"Stop saying my name," she snapped. "You're saying my name like you're expecting me to have a breakdown or something. Which is stupid. Because you're kidding, right?" Her throat ached, sore and stuffed like she'd swallowed a cotton ball. *"Right?"*

Mom looked at Dad and he gazed back, a furtive look passing between them.

Truly screwed her eyes shut. *"I Must Be Dreaming."*

Despite bitching and moaning about this game, this tradition, Truly clung to it. There was safety in the predictability. If Sondheim didn't write it, it couldn't happen.

Someone rested a hand on Truly's knee, fingers gentle, palm soft, metal rings skin-warmed. Mom. "Honey, it's . . . it's not a bad thing."

"It's not," Dad quickly agreed. "Your mother and I, we love each other."

"Very much. And we love you."

"More than anything." Dad's hand came down, warm and solid against her shoulder, squeezing gently. "You are *The Best Thing That Has Ever Happened* to us."

"And *We're Gonna Be All Right*." Mom jostled her lightly. "So, *No Sad Songs*, okay?"

No Sad—

Truly leaped off the couch, knocking Mom's and Dad's hands away in her outburst. *"No Sad Songs?* Are you fucking kidding me?"

Dad frowned. "Buttercup—"

"Did someone—did one of you—"

"No." Mom shook her head. "It's not like that."

"This is no one's fault. Like I said, your mother and I, we love each other very much."

"We do. We've been together for thirty-three years," Mom said. "That's a long time. People change, Truly. Sometimes they grow apart."

People change? Sometimes they grow apart? With all these trite clichés being hurled at her, it felt a little like *she* was getting broken up with.

With Justin, the signs were there. She'd ignored them, yeah, but they were irrefutably there.

But this? This was different. There were no signs. There should've been signs. Shouldn't there?

Then again, she'd been so busy lately, promoting one book and writing another and revising a third, dealing with Justin and everything that entailed. She'd been so wrapped up in herself for weeks . . . a month? Two?

Was it possible there had been warnings and she'd missed them? Jesus Christ, what kind of daughter did that make her that her parents' marriage was on the rocks, and she'd been none the wiser? Absolutely, one hundred percent oblivious.

She was going to be sick, was going to upchuck Aperol all over the pretty green tufted rug covering the glossy hardwood floor. Her stomach heave-hoed and she swallowed down a thick, disgusting mouthful of bitter, citrusy bile.

"Is one of you having a midlife crisis?" she asked, breath sour and voice hoarse. "Because there's a dealership down the road selling convertibles if you're interested."

"No one is having a midlife crisis. I'm certainly not. Are you, Stanley?"

"Can't say I am. Though, even if I were, *If There's Anything I Can't Stand*, it's a convertible. Messes with my hair." Dad ran a hand over the top of his smooth-as-a-cue-ball head.

The bite of bouche de dame she'd swallowed sat like a rock inside her gut. "Then why?"

"Your mother and I, we—" Dad tore off his glasses and rubbed his eyes. "It's a break, Truly. A trial separation. We love each other, dearly, but—"

"But what? If you love each other, then what?" Truly crossed her arms against the rising tide of emotion inside her that had no outlet. *Eighty percent of couples who separated divorced.* It was all she could think about, Colin McCrory's gut-wrenching statistic echoing inside her head. "You're perfect together. You belong together. You have stupid inside jokes, and you dance in the kitchen, and make up lyrics to elevator music and—" They made her believe in love and if her parents, two people perfect for each other, couldn't make it work, what did that mean for everyone else? What did that mean for her? "Are you struggling with intimacy issues? Because that's normal and nothing to be ashamed of. There are therapists you can see. And they make pills for that and—and—and—oh! Lubricant!"

Dad's eyes grew so wide they looked like they were about to fall out of his head. *"Truly."*

Mom fanned her face, cheeks neon. "I am not talking about this."

"There's no shame in using lubricant."

"Let me rephrase." Mom had turned a startling shade of purple. "I'm not talking about this with my *daughter*."

She rolled her eyes. "I'm twenty-seven years old. It's hardly like I'm a virgin."

"*Truly.*" Mom buried her face in her hands.

Dad still refused to look at her head-on. "This is no one's fault. And we don't need to talk to anyone."

Mom shook her head in agreement.

"It's just . . . your mother and I are considering the possibility that maybe . . ." He swallowed hard, eyes growing damp. "Maybe *We Do Not Belong Together.*"

Mom sniffled. "But—but *No One Is Alone* in this. It's no one's fault."

"Certainly not *Your Fault*, Buttercup," Dad said, as if she were twenty years younger and needed the reassurance that this wasn't, in fact, because of her. "*The Reason Why* is just . . . it's complicated."

Complicated?

"Bullshit."

Mom and Dad stared at her, mouths agape.

"People change? Sometimes they grow apart? It's not your fault?" She scoffed. "I'm not *actually* asking for the intimate"— Mom and Dad cringed in perfect synchronicity—"details of your relationship, but I'm your daughter and I think I deserve more than empty platitudes." That was a reasonable ask, wasn't it? "You've been married thirty-three years and I've been alive for twenty-seven of them. Are you just giving up?" She dug her toe into the carpet and blinked up at the ceiling, eyes burning. "Throwing in the towel?"

Over thirty years and a whole life they'd built together, *boom.* Gone.

"We are *not* throwing in the towel." Mom had the audacity

to smile. *Smile.* It made Truly want to bare her teeth and growl. "Your father and I aren't throwing anything away."

"We're taking some time," Dad reiterated, as if she wasn't already committing this entire conversation to memory. As if it wouldn't keep her up tonight. Haunt her dreams. "We've discussed what this time for us means. We plan to sort out what we each want going forward and whether we want the same thing."

"How much time?"

"Three months," he said.

"Three months!"

Any amount of time was too long, but three whole months? Wouldn't that much time apart just make it harder for them if they—*when* they got back together?

"We don't want you to worry," Mom added. "The only reason why we decided to bring this up now—rather, why your father decided to blurt it out—"

"Hey now. Truly deserved to know. We agreed on that."

"I never said she didn't. I'm not taking umbrage with *what* you said, just *how* you said it."

Truly shoved her sleeves up her arms. "Guys, it's not—"

"I didn't hear you telling her, either, Diane. You had an opening and you stalled, talking about your botany club. Someone needed to rip off the Band-Aid."

Christ. Was it hot in here? Or was she just having a hot flash? Could you get those in your twenties? "*Guys.* How you told me isn't the issue—"

"It's a preservation society, not a club."

"Oh, my sincerest apologies."

"Was that sarcasm?"

"Better sarcasm than passive aggression."

Truly scratched at her throat, the pearl-adorned buttoned collar she'd slipped on beneath her sweater suddenly confining. *God*, was that—was that a *rash*? Hives? Had she ever even had hives before? Was she showing a latent allergy to something in Nonna Luzzatto's bouche de dame? Or was she just allergic to conflict?

Mom and Dad never fought.

Never.

"*You* are calling *me* passive-aggressive?"

"If the shoe fits."

"Pot meet kettle, *Stan*."

"Why did you say my name like you're imagining an extra *a* in it?"

"Are you implying that I'm calling you—"

"Just *stop it*!"

Any other time, it would've been comical how Mom and Dad froze, twin expressions of regret and shame etched on their faces. Truly couldn't find any humor in the situation, in her parents looking like scolded children. *She* was the child. Adult child, but child. Not them, *her*.

"Sorry," Dad muttered, shamefaced. "I—Diane—"

"It's fine," Mom said, curt. "I was out of line, too."

"Tensions are running high right now, Buttercup. But we're sorry. Your mother and I were very concerned with how you'd take the news. I don't think either of us got much sleep last night. But we wanted you to know." Dad blinked fast and Truly's chest ached, too small, too tight, everything she felt too big to be contained by fragile bones and paper-thin skin. "Because we love you."

"So much. And no matter what happens, we're always going to love you."

Truly let them drag her into their embrace, let them tuck her into the too-small space between them. Her bones creaked, and her joints protested at being smushed, but she curled up tight like a pill bug with her eyes closed.

"We're in this together," Dad said. "And love . . . *Love Will See Us Through.*"

Chapter Four

Monday, May 3rd
SUBJECT: re: Unhinged w/ Caitlin McCrory
FROM: Caitlin McCrory <caitlinmccrory@caitlinmccrory.com>
TO: Truly St. James <trulystjames@trulystjames.com>
CC: Melanie Morales <melanie.morales@citythatneversleepspr.com>

Dear Truly,

I wanted to reach out and reiterate how sorry I am for Saturday. To put it plainly, it was an epic clusterfuck and I feel terrible for not stepping in before feelings were hurt.

What we managed to record was actually really promising. I know it's a longshot, but if you have time to chat this week, I'd love to buy you a coffee and discuss the possibility of a re-do.

Xoxo,
Caitlin

Monday, May 3rd
SUBJECT: re: re: Unhinged w/ Caitlin McCrory
FROM: Melanie Morales <melanie.morales@citythatneversleepspr.com>
TO: Caitlin McCrory <caitlinmccrory@caitlinmccrory.com>
CC: Truly St. James <trulystjames@trulystjames.com>

Hi Caitlin,

Truly is *so* sorry that she had to duck out of the recording early on
Saturday! While she'd love to reschedule, she's currently on deadline.

I'm so sorry this didn't work out, but if you could keep Truly in mind
for future opportunities, we'd both be so appreciative.

All the best,
Melanie

Tuesday, May 4th
SUBJECT: re: re: re: Unhinged w/ Caitlin McCrory
FROM: Caitlin McCrory <caitlinmccrory@caitlinmccrory.com>
TO: Melanie Morales <melanie.morales@citythatneversleepspr.com>
CC: Truly St. James <trulystjames@trulystjames.com>

Totally understand! Truly's books obviously need to come first!

I've attached the fully edited audio and video files from Saturday
if either of you are interested in listening/watching. Like I mentioned
before, what we recorded is actually really good! With Truly's
permission, I'd love to go ahead and upload this on Friday. Listeners
seemed really jazzed about the episode when I teased it last week and I
honestly think it would be a win-win all around.

No worries if not, but I thought I'd ask.

C

p.s. Truly—Colin wanted me to let you know he's really sorry. I swear I didn't even have to threaten him to get him to say that.

Tuesday, May 4th
SUBJECT: re: re: re: re: Unhinged w/ Caitlin McCrory
FROM: Melanie Morales <melanie.morales@citythatneversleepspr.com>
TO: Truly St. James <trulystjames@trulystjames.com>

Thoughts, T??

I gave the recording a listen and it's *really* not as bad as you made it sound. If you want my two cents, I actually think you and Colin have really great on-air chemistry. The banter was snappy. I was enthralled.

To be honest, it felt like listening to one of your books. 🫠😗

And the plug Caitlin added at the end for your books really doesn't hurt!

xx,
Melanie

Tuesday, May 4th
SUBJECT: re: re: re: re: re: Unhinged w/ Caitlin McCrory
FROM: Truly St. James <trulystjames@trulystjames.com>
TO: Melanie Morales <melanie.morales@citythatneversleepspr.com>

Mel, I love you, but do not *ever* compare Colin McCrory and me to the characters in one of my books again. Colin is *not* hero material.

As for the recording, it was fine. I guess. Trust me when I say Caitlin was generous with the editing and cut the ending before the crap really hit the fan. And you're right, the promo doesn't hurt.

So, sure. She can post it.
T

Tuesday, May 4th
SUBJECT: re: re: re: re: Unhinged w/ Caitlin McCrory
FROM: Melanie Morales <melanie.morales@citythatneversleepspr.com>
TO: Caitlin McCrory <caitlinmccrory@caitlinmccrory.com>
CC: Truly St. James <trulystjames@trulystjames.com>

Hey Caitlin,

Permission granted!
I thought it was such a fun episode! Lots of great banter and compulsively listenable!

All the best,
Melanie

Sunday, May 9th
SUBJECT: Update on Unhinged w/ Caitlin McCrory
FROM: Caitlin McCrory <caitlinmccrory@caitlinmccrory.com>
TO: Melanie Morales <melanie.morales@citythatneversleepspr.com>
CC: Truly St. James <trulystjames@trulystjames.com>

Hi!!

I wanted to let you know this episode has blown my previous record for number of streams within 24 hours out of the water! If this keeps up, this episode is on track to be the most streamed episode of Unhinged on every platform. The response is overwhelmingly positive, and my DMs are out of control in the best way. The people have totally spoken and they love you and Colin. They're pretty much threatening to put my head on a stick if I don't give them more of you.

Look, I know it's a longshot, but is there anything I can do to change your mind about recording another episode and maybe turning this into a series? I totally understand that you're on deadline, but is there anything I can do to make your life easier? I'd offer to cook for you, but I burn water, so . . . I could wrangle Colin into cooking for you? Believe it or not, he's decent in the kitchen. He once put me in a box and tried to give me away to the fire department, so he owes me.

Xoxo,

C

p.s. I'm 100% not above begging 🙏🙏🙏

Monday, May 10th
SUBJECT: re: Update on Unhinged w/ Caitlin McCrory
FROM: Melanie Morales <melanie.morales@citythatneversleepspr.com>
TO: Truly St. James <trulystjames@trulystjames.com>

???

xx,

M

p.s. For what it's worth, your website has had an unprecedented number of hits in the last 72 hours and your newsletter has gained over 400 subscribers. We'd have to contact Jen, but if the number of clicks on your site is anything to go off, I bet your sales have seen a spike, too . . .

Monday, May 10th
SUBJECT: re: re: Update on Unhinged w/ Caitlin McCrory
FROM: Truly St. James <trulystjames@trulystjames.com>
TO: Melanie Morales <melanie.morales@citythatneversleepspr.com>

I like money as much as the next person, Mel, but I just can't. Between you and me, I'd rather stick a rusty fork in my eye than spend five minutes in a room with Colin McCrory.

T

Monday, May 10th
SUBJECT: re: Update on Unhinged w/ Caitlin McCrory
FROM: Melanie Morales <melanie.morales@citythatneversleepspr.com>
TO: Caitlin McCrory <caitlinmccrory@caitlinmccrory.com>
CC: Truly St. James <trulystjames@trulystjames.com>

Hi Caitlin,

That is so fantastic! Truly and I are both thrilled with the episode's success! 🥂🎉

Unfortunately, her schedule really is jam-packed, so at this time she's going to have to pass.

All the best,
Melanie

Monday, May 10th
SUBJECT: Hello
FROM: Colin McCrory <colinmccrory@yahoo.com>
TO: Truly St. James <trulystjames@trulystjames.com>

Truly,

I hope you're not angry that I got your email address from my sister. I just wanted to apologize for getting off on the wrong foot. It wasn't my intention to upset you, but I did, and for that I'm sorry.

I know I don't have any right to ask anything of you, but please don't take your anger at me out on my sister. She's worked extremely hard to build her brand from the ground up and this podcast is her baby. If a baby were exceptionally vulgar. This is strictly confidential, but Caitlin's currently in negotiations with Spotify to ink an exclusive deal. An upward trajectory in streams would go a long way at the bargaining table.

I would give my sister the world if I could so, if there's anything I can do to convince you to give her (and me) another chance, please let me know. I promise to be on my best behavior.

Sincerely,
Colin

p.s. my sister didn't put me up to this. I swear.

Chapter Five

I mean, who even has a Yahoo address anymore?"

"I don't know, hon." Lulu looked away from the box of brightly colored butt plugs she was inventorying, clipboard in hand. "People over the age of seventy-two?"

"Or sociopaths." Come as You Are was dead this time of day and since Lulu was the manager, there was no one there to fuss at Truly for sitting on the counter.

"Hey, hey! Or work with me here." Lulu threw a dented box at her and Truly just barely managed to catch it. "Luddites."

"He was wearing an Apple Watch." Truly turned the package over in her hands. "Why'd you throw me this?"

"Damaged goods. You want?"

"Is this your way of telling me I need to get laid?"

"I was trying to give you a gift, but hey, if you want to talk about your sad sex life, I'm game."

"Shut up," Truly said without any real heat. "It's not *sad*, it's *solo*."

"*Hence* the Booty Bling Wearable Silicone Beads." Lulu wrinkled her nose. "A terrible name, but the reviews are great. You're welcome."

Truly set the box aside. "I'd rather not talk about my sex life at all."

"No, *apparently* you'd rather bitch about Colin McCrory."

"Am I not allowed to vent anymore?"

Lulu held up her hands. "All I'm saying is you've spent more time complaining about Colin McCrory, a dude you spent less than an hour with, than Justin, a guy you dated for six years. Don't you think that says something?"

It said that Justin wasn't worth talking about. "I've said everything there is to say about Justin."

"And your parents?" Lulu frowned. "Do you, I don't know, maybe want to talk about them?"

And say what that she hadn't already said?

Not even two weeks had passed since her parents had flipped her whole world upside down and it was already starting to look like this . . . *trial* separation? Might not be as temporary as they had led her to think.

Dad had moved into a short-term rental across town that was closer to the theater where he worked. A fact of which Truly had only been made aware when she'd beaten him home for their regularly scheduled Sunday brunch. A Sunday brunch Mom and Dad were adamant that they not cancel because, according to them, they were still a family and nothing among the three of them had to change.

Wishful thinking had to run in the family because everything *felt* different. *Badwrong* in a way she could barely put her finger on but made her feel like her skin didn't fit right.

Mom's and Dad's hands didn't brush when he dished out plates of delicious-smelling apricot and pancetta strata and they sat farther apart on the couch than they usually did and they were so polite, so careful, acting more like strangers than a married couple. Truly had wanted to rip her skin off and go running out the front door, but she'd stayed longer than usual, desperately hoping she'd blink, and everything would right itself.

Of course, it hadn't. She'd gone home and thrown herself into work, hammering out a new chapter in her book. Only that hadn't worked out for her, either.

It was hard to write a convincing happily ever after when her own faith in those was turbulent at the moment.

If she didn't get her shit together, she was going to have to beg her editor for an extension, something she hadn't had to do in years.

"I'd rather not talk about the nightmare my life has turned into, thanks. Been there, done that, already went through half a box of Kleenex sobbing my soul out to you on the phone." She grabbed the Booty Bling Wearable Silicone Beads box and turned it over in her hands, just for something to do. "Anyway, do you think he's using a fake email address? Like, I get not using his work address for personal shit, but do you think he—"

"Do I think a guy you met once crafted a burner account just to email you?" Lulu stared at her. "Truly. Babe. Honey bun. This is getting ridiculous. Just call the dude up and set up a time and a place to hate-fuck him. No one, and I mean *no one*, deserves to be living rent free inside your head if they aren't making you come so hard your brain leaks out your ears."

No one had ever made her come so hard her brain had leaked out her ears. But the idea of her and Colin— "Don't be gross."

"Just saying. Sounds like a textbook case of unresolved sexual tension, to me."

"You're terrible," Truly complained, halfhearted at best.

"And yet you love me anyway." Lulu brightened. "Hey, I know

what'll cheer you up. You want to hear about the gallon of lube I had to clean up with a push broom on Friday?"

That sentence made very little sense and yet she was intrigued. "They make gallon-size lube?"

"Well, sure." Lulu swept her long, glossy black hair up in a bun. "Some folks like to buy in bulk."

Truly couldn't fathom what someone had to be doing to go through enough lube on the regular that buying a gallon was economical. "Tell me everything."

Lulu was in the middle of regaling her with the tale of three inebriated college students, a gallon drum of silicone-based lube, one pair of vintage Heelys on the fritz, and a leather crop—whose role in this whole charade Truly *still* didn't quite understand—when the bell above the door chimed.

"Hello and welcome to Come as You Are, the one-stop shop for all your sexual healing needs. Don't procrastinate; let us help you masturbate," Lulu recited the god-awful greeting that Benny, the shop's owner, had written himself. Truly had offered to help him retool the greeting but upon hearing *retool*, he'd fallen into a fit of giggles, rendering her offer useless. "My name's Lulu. What can I help you find on this glorious hump day?"

"Truly?"

"*Colin?*"

There, in all his Bambi-eyed glory, was Colin McCrory. As if she'd manifested him, conjured him through sheer . . . bitching.

"Hi." He tucked his hands inside the pockets of his black dress pants and rocked back on his heels, inadvertently causing the bell to chime when his ass bumped the door. His cheeks flushed and if a twisted thrill shot through her at Colin looking caught off guard, well, being petty wasn't a crime.

Lulu's jaw dropped.

That's Colin? she mouthed.

Truly nodded and Lulu crudely pantomimed slapping the rear of *something—someone?*—in front of her.

"What are you doing here?" Truly demanded, sliding off the counter.

"A guy can't visit his neighborhood, uh, sex shop?"

Truly's brows rocketed to her hairline. Neighborhood? Bullshit.

"We prefer the term *adult boutique*," Lulu said.

Truly harrumphed. "Are you stalking me now?"

Colin blanched. "*Stalking you?* Why would I be stalking you?"

"Who knows? Maybe calling me reductive wasn't enough. Maybe you felt the need to accuse me of being something else patently false to my face."

"Wow," Colin intoned. His soft, sunshine-yellow button-down stretched obnoxiously across his shoulders when he crossed his arms. "Someone thinks awfully highly of themselves. And for the record, I never called *you* reductive. I implied that your viewpoint was reductive."

Truly was an amalgamation of all her viewpoints, so how exactly was that any different? "What else would you be doing here?"

"Maybe he came in to do a little light shopping," Lulu said. "All penis pumps are currently thirty percent off."

"I'm actually *not* in the market for one of those, but thanks?" The pink flush sweeping across his cheeks was not adorable.

Lulu shrugged. "Yeah, I can't really imagine anyone needing more than one."

He blinked, absurdly long lashes fluttering. "That's, uh, that's not why I don't need—"

"Hey, man." Lulu held up her hands. "This is a safe space. I'm not here to judge what you do with your junk."

"That's, um, big of you."

Lulu bared her teeth in a sharklike grin. "That's what she said."

Truly snorted. A mistake because it made him look at her and—those eyes were a weapon. It should be a class A felony to possess eyes that pretty a shade of brown and lashes that thick. All he had to do was flash those Bambi-eyes and people probably swooned. Not Truly, obviously. Other people. He was probably hell to go up against in court.

It took a second to realize he was just staring at her and not saying anything. Unless he'd said something, and she'd missed it? "Why are you looking at me like that?"

The corners of his eyes creased when he smiled. "Is looking at you a crime now?"

Stupid stomach of hers just had to swoop. A distant cousin of the swoon. Extremely distant. Several times removed. Truly crossed her arms. "Maybe it is."

Colin laughed, ducking his head, toe of his loafer scuffing the mat in front of the door, looking as close to sheepish as she'd seen him. "Look, I really was in the neighborhood, okay? I work on Leary Way, and I live up on Baker Avenue near 45th. I drive past this place every day." He looked up at her through his lashes. "I swear I'm not stalking you, Truly."

She sniffed. "So, this is all just a big coincidence? You expect me to believe you come here often?"

One of his brows rose. "Do you?"

Touché. "*That* is none of your business."

"I saw your car," he admitted. "In the parking lot. I remembered seeing it in the garage at the studio. There aren't that many 1968

Volkswagen Beetles painted like Herbie the Love Bug adorned with eyelashes driving around town."

"It's a '69, actually."

Lulu broke out into giggles. *Perv.*

"But good eye. So, what? You recognized my car and decided to come in here? You realize you aren't doing much in the way of convincing me you weren't stalking me, right?"

"Stalking would imply I'm following you and I think I established this was a complete coincidence." He held out his arms, palms up. "Come on. You're going to tell me you, of all people, don't believe in fate?"

"*'You of all people'*?" Truly wrinkled her nose. "Why, because I write romance novels I must believe in fate?"

"Now you're just putting words in my mouth."

"Are *you* suggesting it was fate that we happened to cross paths in a sex shop?"

"Adult boutique," Lulu whispered.

"When you put it like that," Colin deadpanned, regaining his footing. The color in his cheeks had mostly dissipated, the tips of his ears still pink. "You ignored my email."

She scoffed. "I did no such thing."

"You're telling me you were planning on responding?"

At some point in the near never. "I'll have you know that I am extremely busy."

Colin looked around the empty store. "I can see that."

Brat. "Lulu, here, is not just my best friend, but she helps me brainstorm. She's my—my research assistant. It might not look like it, but I'm working."

Lulu waved her fingers.

Colin's brows knit. "You write historical romance."

"And you think they didn't have sex in the Regency?"

Lulu dissolved into giggles. "You sweet summer child."

Colin huffed. "Of course, people had sex. I just wasn't aware they had"—he leaned closer to the counter, peering over Truly's shoulder, smirking—"Booty Bling Wearable Silicone Beads."

Her face flamed. "*Be that as it may*, you still haven't addressed what you expected to happen when you walked in here. What if I had been shopping?"

Colin shrugged. "I suppose I would've learned whether you ever replace that stick up your ass with something a little more fun."

His eyes drifted pointedly to the box over her shoulder.

Oh, that son of a bitch.

"One, I do *not* have a stick up my ass," she said, ticking points off on her fingers.

Colin grinned. "Could've fooled me."

Asshole. "And *two*"—she grabbed the box off the counter and shoved it against Colin's chest. He barely budged. "That's not mine."

Colin nodded and took the box, turning it over in his hands. "I'm sure that's what everyone says. Just doing research, right?"

Unbelievable. "And *three*—"

"Please, I'm on tenterhooks," he said, and she wanted to wipe that insufferable smirk off his face. "Don't leave me hanging."

Her pulse thundered in her temples, and it took every iota of self-control she had not to place her palms flat against his chest and *push*. To find out just how hard she'd have to shove Colin to make him move. She crossed her arms instead, the safer, saner option. "If my memory serves me, and trust that it does, I believe you promised to be on your best behavior the next time we met?"

Colin grinned and rocked back on his heels, cheeky. "Who says this isn't my best behavior?"

Oh, he was on thin ice. "For someone who wants something, you aren't doing very much to endear yourself to me."

Colin leaned in, dropping his voice. "Tell me you aren't having the time of your life right now."

Truly gulped. Audibly. She covered it with a scoff. "I have no idea what you're talking about."

"Sure you don't." Colin smiled. "Now, this time, say it like you mean it."

She sucked in a breath. "Are you *always* such a brat?"

Colin shrugged, much closer than she'd realized. Close enough that his shirtsleeves brushed her arms. "Maybe you bring it out in me."

She scoffed. "How convenient."

"Maybe it is," he murmured, lashes casting shadows against his cheeks as he blinked down at her. "What are you going to do about it, Truly?"

A shiver raced up her spine.

"Don't give me ideas," she warned.

"*Give* you ideas?" Colin tutted. "Like I'd give myself that much credit. I bet I just . . . bring them out of you. Isn't that right?"

Goose bumps erupted along every inch of her skin.

"This is better than Pay-Per-View," Lulu whispered.

Truly jumped back and—*ow*—bumped her hip against the counter.

At least Colin looked equally worse for wear, dazed and embarrassed, one hand gripping the back of his neck, his head ducked, eyes averted. All the better; those things were as dangerous as she'd suspected, practically hypnotic.

"Boo," Lulu huffed. "Just when things were getting good."

Colin shot her a weak glare before turning back to Truly. "Truly—"

"You know," she said, trying to find her footing. Better not to let him finish when her name in his mouth was as good as a weapon. "I'm not sure you're really sorry."

What had he apologized for, exactly? That's right—he was sorry *if* he'd upset her. Hmph. *If.*

"Well, that *is* a conundrum," he said, tongue pressing against the inside of his cheek.

"Isn't it?"

"Colin," Lulu called out, batting her eyelashes sweetly. "Hate to break it to you, buddy, but this store is for paying customers only."

She looked at Truly and smiled deviously.

Oh, brilliant, devious Lulu. Truly owed her big-time.

"What about her?" Colin jerked a thumb over his shoulder at Truly.

"What *about* her?" Lulu asked. "Truly buys shit here all the time."

"Oh, yeah?" he asked, interest clearly piqued. "Like what?"

"None of your business." Truly sniffed. "I think what Lulu here is trying to say is that if you'd like to patronize this store, you're going to have to make a purchase."

Lulu snapped her fingers. "Bingo." She wandered over to the front window and flicked the sign that read No Loitering. "If you'd like to talk to Truly, you're going to have to pay the piper."

Colin stared at her. "If I want to talk to Truly, I have to buy something? That's what you're telling me?"

"Beauty *and* brains." Lulu grinned. "Who said they can't coexist?"

Colin laughed. "Wow. All right." He sauntered over to the counter, selected a pack of candy, and slapped it down on the counter. "Fine. I'd like to make a purchase."

Lulu circled the counter. "Ooh, penis-shaped hard candy, nice. That'll be $5.99."

Colin whipped out his credit card.

Lulu hissed. "Oof, sorry, we've got a ten-dollar credit card minimum."

"*Ten dollars?*" Colin scoffed. "That's ridiculous. And not even legal."

"Them's the breaks, dude," Lulu said. "I don't make the rules, I just enforce them."

Colin sighed and grabbed another bag of the same pastel, dick-shaped candy confections.

Lulu beamed. "Lucky for you, we've got a buy one, get one free deal happening."

Colin sighed. "You're kidding."

"I'd never kid about BOGO sales," Lulu said, hand to heart.

Colin rolled his eyes and slapped yet another bag of dick-shaped candy down onto the counter. "Three bags, then."

Lulu scanned it and hummed. "Oh, no. Did I say buy one, get one free? I meant buy one, get two free."

"Are you pulling my leg?"

"Do I *look* like the type of person who would joke about a buy one, get two free sale on cock-shaped candy?"

Colin rapped his credit card against the counter. "This is ridiculous."

"Pony up the cash, cowboy, or else get the hell out of Dodge," Lulu said.

Instead of walking out, Colin walked over to the carousel of condoms and grabbed a package of *ribbed for her* off the hanger, tossing it onto the counter. "How's that?"

"Wouldn't you know, we're running a *safe sex savings*. A free pack of condoms with every purchase. Your grand total is still . . . $5.99."

Colin slumped against the counter. "You're killing me."

Lulu grinned, all teeth. "Hop to it, hot stuff. We're burning daylight here."

Colin set off into the store like a man on a mission.

"You're not actually running any BOGO sales, are you?" Truly asked, pretty sure of the answer.

"Do I look new to you?"

Five minutes later, Colin returned, promptly dumping two items onto the counter. "Ring me up, Scotty."

"A nerd. I dig it. Now, let's see what we have here." Lulu started ringing up his items. "We've got four packages of novelty penis-shaped hard candies, one package of Trojan condoms, one Happy Rabbit vibrating cock ring"—Colin flushed—"and a four-ounce bottle of Sliquid Swirl Natural Water-Based Lubricant in the flavor"—Lulu squinted at the label—"pink lemonade." She grinned. "You get down with your bad self."

The way he flushed from his hairline to his starched collar made Truly's stomach twist. She refused to investigate the feeling further.

"Your total comes to $115.72 with tax."

Colin choked. "One hundred and—what happened to buy one, get three free?"

"Aw, shoot." Lulu shrugged. "Your purchases must not have been applicable after all."

He sighed and slipped his card into the reader like a good sport.

Lulu started bagging his items.

"Do I have permission to speak, or do I need to submit a written request?" Colin asked.

"You're barking up the wrong tree, baby boy." Lulu grinned, passing him his receipt and a pen. "Ask Truly."

Colin signed the receipt with a swooping flourish. "Truly?"

This entire interaction had been . . . not entirely awful. But it didn't magically erase the fact that Colin McCrory had hurt her feelings. That wasn't something she could just laugh off or pretend away.

"Color me surprised you're waiting for my answer. Instead of, you know, running roughshod all over me the way you did during the podcast."

Lulu cleared her throat. "You know what? I'll be in the back. Inventorying ball gags and blindfolds. It was a pleasure meeting you, Colin."

Colin nodded, but waited to speak until Lulu had wandered out of earshot. "Running roughshod over you how, exactly?"

"You're kidding."

A furrow appeared between his brows. "I'm not. You told me you weren't sure whether I was truly sorry, so I'm trying again. But in order to apologize sincerely, I need to know exactly what it is I'm apologizing for."

Jesus. She'd expected him to just—just say he was sorry so he could get it over with before moving on to hounding her about recording another episode. She hadn't expected an actual attempt at contrition.

"That's . . . big of you," she conceded, crossing her arms like a shield because she hadn't accounted for the vulnerability this would require of her. "Fine. You interrupted me."

Colin nodded slowly, as if he were filing her words away. Actually listening. *Actively* listening. "Okay. And?"

He expected her to keep going? Air all her grievances? Fine, she could do that. "You . . . you trivialized my"—*feelings*—"point of view. We might have had differing opinions, but that didn't make my opinion any less valid than yours." Even if he had turned out to be right. "And it absolutely didn't excuse you calling me— sorry, my *viewpoint*—reductive. That was rude. And shitty. And out of line."

And a dozen other adjectives she could rattle off if she felt like being redundant for the sake of making her point. And she didn't. If Colin hadn't gotten the gist by now, there was no hope for him.

"Are you finished?"

"For now."

His lips twitched. "Okay." He took a deep, bracing breath in through his nose, broad shoulders rising and falling. "You're right—I did cut you off and for that I apologize. Not only is interrupting rude, but it demonstrates a lack of respect. My actions were antithetical to my feelings because I *do* respect you. I got caught up in the moment and my passion got the better of me, but that doesn't excuse my poor behavior. I can't promise it won't happen again, but I do promise to try harder in the future." Colin grabbed a feather tickler off the counter, smile going lopsided as he whacked it against his palm. "Just smack me the next time I interrupt you."

"That's for tickling, not flogging." She snatched it away from him with a laugh. "And it hardly counts if you like it."

For a moment, Colin just stared at her, smile disconcertingly soft. Being the subject of his undivided attention made her stomach twist and her toes curl and uncurl inside her sandals. "You have a nice laugh."

Her stomach went into free fall. "That—that doesn't sound like an apology."

Colin ducked his head. "Apologies, right. I—shit." He ran his hand over the top of his head, messing up his hair. "Okay, yeah, I could've disagreed with you without belittling your stance, and for that I'm sorry. It was a dick move on my part, trivializing your viewpoint." There he went again, looking up at her through his lashes. Colin was taller than her but when he did that it made her feel like she was towering over him. "I promise I won't do it again."

And just like that, what lingered of her ire was gone, the hollow in her chest where her anger had resided filled with a burning need to meet Colin's sincerity with her own. "To be fair, the topic is—was?—sort of a sensitive one for me. It doesn't excuse what I said about your career clouding your judgment or the fact that I lashed out at you, but I hope it explains it."

Colin's gaze swept across her face like he was trying to put together a puzzle with only half the pieces. "Was?"

Was what? "Sorry?"

"You said *was*." Colin reached out, plucking the tickler from her clenched fist. She'd honestly forgotten she was still holding on to it. "The topic *was* sensitive?"

"You, uh, caught that, did you?" She wished she was still holding that silly tickler, if only for something to do with her hands. "My fiancé—*ex*-fiancé—and I were on a break."

The tickler hit the floor with a whisper of a thud, landing feather-side down before falling onto its side. Colin bent at the waist, snatching it off the ground. When he rose, his cheeks were pinker than they'd been before. "Oh."

"Yeah, *oh*." Truly snorted and rolled her eyes. "It was his idea. The break, not the breakup. That part was all me. See, Justin, he's in a band and they're on tour. He told me he didn't have the time to devote to our relationship, but that it was temporary and that it wasn't because he wanted to see anyone else. Only, the morning of the podcast, I stopped by his place and caught him . . . well, he wasn't on tour yet and he wasn't alone, if you catch my drift."

Colin frowned. "I'm sorry, Truly."

She laughed. "Whatever. I'm not even that upset about it."

Not as upset as she probably should've been, at any rate.

It was all more than she'd planned to say, but when he wasn't driving her up the wall, Colin was easy to talk to. Something about those Bambi-eyes loosened her tongue, made her want to spill her guts. Throw her well-whetted sense of self-preservation right out the window.

"Still. That's a shitty way to find out the truth. I wouldn't wish that on anyone."

"Not even an enemy?" Truly teased.

Colin smiled warmly. "You're not my enemy, Truly."

No, she supposed they weren't. She wasn't in the habit of wanting to study her enemies' eyelashes, *so*.

"I didn't exactly memorize the email you sent, but I believe you said something about convincing me to give the podcast another shot. So, go on." She cocked a brow. "Convince me."

Chapter Six

Truly arrived at the studio before Colin.

"Come in, make yourself at home." Caitlin all but shoved her down onto the couch, the very same couch where she'd lost her cool three weeks prior. "Can I get you something? Maybe that martini this time? Don't tell my brother, but I've got it all—gin, vodka, olives, twists. Name it."

Truly laughed. "I'm good, thanks."

As tempting as it was to take Caitlin up on her offer, she wanted to keep her head about her more than ever.

Caitlin took a seat kitty-corner to her on the chaise side of the sectional. "You have no clue how surprised I was when my brother told me he'd convinced you to give me another chance."

Probably as surprised as Truly was when she'd agreed. "It wasn't you who needed the second chance. But your brother and I talked it out. It's . . . water under the bridge."

"Thank God." Caitlin beamed. "I was trying to play it cool last time, didn't want to gush, you know? But you're seriously my favorite author. Like, you renewed my hope in love."

Caitlin was what? Twenty-two? What exactly was there to renew?

"I mean it. You're my icon."

Icon? Truly snorted. "That's *way* too generous of you."

"Hardly. You're amazing. And my brother—"

The studio door opened, and Colin shouldered his way inside, eyes immediately landing on Truly. A smile lit up his face and wow, the Chipotle she'd had for lunch was *not* agreeing with her. That was why her stomach somersaulted. Bad beans or expired sour cream . . . too much fiber. "Hey."

"Speak of the devil," Caitlin said. "You're late."

"By what? A minute? Kiss my ass. I brought you coffee."

"Did you even get my order right?"

Colin sighed, aggrieved, broad shoulders rising and falling, and her stomach flipped all over again. Bad beans for sure. "Iced venti sugar cookie latte with three pumps hazelnut syrup and sugar cookie cold foam."

"Sprinkles?" Caitlin asked, reserving judgment.

"You and your fucking sprinkles." He huffed. "It's May, Caitlin, and while it might be Christmas year-round for you, it's not at the coffee shop."

Caitlin's bottom lip jutted out. "Whatever."

"*So*, I had to stop at the grocery store on the way over here to buy you your goddamn red and green sprinkles." Colin thrust the drink at Caitlin. "You're welcome."

Caitlin made grabby hands. "Best big brother, *ever*."

Colin laughed. "You want to really show your appreciation? Say that in front of Caleb the next time I'm around."

Caitlin grinned. "Consider it done."

"Who's Caleb?" Truly asked.

"Our brother," Caitlin said.

Colin shook an iced drink in Truly's face. "Here."

She studied the Sharpie scribble along the side of the plastic cup. Iced quad grande oat milk latte with two pumps of vanilla syrup. She took the coffee from him. "What is this?"

"Other than an egregious amount of caffeine?" Colin dropped the gym bag he was carrying and sat beside her. "It's your order, isn't it?"

"You knew that *how*?"

"He fished it out of the garbage after you left," Caitlin said, tapping away at her phone. "Like the total freak he is."

"Jesus H. Christ, Caitlin," he complained. "Is nothing sacred?"

"Whoops." She looked up from her phone and grinned, chewing on her straw. "Was I not supposed to say that?"

Truly stifled a laugh. "Circling back to you being a stalker . . ."

"How'd I know you were going to say that?" He groaned, head flopped back, and eyes pinched shut as if he were in pain. "I just wanted to do something nice, okay?" He cracked open one eye. "Consider it a gesture of goodwill."

She took a sip and—*oh, yeah*. That was the shit. Nectar of the gods in a plastic cup. "As long as you continue to use your creeper powers for good, not evil, who am I to complain?" Truly swallowed another mouthful of iced coffee deliciousness and with it, a groan. So good. "Whatever you're preemptively apologizing for? Consider it forgiven."

"Bold of you to assume I'll be the one apologizing today," Colin said. "But on the off chance things do get heated . . ."

He unzipped his gym bag.

"No one wants to sniff your sweaty gym socks." Caitlin wrinkled her nose.

"Hey," he warned. "I bet my gym socks could fetch a high price on some fetish site."

Caitlin gagged. "I don't wanna yuck anyone's yum, but *barf*."

Truly covered her giggle with another sip of her latte.

"You'll be eating those words when my gym sock OnlyFans makes us millions."

"I'll pay you to say the words *gym sock OnlyFans* at our next family dinner." Caitlin chortled. "Mom'll have a conniption fit."

"As if she doesn't have one every time we all get together?" Colin's smile was thin, his voice tight. Curiously so.

Caitlin wiped tears from her eyes. "Yeah, but about normal things. Like how we're both awful disappointments and she wishes we were more like her precious Caleb. Not her son selling his sweaty socks on the internet for kinksters to fap into."

In what universe were Colin, a successful lawyer, and Caitlin, a semi-famous internet personality, awful disappointments? They both had health insurance, which was a sad, sad barometer for success, but more than Truly could claim.

Colin rolled his eyes. "I didn't bring my gym socks. I didn't even go to the gym today."

Truly leaned forward, peering curiously into the bag that contained a—football helmet? No, *two* football helmets. "Um."

Without warning, Colin grabbed the smaller of the two helmets, a scuffed mustard-yellow eyesore, and plopped it onto her head. It smelled faintly of gym socks.

Truly glared.

"You know." Colin grinned. "In case things come to blows."

"You guys cool if we take five?" Caitlin rattled the ice in her otherwise empty coffee cup. "Truly? You want to do that weird thing girls do where we go to the bathroom together and listen to each other pee? I promise to tell you embarrassing stories about my brother."

Colin yanked off his helmet. "You're a menace."

"That just might be the kindest thing you've ever said to me." Caitlin pretended to wipe away a tear. "Truly?"

As tempting as the offer was . . .

"I'm good." She held up her half-full coffee. "But rain check on those stories?"

"You got it." Caitlin winked on her way out the door. "Don't kill each other while I'm gone. It would be a bitch to get bloodstains out of this carpet."

The studio door shut, leaving Truly alone with Colin.

"Sisters." Colin sighed.

"Can't live with them, can't live without them?"

Colin looked thoughtful. "I don't know. I once tried to surrender Caitlin to the fire department, so can't say I didn't try to live without her."

She tugged off her helmet and set it down on the cushion beside her. "I thought Caitlin was kidding when she told me that."

"Nah." He grinned. "Guilty as charged."

"Come on," she cajoled. "Having a little sister must've had its perks. Occasional hero worship, at least."

He laughed. "Let me guess—no younger siblings?"

"Only child," she admitted.

"Ah." He nodded. "Should've known."

"What's that supposed to mean?"

"Hard to say." He cocked his head, studying her. That squirmy feeling in her stomach returned, the one she got each time Colin stared at her. As if with every question she asked *him*, he managed to peel back another one of *her* layers. "I guess you just have that look about you."

"*Look* about me?" She dared him to say something offensive. That she seemed spoiled or bossy or maladjusted or any of the other stereotypes she'd heard about only children. "What sort of look?"

"Like you've never known the pleasure of waking up to a spit-covered finger in your ear before? That look."

She laughed, shoulders relaxing. She hadn't woken up to that. Small favors. "That does sound disgusting."

"You have *no* idea."

"You have a brother, too? Older or younger?"

"Twin, actually." He studied the dent at the back of his helmet. "Technically, I'm twelve minutes older. Last time I ever came first at anything."

He laughed, passing it off as a joke, but Truly wasn't an idiot. Which was why she didn't push. People didn't often like to have their bruises pressed.

"And your parents? Do they live around here?"

"Sure. They still live over in Woodinville where I grew up."

"Ah, Woodinville." She nodded. "Nice place. Um, good wine."

"Oh, yeah. The wine really was the highlight of my childhood." She sputtered. "I'm trying here."

"Trying? My, my, Truly St. James," he admonished, tutting softly. "You wouldn't happen to be trying to get to *know* me, would you?"

"Yeah, well, you aren't exactly making it easy." She huffed, eyeing the orange eyesore on Colin's lap. "Maybe you should put that helmet back on."

"Is that a threat?" He smiled, a hint of teeth appearing between his full pink lips.

She crossed her arms and looked away from his mouth, his face, his—everything.

"More like a warning."

"Hey." He bumped her with his elbow, a gentle nudge. "I'm teasing you. It's a thing people do."

"Oh what, like pigtail pulling?" She scoffed. "Only child here, remember? I wasn't exactly raised to play nicely with others."

Colin hadn't moved his arm and it was warm against hers, heat bleeding through the cotton of his shirt. Her sundress left her own arm bare, and goose bumps rose along her skin, not because she was cold but because there was something startlingly intimate about feeling Colin's shoulder brush hers with every breath he took.

"Maybe I don't want to play nicely with you."

That was—*he* was—she—*play*—with—*hnggg*?

Her brain glitched.

Holy shit.

Had Colin McCrory just come on to her?

Her heart stuttered then sped, hurling itself against her rib cage.

She wasn't an idiot.

They'd flirted. *Pigtail pulling*. But that's all it had been. Nonsense.

This felt different. Like he was suggesting *more*. Proposing their flirting actually lead to something.

For the second time in less than a minute, her mind glitched, thoughts of what that *something* might be clogging up her brain like a traffic jam.

Colin winced and—why was he wincing? Oh yeah, that's right,

because he wasn't inside her head. Because he'd probably taken her silence as a rejection rather than speechlessness.

She opened her mouth—

"You know, I just meant, you're not very good at small talk."

Oh. *Ouch*. Never mind, *not* hitting on her. Just casually insulting her.

"Shit, that came out wrong. You aren't bad at small talk, I just meant . . . do you really want to talk about my brother or where my parents live, or do you want to ask me whatever it is you've clearly been dying to ask?"

"I was raised with manners, you know," she said, finding her footing after the one-two punch of believing she was being hit on, only to realize . . . not so much. Honestly, she didn't even know anymore. "I didn't think asking point-blank about potential childhood trauma would be very polite."

He flashed her another smile. "I think I like you better rude."

She stomped ruthlessly on the fluttering in her stomach. "Well, since you asked. Are your parents still together?"

Colin nodded and settled deeper into the couch. She found herself sliding farther into his side. The cushion was uneven, that was why, but it also felt a little like Colin had his own gravitational field. "Married thirty-two years."

"Happily?"

At that, he laughed. "You really don't fuck around, do you?"

"Hey, *you're* the one who said I could—"

Colin McCrory had the gall to press his finger against her lips, physically shushing her. Screw personal space, right?

For a second, she was tempted to meet his daring with her own, to nip the tip of his finger, maybe press the tip of her tongue against the pad. She could only imagine what his face would do, how his big brown eyes would grow huge, might even darken from chestnut to chocolate.

A strange thrill shot through her and it took every ounce of self-control she possessed to not act on that unwelcome, intrusive thought.

"I didn't say it was a bad thing." He lowered his hand, index finger grazing her chin. Her lips tingled where he'd touched. "I'm impressed, to be honest. You go straight for the throat. Anyone ever tell you you're brutal?"

"Maybe." No one had ever made it sound like a compliment before. "But whatever," she said, flippant tone at odds with her racing heart. "You like me better rude, remember?"

Colin nodded slowly. "Yeah. I guess my parents are happy."

"You *guess*?"

"I mean, I've never asked?"

It wasn't something someone should have to ask to know. It was obvious. Or it should be.

She frowned.

Maybe not. What did she know, right? "Huh."

"Next question?"

"You're assuming I have one."

Colin simply stared at her.

Truly rolled her eyes and swallowed hard. "Fine. What about you? Have you ever been married?"

"No," he answered without hesitation.

Hm. Interesting.

"Not what you were expecting? You've got sort of a . . ." He pointed at the space between her brows. "Wrinkle happening there."

She smacked his hand aside. "It's rude to talk about a lady's wrinkles."

His teeth sank into his bottom lip, doing a piss-poor job of hiding his smile. "My sincerest apologies."

She rolled her eyes. "I'm surprised, is all."

"That I've never been married?" He held a hand to his chest, no longer even trying to hide his smile. "I'm flattered you think I'm such a catch."

She elbowed him in the side, not nearly hard enough for the theatrical *oof* he let out. "I'm surprised you've never been divorced, actually."

He sputtered out a laugh that trailed off into a pained groan. "You're killing me."

For being killed, he sure sounded like he was enjoying himself.

"No offense. I'm just trying to understand what's wrong with you."

"Oh, sure." He laughed. "No offense."

"You know what I mean."

His brows rose. "Do I?"

"Don't act like you don't have baggage. No one reaches the age of twenty-five without at least a carry-on's worth of issues. And you're—how old *are* you?"

"Thirty-two," he said, looking thoughtful. "So what's wrong with you?"

She wasn't blind to her own flaws. If anything, writing romance and constantly creating realistically flawed characters from scratch had made her intensely aware of her own. But that didn't mean she relished talking about her own imperfections. If that made her a hypocrite, add it to the list. "We're not talking about me. We're talking about you."

"Fine. What is it about me that screams *flawed* to you?"

It wasn't so much *flawed* as it was, well . . . "Let me back up."

"By all means." He swept out a hand, giving her the floor.

"When I come up with my characters, I think about what's happened in their past to make them who they are. They have wounds that cause them to develop fears, and those fears lead to false beliefs. Misperceptions about who they are and the world around them and—and love. Obviously. Everything they do, every choice they make, it all comes back to that. What they want, what they're willing to do to get it, their personality traits, the choices they make, even their jobs. Sometimes especially their job. And I don't think we, as people, are any different."

She grabbed her coffee off the table and shoved her straw down into the ice, crushing the cubes to bits. "Being a romance writer is more than what I do. It's who I am." To the point where her self-worth was tied up in it, which couldn't be healthy, but that was for her to unpack some other time and maybe under the guidance of a trusted professional. "And you're a divorce attorney—"

"Family lawyer," he corrected. "But sure, that's part of it."

"I'm trying to understand *why*."

His teeth grazed his bottom lip. "Sometimes a job is just a job, Truly."

She frowned. Sometimes, sure.

"Don't get me wrong. I like what I do."

How could anyone enjoy being a divorce lawyer? Family lawyer. Whatever. "See, I don't get that. No offense, but what you do sounds *awful*."

Day in, day out, all that divorce. It made her queasy.

"Truly." He bumped his shoulder against hers. "You do realize I'm not the grim reaper of relationships, right?"

Well. Of course not. That would be ridiculous. Even if the thought of Colin carrying a scythe into a courtroom did make her smile. "No, but I assume divorce tends to bring out the worst in people. Couples fighting, their lives and love reduced to assets. Kids caught in the middle, bargaining chips. Doesn't it all get exhausting?"

How had he not lost all faith in love?

The clock on the wall over the door continued to tick faithfully as Colin silently weighed her words, or maybe his, with a thoughtful frown.

"Divorce can absolutely bring out the worst in people, but just because it can doesn't mean that it always does," he finally said. "I've been doing this for seven years. I know I haven't seen it all, but I've seen enough to know that sometimes letting someone go can be the greatest gesture of love a person can make."

His answer was predictably heavy, less predictably poignant. Something to chew on, even if she didn't necessarily agree with it. Or like it.

"Some days, some cases, are worse than others. Mediation, listening to couples bicker over who gets what, that's never fun. Washington's a no-fault state, meaning neither spouse has to prove the other is to blame for the separation, but that doesn't mean my clients don't like to air their grievances. I get told *a lot*, more than I need to know, more than I want to know." He ran his knuckles along his jaw, the faint shadow of scruff there rasping softly against his skin. "But I also handle adoption and guardianship cases, so it's not all doom and gloom. It's just my job." He smirked. "Doesn't hurt that I'm damn good at what I do."

"Oh, yeah? What's that?" she taunted, teasing a two-way street. "Arguing?"

"So, you admit it?" He flashed his teeth, smile triumphant. "You think I'm good at arguing?"

She *had* implied that, hadn't she? "Point proven, I suppose."

His smile softened into something slightly less smug, but no less mischievous.

"What?" She looked at him askance. "Do I have something on my face?"

He laughed. "Other than that persistent wrinkle between your brows?"

She smacked his arm, a little harder than she probably ought to have, too playful, too familiar for two people who were practically strangers, but Colin just laughed harder. "What did I say about mentioning those?"

He caught her hand before she could smack him again. Caught it and held it and didn't let it go. "I'm sorry."

Prove it, she wanted to say. *Show me just how sorry you are.*

If thinking the words was weird, saying them out loud would've been—unhinged. Her sense of self-preservation wasn't anything to scoff at, so the only halfway decent explanation for her temporary foray into insanity had to be that Colin was still holding her hand.

She tugged her hand from his and tucked her fingers beneath her thigh for good measure, shoring up her—newly—tenuous self-control. All the while dutifully ignoring how her body had gone bloodless, half of it gathering in her cheeks, the rest rushing *down*. "You were saying?"

"I was going to ask if you're the only one allowed to ask questions," Colin said, looking so much calmer, cooler, more collected than she felt. Like her touch hadn't just woken something within him the same way his had her.

Maybe Lulu was right. Maybe Truly needed to get laid.

Skin-starved was a thing, wasn't it? Maybe that was it, maybe she was just skin-starved. *That* made infinitely more sense than Colin's skin, in particular, being a drug. It had nothing to do with him at all. Skin was skin was skin and Colin just happened to be the one who had touched her. Wrong time, wrong place, wrong person.

The thought was a cold comfort when it felt like she had an auxiliary heartbeat between her thighs. "Was there, um, something you wanted to ask me?"

"How long were you and your ex together?"

An ill-timed inhale had her sputtering, coughing. "*That's* what you want to know?"

"Turnabout's fair play," he said. "If I have flaws, surely you do, too."

She was really starting to regret explaining her thought process. "Six years."

His brows rose. "That's a long time."

Long enough that she'd convinced herself Justin was *the one.* Amazing how easy it was to lie to yourself when you desperately wanted something.

"I guess it is. Next question?"

"Assuming I have one?" He volleyed her own words back at her, serving them to her with a knowing smile.

"Ha, ha." She jostled him lightly, careful to keep her hands to herself this time. "Just ask."

"Okay, fine. Where'd you grow up?"

"Shut up." She laughed.

"I'm serious! Unlike you, I actually want to know the answer to that question."

"*Ouch.* And you call me brutal?" She held a hand to her chest in mock affront. Beneath her palm, her heart rabbited. "I was curious, too."

Colin arched a single brow, calling *bullshit* without opening his mouth.

"I was! I was just, you know, more curious about other stuff." Her ears burned. For some bizarre reason, copping to curiosity felt different than being curious. Like it was one thing to push and prod and press Colin, to put him on the spot, a horse of a totally different color to admit that she'd spent time thinking about him, enough to want to puzzle him out.

"If you don't answer the question, you're going to make me think you're hiding something. Witness protection? Nah, that doesn't feel right. I bet you're on the lam."

"The lam?" She snorted. "What are you, a 1920s mobster? Who says that—*the lam*?"

What a dork.

He shut one eye and pursed his lips. "I've got your number, St. James. Bet you're wanted in, like, twenty states."

"Wanted for what?"

She dared him to say something disgustingly corny like *being criminally sexy* or *arrestingly beautiful*. *Stealing hearts* or *having killer wit*.

"Given what I know about you?" Colin's eyes raked over her, appraising in a way that made her squirm inside. "Killing a man, obviously."

"You realize blue balls aren't lethal, don't you?"

The look he gave her was gratifying, narrowed eyes glinting in the glow of the ring light his sister had left on, lips thinned like he was struggling not to laugh. "You're not at all what I expected, St. James."

If anything was criminal, it was the way he said her name, emphasis on *saint*. Teasing her with her own name, a name she'd chosen, a name that sounded sacrilegious rolling off his tongue. The way he made her feel with a single look?

Truly was no saint.

She disguised her shiver with a long sip of iced coffee. "You're . . . maybe not what I expected, either, Colin McCrory."

"Oh yeah?" He grinned. "Realizing I'm not so bad after all, huh?"

"No," she deadpanned. "You're worse."

His tongue clicked against the back of his teeth. "Just when we were starting to get along. So?"

"So, what?"

"Where are you from?"

Oh, right. "I grew up in Laurelhurst."

"And I already know your parents are still together."

Her heart shrunk and sank inside her chest.

"Um, no. They're separated, actually." She stabbed at the ice in her cup, sending milky coffee splattering against the lid. "It's—it's new."

Air hissed between his teeth, his grimace sharp. "I'm sorry. That's . . . damn."

"Yeah. *Damn.*" An awkward laugh escaped her. "But you see couples separate all the time, so I'm sure it's nothing new for you."

He could stop looking at her like that, eyes gentle like he could tell how—how hopeless she felt. How heartbroken.

"How are you coping? Do you have someone to talk to? What about your friend? The, uh, scary one?"

"Who? Lulu?" She laughed. "Don't let her hear you call her that. Her ego doesn't need inflating."

"Neither does my dick, for the record."

That was the wrong moment to take a drink, iced coffee burning in the inside of her nose. Colin pressed a wad of tissues into her hand, and she blotted her face. "That's nice?"

"I meant because Lulu tried to sell me a penis pump the other day and I said I wasn't in the market for one, not because I already have one, but because I'm not in need of, you know"—Colin cleared his throat—"help with the, uh, inflating? Engorgement?" He made a vague downward gesture. "Not that there's any shame in needing assistance! But I don't. And I'm going to stop talking right now. In three, two . . ."

Colin mimed zipping his lips.

She hid her smile behind her napkin. "Good to know all your systems are a go, McCrory."

He groaned. "Can we please forget I said that?"

"And hamper my joy?" She tutted. "You're delusional."

"So glad you find my humiliation amusing."

"I really, truly do," she said. "But don't worry. We can keep this strictly confidential. Just between you and me."

"Oh good. For a second there I was worried you'd immortalize my shame in the pages of one of your books."

"Hey now. I would at least change your name first. Protect the innocent and all that."

Colin swayed to the side, his shoulder knocking into hers. "What if I'm not so innocent? You ever think about that?"

Another thrill shot through her, making her swallow hard and grip her knees, her whole body buzzing, and not from the caffeine. Did she think about that? More often than she was willing to admit on pain of death. "I'll definitely use your real name, then."

His smile softened. "Seriously—do you want to talk about it?"

"I'm sure your penis is nice, Colin, but I don't know if we need to discuss it."

"Your parents." He laughed. "I'm talking about your parents."

"I doubt I can afford your hourly rate, whatever it is."

"Come on. I'll give you the friends and family discount."

"Oh, so we're friends now, are we?"

"Considering we were just talking about my dick, I hope so."

"You don't really want to hear about my parents."

"I asked, didn't I?" He nudged her with his arm. "Come on. I'm a great listener and not to brag, but *the* Truly St. James said she was impressed by me."

She snorted. "The bar was on the floor, trust me."

He clutched his chest dramatically and she laughed.

As loath as she was to admit it, as a divorce lawyer, Colin did have experience she didn't. With as many failed marriages as he undoubtedly had encountered in his career, maybe he could provide an alternative perspective. Help her see the forest for the trees.

"Okay, this is going to sound corny, but my parents have always been able to look at each other across a crowded room and have a whole conversation with just their eyes. No words. A single glance. While all my friends were dreaming of Prince Charming or whoever, I was dreaming of someone who would look at me the way my dad looked at my mom. Someone who would love me the way he loved her. I don't know how you go from him buying her sunflowers every week and her secretly taking cooking classes so she could make this obscure soup his great-grandmother made him when he was little to them telling me that maybe they've grown apart. Maybe they don't belong together anymore. It doesn't make sense. There should've been signs, right? People don't decide to separate without there being signs."

"Is it possible you only saw what they wanted you to see?"

She frowned. "Are you suggesting their marriage wasn't as perfect behind closed doors?"

"A lot of parents hide the truth from their children, even their grown children, because they believe they're protecting them. I'm not saying that's what's happening, but . . ." He rapped his knuckles against his knee and winced. "Do you think it's possible you only saw what *you* wanted to see?"

She hugged her arms around herself. "You think I'm looking at their marriage through rose-colored glasses?"

He smiled softly. "Only you can answer that question, Truly."

"*Wow.*"

His brows rose, his forehead scrunching. "What?"

"That was rather insightful." She pretended to glower. "I kind of hate it."

Colin laughed. "I'll try to be less astute next time."

She smiled and—she was smiling. She was talking about her parents possibly divorcing, and she was smiling.

Just like that, her face fell. "Insightfulness aside, I don't think that's it."

"No?"

"They don't fight. They've *never* fought. And okay, maybe it's possible I've put their relationship on a pedestal, but only because if any relationship deserves to be on one, it's theirs. But I'd notice if they were suddenly at each other's throats."

"Hm."

There he went again. "What does that mean? *Hm?*"

"Maybe that's the problem. Look, I don't know your parents, but communication problems contribute to over twenty percent of divorces. If you consider underlying causes, that number is probably significantly higher. Sure, that can often mean fighting too much, but a lack of communication can be just as lethal to a rela-tionship as poor communication."

She scowled. "I understand the significance of communication." She wasn't *new*. But in what universe was conflict an indicator of relationship success? "Are you seriously telling me you think it's a bad thing my parents don't fight?"

Coming from the guy who claimed to like her better rude, maybe she shouldn't be surprised.

"I'm not suggesting your parents ought to be having scream-ing matches," he said. "But disagreements are natural. Normal. The fact that you've never seen them fight makes me think they're either keeping those arguments behind closed doors or sacrificing communication for the pretense of peace. But peace doesn't mean the absence of conflict. That's not realistic. It's about being able to have those inevitable disagreements without being contemptu-ous or defensive. You're telling me you and your ex—Jake?—never fought?"

At first, no, they hadn't. For the first year, year and a half, she'd have been hard-pressed to name a single meaningful flaw of Jus-tin's, a flaw she couldn't see past or couldn't embrace as a perfect imperfection. His snoring? Charming. His inability to match his socks? Adorable. The fact that he was often late, claiming the need to scribble down a new chord progression? A sign of his creative genius.

Of course, the honeymoon period had ended, just like she'd known it would. His snoring had gotten old, his mismatched socks started to look sloppy, and his constant tardiness led her to buy him an absurdly expensive watch with her first-ever book advance, a watch that gathered dust on his desk because it wasn't *metal* enough. Still, she shrugged off how, on occasion, Justin would party with his friends all night and be so hungover the next day that he'd cancel a date. Or how he'd still been drunk the morning he met her parents or how he hated going anywhere he couldn't wear jeans and that he always bitched about how expensive going to the movies was and why couldn't they just torrent something at home?

Choking down the little things didn't make them go away; the problems snowballed, and her frustration mounted, ire leeching out in eye rolls and snark and passive-aggressive quips, pretending to be asleep when Justin would stumble home at three in the morning because she didn't want him touching her when he was wasted and reeking of bottom-shelf tequila and cheap perfume, but she didn't want to argue, either. Especially when he wouldn't remember in the morning, when she'd be the only one weighed down by the aftermath of a fight.

Because when they did fight? Those fights never led to any sense of harmony let alone to resolution. Change. Growth. They only left her feeling like a failure because happy couples? Happy couples didn't fight. Her parents didn't.

"His name's Justin," she said. "And we're hardly a great example. Clearly."

Colin held up his hands. "Fair enough."

Fair enough wasn't good enough. He couldn't just make her question what she thought to be true and leave it at *fair enough*.

"What would you say?" she asked. "If my mom or dad walked into your office? Or any other couple who was . . . considering their options."

Colin pressed his shoulders back against the couch and sighed. "By the time most people are ready to seek legal representation, their marriages have been effectively over for months, if not years. But sometimes that's not true. You're right. Sometimes people do just want to understand their options. They don't always know who else to talk to. Which is why I always ask my clients if they've gone through any marital counseling. If they think there's a chance of reconciliation. Because if there is, even a small one, I always encourage them to consider."

"Couple's counseling, huh? You actually recommend that to your clients? Doesn't sound like a great business model to me."

Colin laughed. "If I was in it strictly for the money, I'd have gone into corporate law."

"Because divorce law is *so* altruistic."

"*Family* law. And I never claimed to be a saint. The divorce cases I handle are my least favorite, but they're what allow me to take on pro bono adoption and child custody cases while still paying my rent."

Pro bono adoption cases? Well, she'd be damned. Maybe this man *was* a saint.

"Look, I appreciate the insight. Really, I do. It's good advice. But I already suggested they talk to someone. And they shot me down." Technically, she'd implied they should speak to a sex therapist, but she had a feeling they wouldn't be keen on going to the regular sort, either. "I'm just frustrated. They belong together. I know it. I only wish I could make them see it." Remember it. "If I thought I could lock them in a room together until they worked things out, and get away with it? I probably would."

Colin laughed. "Bet you wish you were the one with the twin right about now."

"I—what?" She didn't follow.

"You know, *The Parent Trap*? Lindsay Lohan? Twins separated at birth who meet at summer camp and switch places?"

"I'm familiar with Nancy Meyers's oeuvre. I just don't know what it has to do with me or my parents."

"You know! They, uh . . ." He snapped his fingers twice before shooting finger guns at her. "They re-create the night their parents met on the boat to rekindle the"—he razzle-dazzled his fingers, putting Sparky Polastri's spirit fingers to shame—"spark and later, they refuse to reveal who's who until the whole family goes on a camping trip and—I sound crazy." Colin palmed his face and laughed. "Sorry, it's just, you were talking about locking your parents in a room together and my brain jumped to *The Parent Trap*."

"Better that than *Gerald's Game*, I guess."

He laughed, a rich, deep sound that did *not* make her shiver. "Yeah, I'm going to have to advise that you *don't* handcuff your parents together. That would be crazy."

"No crazier than having some secret identical twin from whom I'd been separated at birth." She sighed. "And seeing as I don't have one of those—"

"That you know of."

"Cute."

He grinned. "I try."

Colin McCrory didn't have to *try* to be cute. He just was. And he knew it. Which should've lessened the effect his smile had on her and *yet*.

"I can't exactly Parent Trap my parents by myself. I mean, that would be insane."

Colin laughed, dark eyes crinkling and the smile lines along the sides of his mouth deepening and don't even get her started on his dimples. "Pretty wild. Assuming you could even pull it off."

"Right?" Her voice cracked. Stupid, pretty dimples. Stupid,

pretty eyes. Stupid, pretty *everything*. You'd think she'd never kissed a pretty boy, let alone gotten railed by one. "*So* wild."

Except . . .

What if she *could* pull off her very own Parent Trap?

Would it really be that difficult to convince Mom and Dad—separately, obviously—to be in the same place, at the same time?

If anyone was in the position to do it, Truly was.

She'd have to get them somewhere remote. But not *too* remote. She was shooting for Nancy Meyers, not Stephen King. Somewhere Mom and Dad would have no choice but to talk. Somewhere they'd be reminded of what Truly already knew to be unequivocally true—that they belonged together.

Dennis Quaid and Natasha Richardson had a boat, the *Queen Elizabeth II*, and her parents had—

The lake house.

Six hundred magical square feet located directly on Lake Chelan. Two bedrooms, one teeny-tiny bath, and the ittiest-bittiest still glamorous kitchen that Nancy Meyers would've drooled over. Landlocked, lake-life paradise.

Truly was a freaking genius.

From the time she was two until she was twenty, she'd spent a month each summer in Chelan with her parents. Then she'd started seeing Justin and summers that had once meant sunburns and marshmallows roasted over a fire, watching her parents always touch, shameless in their inability to keep their hands off each other, became days spent drafting in the back of a van that smelled like BO and nights spent sleeping in grody motels in Puerto Vallarta, Panama City, Pensacola, Daytona Beach. Anywhere Justin's band could plug an amp in and play for wasted college kids because he had gas money from his daddy and a *dream*.

A dream Truly had supported body, mind, soul, heart, and wallet because that gas money? Only went so far when it was spent on drinks instead of actual gas.

Just the thought of a summer spent in Chelan sent a pang of longing through her. If she missed the lake house, there was no way Mom and Dad didn't. Right?

How hard could it be to convince them to spend a little time with their only child?

She'd have to spin it just so. Ask Mom to spend two or three weeks tasting her way with Truly through north-central Washington's wine country. Guilt Dad into the father-daughter vacation he'd owed her since the time he got food poisoning the week he was supposed to chaperone her senior trip to DC. Tell them both, separately, that she needed a little time outside the city to get over Justin. That the fresh lake air was just what she needed to power through her deadline.

Maybe it was underhanded, but Truly cared. Cared so much she didn't give much of a damn about right or wrong as long as it worked. All's well that ends well. Her parents might be giving up on their marriage, but Truly?

She'd be damned if she did the same.

Chapter Seven

B abe, I love you, but this is quite possibly the dumbest idea you've ever had."

Truly snatched her pint glass from Lulu with a glare, accidentally sloshing beer on the table. This whole bar was grody—floors sticky with God knew what, band posters stapled on top of each other an inch thick off the wall, graffiti covering the bathroom stalls, layers of lipstick kisses on the mirror, cigarette smoke drifting inside from the alley. Some spilled beer would go unnoticed.

"What's so dumb about wanting my parents to be happy?" she shouted over the noise. *Music* was too generous to call whatever was happening on the stage, but that's what they got for going out for drinks on a Monday. Subpar, shitty bands. But sitters were cheaper on weekdays than weekends so Truly couldn't really complain.

Lulu frowned and pointed at her ear. *"What?"*

Mercifully, the guitarist's earsplitting riff ended, and the music stopped, the song over. Truly could hear herself think again. "I *said*, what's so dumb about wanting my parents to be happy?"

Dad had been an easy sell. Not only did he have plenty of PTO saved, the Lake Chelan Concert Hall was hosting a one-night-only production of *Repo! The Genetic Opera*, one of Dad's all-time favorites. All Truly had had to do was look at him with big eyes and a slightly jutted lower lip over FaceTime, ask if he'd be interested in spending a little quality father-daughter time in Chelan, and he'd readily agreed.

Mom had been slightly harder to convince, claiming to be extraordinarily busy with the fund-raiser the horticulture society was planning, but as soon as Truly had mentioned that the annual Lake Chelan Arts Festival was coming up and it would be fun to get out of the city, drink a little wine, and hit up the silent auction? Mom had folded like a house of cards.

Stage two of Operation Get Mom and Dad Back Together was a go. In a little over two weeks, they'd all be in Chelan and she'd be one step closer to achieving her goal.

Lulu rolled her eyes. "That's the thing, you don't want your parents to be happy; you want them to be together."

"It's the same thing."

"Is it?"

Truly sipped her beer and tried not to make a face. Next round, she was totally ordering a Dirty Shirley. "Obviously."

"Look, babe, light of my goddamn life, I love you and I know your heart is in the right place, but your brain? Babe, it's all kinds of fucked-up."

Yikes.

"You sure know how to make a girl feel special."

Lulu waved her off. "Oh shut up. We're all a little fucked-up. It's just that your brand of fucked-up is a little more"—she clenched her fingers like she was choking someone—"hands-on."

Her brows rose. "Are you insinuating that I'm some kind of control freak?"

"Hon, you waved goodbye at *controlling* as you passed it *miles* back." Lulu wiped beer foam from her top lip. "I'm not saying it's a bad thing. It's just a thing. You like to call the shots. You can't help it any more than you can help that your eyes are brown."

"You just literally called my brain fucked-up."

"Ugh, I hate it when you pay attention to what I say." Lulu nudged Truly's beer toward her, urging her to drink up. "I'm just saying, there should only be two people in your parents' marriage." She cocked her head. "Unless they're game to add a third. Your dad *is* a stud."

Truly wrinkled her nose. "Gross."

"Objectively, your father's a silver fox."

"*Objectively*, my father has no hair on his head."

Lulu looked at her and they burst out laughing.

"He looks like Stanley Tucci!" Lulu argued. "He fixes a mean Aperol Spritz! It's hot."

"He's my father!"

"I have eyes and a functioning libido." Lulu sniffed. "Your daddy's dead sexy, live with it."

Truly shivered. "I will *pay* you to never call my father *daddy* ever again."

"Get the next round and I'll try to restrain myself. My point stands. I know you love your parents, but it's their relationship. Not yours, theirs. I say this with all the love in my heart, of which for you I have an abundance, but this isn't yours to fix. Quit meddling; that way madness lies."

"All I'm doing is making sure the circumstances are conducive for communication. That's it! The rest is up to them."

Lulu stared, looking unconvinced. "You're literally tricking them into being at the same place at the same time. The same itty-bitty lake house. You called it *forced proximity*. You want to know what I heard when you said that? Captivity."

Beer dribbled out the sides of Truly's mouth. "Lulu!" She scrambled for a napkin and of course there were none. She wiped her chin with her hand. "Way to make it sound like my parents are Ling-Ling and Hsing-Hsing. I'm not a zookeeper."

"Come on. You're engineering the perfect environment for them. A place they can't escape—"

"They each have cars. Freak."

Lulu flipped her off. "Oh, like you haven't considered leaving out a little guest basket for them. Massage oils and flavored lubricants and teas to stimulate their libidos. You're probably going to show up to the cabin early just so you can douse their bedroom with black market pheromones you bought online."

"Your brain is a scary place."

"No worse than yours, you hypocrite."

"Contrary to whatever goes on in your wildest, weirdest fantasies, I have no intention of forcing my parents to do anything they don't want to do." Other than, you know, be in the same place at the same time and talk. "I just want to encourage . . . togetherness. Communication. This isn't about me. I just want them to remember all the reasons they love each other."

"Parent-trapping your parents is a bad idea," Lulu singsonged, reaching for her beer.

"It's brilliant," Truly singsonged right back. "I'm sorry you don't have the vision to see it."

"Oh, I've got vision." Lulu waggled her brows.

"Pervert." Truly giggled. Maybe she'd skip the Dirty Shirley. This second beer was hitting her hard and fast. "If you're going to blame anyone, blame Colin. He's the one who gave me the idea."

Kind of. Technically, she'd come up with it on her own, but Colin was definitely the one who'd planted the seed.

"Whoa, whoa, whoa. Hold the phone. *Colin?*" Lulu leaned her elbows on the sticky table. "The dude you want to hate-fuck?"

"If you mean the guy I'm doing the podcast with, then yes," Truly said primly. "I do not, nor have I ever wanted to, *hate-fuck* anyone."

Lulu burst out laughing.

"I don't! I—his advice isn't half bad, all right?" She squirmed atop her barstool. "Maybe he's not entirely awful, either. He's actually kind of clever. Funny."

"Oh, you *so* want to sit on his face." Lulu grinned. "I fucking knew it. Slut."

"*Lulu!*"

"I say that with all the love in my heart. Reclaim the word, hon. Seize that bull by the balls."

Truly balked. "Horns. It's seize the bull by the horns."

Lulu smirked. "Isn't that what I said?"

Truly brought the glass to her lips and chugged. She was not *nearly* inebriated enough for this. "You're ridiculous."

"What's ridiculous is the chemistry you two had." Lulu fanned herself. "If I could bottle that shit up and sell it, I'd make millions. *Millions.*"

"It's not like that. Colin and I aren't like that."

Lulu rested her chin on her folded hands. "And whose fault is that, hm?"

"No one's. It's—" Her phone buzzed, lighting up with a text from an unknown number. Great. Probably another of those *we've been trying to reach you about your vehicle's extended warranty* spam texts. "Sorry. One sec."

She pried her phone off the sticky tabletop and swiped at the screen.

The fuck?

Her heart stopped.

Dark and slightly blurry, that was clearly a snapshot of someone's Kindle. A Kindle with two of her most recent books downloaded.

Truly flashed Lulu the screen. "That's weird, right?"

Her number wasn't public. It wasn't on her website. Her publicist had it, yeah, but Mel wouldn't give it out all willy-nilly.

Lulu frowned. "Local number?"

206. "Yup."

Lulu looked over her left shoulder, then her right. Like anyone in this dive had their fucking Kindle out. "Ask 'em what they want."

Truly rolled her eyes fondly.

> **TRULY (10:15 P.M.):** Who is this?

There, direct and to the point.

"I asked who they were."

Lulu scoffed. "They could lie."

Now who was being ridiculous?

Her phone buzzed with a reply.

> **UNKNOWN NUMBER (10:16 P.M.):** Colin.

> **UNKNOWN NUMBER (10:16 P.M.):** McCrory. In case you happen to know another Colin.

UNKNOWN NUMBER (10:16 P.M.): Plausible, considering it was in the top 200 names from 1982 to 2016.

Truly smiled.
Colin freaking McCrory.

TRULY (10:17 P.M.): Did you Google that?

COLIN (10:18 P.M.): Would you judge me more if I said yes, or no, that I just had that fact in my back pocket?

TRULY (10:18 P.M.): Don't worry. I'm going to judge you either way.

"What has you grinning like that?"

She dropped her phone, caught red-handed. "Um, nothing?"

Lulu glared. "Bullshit. Fess up. Did your mystery texter send you a dick pic? Is it good? Share with the class."

"No! It's nothing like that." Fessing up to this felt worse. "It's, um. It's just Colin."

Lulu grinned. *"Just Colin.* Speak of the devil, huh?" She froze. "Holy shit. He's reading your books? *Truly."*

"Kind of weird, right?"

He didn't need insight into the inner machinations of her mind, and that's exactly what her books would give him.

"Kind of hot, I think you mean," Lulu said.

Her phone buzzed and damn it if her heart didn't lurch. "Hold on."

COLIN (10:19 P.M.): Rude.

Her face went instantly hot.

TRULY (10:20 P.M.): I thought you liked me rude. Or was that just sweet talk?

Her phone buzzed almost immediately.

COLIN (10:20 P.M.): You think I'm sweet?

She took a greedy gulp of room-temp lager. Nothing she'd tried so far had gotten rid of the butterflies fluttering in her stomach. Might as well try drowning them.

"How'd he get your number, anyway? Did you give it to him? Truly, have you been holding out on me?"

"*No*, you nosy freak. I don't know how he got my number." Lulu kicked her under the table. "Well, *ask*."

TRULY (10:21 P.M.): How'd you even get my number?

COLIN (10:22 P.M.): My sister.

Of course.

COLIN (10:22 P.M.): Don't blame her. I asked her for it.

COLIN (10:23 P.M.): She told me not to be weird. Whatever that means.

Lulu snatched the phone from her.

"Hey! Boundaries, much?"

"You were literally in the delivery room when I had Mai. You have seen my vagina at its absolute worst. We have no boundaries." Lulu swiped at the screen. "Damn. Please, for me, tell him he's been a very good boy and put him out of his misery?"

She buried her head in her hands and groaned. *"Lulu."*

Lulu kicked her under the table. "The guy's gagging for it. He's humping your leg. Virtually. *Textually.* Throw him a bone, I beg you. Do it for me. Pretty please with a cherry on—"

"Fine. I'll throw him a bone."

> **TRULY (10:26 P.M.):** If you wanted to impress me, you should've started with my backlist, McCrory.

She showed Lulu the screen. "How's that?"

"Damn." Lulu whistled. "Making him work for it. You're a sadist, St. James."

A sadist? Oh, as if. "I am not."

"Tell me you're not deriving pleasure from making this boy jump through hoops for you and then get back to me."

No one was making anyone jump through any hoops. "I don't—"

"So help me God if the next words out of your mouth are *I don't want him.*"

Truly shut her mouth and stared at the sticky table. Someone had gouged a set of initials into the wood inside an ugly lopsided heart, which she traced with a finger.

For the first time in years, Truly didn't have a clue what she wanted.

It had always been simple.

Work hard doing something she loved, meet someone, fall madly in love, get married. Have a home, a life, as full of love and laughter as her parents had.

Everything she'd ever wanted had hinged on her belief in happily ever afters, but now she had doubts she'd never had before. She wanted to believe, did she ever, but . . .

She just didn't know anymore.

"I just got out of a six-year relationship, Lulu."

"*Exactly*. You just got out of a six-year relationship with a man-child you gave a lot of yourself to and got next to nothing from in return. You deserve to be happy."

Truly shifted uneasily on her barstool. "I don't even—he's not—okay, Colin's . . . nice to look at."

Fun to—to tease. Flirt with. She hadn't flirted with anyone in too long and it was novel. That was it. It was new. Of course she was enjoying it. It didn't mean anything.

Lulu looked thoughtful. "Not my usual type, a little too pretty, but he does have a very sittable-looking face and a slutty little waist working in his favor."

"Be serious, please."

Lulu rested a warm hand atop hers. "I love you, Truly, I do, but that's your problem. You're so serious these days and I could strangle Justin because I know he's the reason. Because you always had to be the responsible one. I don't know when it happened, but somewhere along the line he stopped treating you like a partner, and he expected you to—to practically be his mother."

Truly wrinkled her nose. "That's not—"

"It's true and you know it. And I know you did it because you loved"—it must've taken a lot for Lulu to say the word, her nose wrinkling and lips pursing distastefully—"Justin and because you have a big heart and you wanted so badly to see the best in him. You wanted to believe he could be better, but you? You deserve so much more than six years wasted waiting on a pumpkin to turn into Prince Charming."

Truly sniffled into the dregs of her beer. "You're the best. Really you are, but I—I'm kind of a mess right now, if you hadn't noticed. I'm far from being in the right headspace for a relationship."

Even if she was ready for one? A divorce—sorry, family lawyer and a romance author? Everyone knew that, like enemies to lovers and secret babies, opposites attract only worked well in fiction.

Lulu scoffed. "He's cute, but Christ, who said anything about a relationship?"

Truly frowned.

"Sweetheart, I'm not suggesting you marry the guy. I'm suggesting you go get your back blown out by the dude who's currently sitting at home reading books you wrote and texting you after asking his sister for your phone number."

Truly pressed a condensation-covered hand against her burning cheek.

After she and her high school boyfriend had amicably broken up after graduation, she'd gone on a string of disastrous dates with guys who'd made it clear they were more interested in getting in her pants than remembering her name. She'd put herself out there, gone to parties, joined a few of the supposedly less sleazy dating apps, and just when she was ready to call it quits and take a break from the dating scene? She'd locked eyes with Justin across the campus quad and the rest, as they said, was history.

Truly hardly thought her heart was located inside her vagina, but she'd never had a one-night stand, a fling. She didn't know if she was built for casual, let alone whether that was what she wanted.

"I don't even know if Colin's single. I don't even know if he likes women. Even if he does, that doesn't mean he likes me. The point could be entirely moot."

"Don't be dumb." Lulu drained her beer, stood, and pointed at Truly. "I'm going to hit the head. While I'm gone? You, missy, are going to ask that boy if he's single, you hear me?"

No. No way. She shook her head. "I am not doing that."

"Come on." Lulu rolled her eyes. "At least check his Instagram for clues."

"Clues? What kind of—"

"You're smart. Figure it out."

"Lu, I can't just—"

Lulu threw up deuces as she disappeared down the hall.

Truly sighed and slumped against the sticky table.

Screw Lulu.

She was *not* going to open Instagram, and she definitely was *not* going to search for Colin.

Truly glanced at her phone. She *wasn't*.

What were the chances of him being on IG, let alone his profile even being public?

Truly picked up her phone and set it right back down.

The chances didn't matter because she wasn't going to look because she didn't care. She *didn't*.

Her thumb hovered over the IG icon on her home screen, but she wasn't going to do it. She *wasn't*. She was just going to scroll her feed, maybe watch a few stories, and—

Search: Colin Mc—

He was the number one search result. Algorithms were terrifying and Truly? Truly was weak.

She didn't know what she was looking for. The same person cropping up in multiple photos? Heart emojis in a caption? Colin looking at them all gooey-eyed? His hand a little too low on their waist to be friendly?

Caitlin made several appearances in his feed, and so did a guy with piercing green eyes and a birthmark over his left eye who was almost as pretty as Colin. His handle was @cillianmccrory so she was willing to bet they were related. Hence, *pretty*.

Otherwise, it was all awkwardly framed selfies and group shots with girls seated atop Colin's lap. Gorgeous girls. Lots and lots of gorgeous girls with their hands in his hair or their lips pressed to his cheek, and it was never the same girl, either. Which didn't rule out the possibility that he was seeing someone, but it didn't confirm it, either.

Seven weeks back and Truly had learned nothing.

. . . other than the fact that Colin looked ridiculously hot in a three-piece suit. Big surprise there.

She clicked on the photo, a group shot taken at some fancy shindig. A wedding, maybe. Even though all the guys in the photo were dressed similarly, her eye was drawn to Colin, left of center. His smile was just a little brighter; he was just a little bit *more*.

She scrolled to read the caption.

It was an honor to be named the recipient of the Emerald City Family Defense Fund's Volunteer of the Year Award at last night's Santa Claus for a Cause Toy Drive and Auction benefiting children and families in King County.

Unreal.

Against her better judgment, she scrolled to the next picture on Colin's profile and—

Hello, sailor. That was a lot of skin on display.

His pale blue swim trunks revealed more of him than she'd had the pleasure of seeing before.

And what a pleasure it was.

Dark hair trailed down from Colin's belly button—an innie—and disappeared down into those swim trunks that looked about a size too small, as if he'd borrowed them from someone else. His thighs, paler than his calves by a shade, were on full display, sprinkled with downy brown hair, flattened against his dripping wet skin and—

Truly choked on air.

She didn't have to guess anymore. The rest of Colin was just as mole-splattered as his face, his neck. There were two beauty marks resting just above each collarbone. Like a matched set. Truly wanted to draw a line between them. With her tongue. Fuck, she wanted to wrap her hand around his throat, *gentle*, and measure the distance between those two spots with her thumb and pointer finger.

Oh, she was so screwed.

She needed to talk to Lulu, stat.

Truly squinted down the hall. A line had formed outside the bathroom and considering how long it was? Chances were, Lulu was caught up in it.

Screw waiting. She took a screenshot and sent it to Lulu, needing to get this off her chest.

> **TRULY (11:04 P.M.):** He's so pretty it pisses me off.

She hit *send* and slumped against the wall. Save for the push-pin digging into her shoulder blade, she felt so much better. Lighter.

Her phone buzzed and she took her time reaching for it.

> **COLIN (11:10 P.M.):** I don't think you meant to send this to me?

Her brain snagged like it was caught on blackberry brambles.
Didn't mean to send *what* to him?
She scrolled back through their messages and—
Oh shit.
Her stomach went into free fall.
Fuck.
Oh fuck.
No.
No, no, no.
She didn't. She couldn't have.
Oh God. She had.
The proof was right there, staring her dead in the face.
Instead of texting Lulu, she'd sent her screenshot and incriminating message to Colin. Because *he* was her most recent contact. Because she was just tipsy enough to do something as careless as press *send* before double-checking who she was texting. What a rookie move.

Her hands shook as she typed.

> **TRULY (11:13 P.M.):** please forget i sent that

Shame curdled in her gut like spoiled milk as those dumb little dots danced across her screen, proof that Colin had seen her text and was typing back.

COLIN (11:15 P.M.): If that's what you want?

What did he mean, if that's what she wanted? It was mortifying. Of course she wanted him to forget. She wished *she* could forget. Wished she could wipe this whole encounter from her mind, *Men in Black*–style.

TRULY (11:18 P.M.): i'm out with lulu and i'm a little drunk right now srry!!

If she made sure to add in a typo so she'd seem drunker than she was? That was for her to know and Colin McCrory to never, ever find out.

COLIN (11:20 P.M.): Ah. Haha. Okay.

Haha? She whimpered softly into the palm of her hand. Kill her now.

COLIN (11:21 P.M.): Have fun and uh, drink water?

COLIN (11:21 P.M.): Good night, Truly.

She was contemplating hurling herself off the roof of the bar when Lulu threw herself into her seat with a beatific smile that waned as soon as she actually looked at Truly. "What'd I miss?"

Chapter Eight

Truly was handling last night's epic gaffe remarkably well.

If, by *remarkably well*, you considered putting your phone on "do not disturb" and hiding under the covers of your bed until noon, which she did.

Avoidance was a completely natural coping mechanism no matter your age, thank you very much. But she couldn't avoid her phone forever. She had a call scheduled with her agent at two and she needed her phone for that.

With one eye shut and her teeth sunk borderline-painfully into her bottom lip, she flipped her phone off "do not disturb" and watched with bated breath as her emails and texts flooded in.

Colin's name crossed her screen and her heart stopped.

COLIN (8:15 A.M.): <link>

A link. That was it. No context, nothing. Not even a preview because it was hit or miss if those even showed up.

She clicked it and held her breath, waiting for . . . she didn't know. An article to wikiHow's *How to Take a Hint: He's Just Not That Into You*? Stupid, stupid, stupid. Truly was never going out drinking with Lulu again. She was a bad influence, the worst, most meddlesome—

The page loaded and Truly frowned.

It was an article on hangover cures. Specifically, *15 Wacky & Wonderful Hangover Cures from Around the World.*

She scrolled and—tried not to gag.

Pickle juice she could get behind. Hair of the dog? Probably not a smart choice, but a fair one. Raw eggs? No thanks, though if it worked for Rocky, it had to have some merit, right? But some of the items on this list? Sparrow droppings in brandy? Deep-fried canary?

> **TRULY (12:18 P.M.):** Pizzle? You're cracked, McCrory.

She wasn't expecting a near instantaneous text back but—

> **COLIN (12:20 P.M.):** Centuries of Italians swear on bull penis, Truly. Don't knock it 'til you try it.

Centuries of Italians, her ass.

> **TRULY (12:21 P.M.):** My nonna is rolling in her grave. I'm not a pit bull. I don't need a bully stick.

> **COLIN (12:22 P.M.):** Your bark suggests otherwise.

She scoffed into the silence of her apartment, her heartbeat obnoxiously loud inside her head. Asshole. She smiled as she typed.

TRULY (12:23 P.M.): You're a real piece of work, you know that?

COLIN (12:25 P.M.): You happen to look in a mirror lately, sweetheart?

Her insides fluttered. Stupid, traitorous body just had to go and have the most obnoxious reactions where Colin was concerned.

TRULY (12:27 P.M.): Jerk.

Admittedly, not her best comeback. But—

COLIN (12:27 P.M.): Jerk? Really? Is that the best you got?

TRULY (12:28 P.M.): You can't handle my best.

COLIN (12:30 P.M.): I think you'd be surprised what I can handle.

Her breath vanished and heat filled her chest.

She was playing with fire, flirting with Colin when she didn't know what she wanted. Except she knew one thing she *didn't* want, and it was to stop.

Words were her *thing*, and Colin gave as good as he got. She hadn't felt this keyed up just from talking to someone in . . . that she even had to think about it was tragic.

TRULY (12:33 P.M.): Famous last words.

COLIN (12:35 P.M.): Sounds a little like you don't believe me.

TRULY (12:36 P.M.): Why should I?

COLIN (12:42 P.M.): Because I'm a man of my word.

COLIN (12:42 P.M.): And I know what I want.

Her heart hurled itself against the wall of her chest as she read his text two, three, four times, starting to suspect she was the one who'd bitten off more than she could chew.

What was she supposed to say? *Duly noted? Good to know?*

The obvious answer would be to ask him what it was he wanted, but she couldn't just come out and do that. If she asked Colin what he wanted, she'd need to dig deep and figure out what the hell it was *she* wanted and she wasn't ready for that. She didn't know if she'd ever be ready.

She didn't want to stop, but this? Whatever it was they were doing was safe. No need to ruin a good thing by taking it any further.

TRULY (12:48 P.M.): Sorry again for anything offensive I might have said last night. I don't usually cut loose like that.

She wasn't a coward. She *wasn't*. She was just . . . exercising self-preservation. Being responsible and—and mature.

Fifteen excruciating minutes passed without a reply. Fifteen excruciating minutes during which Truly worried her thumbnail down to the quick while waiting for her ancient-ass coffeepot to sputter out twelve ounces of sludge.

Her phone dinged and she leaped across the kitchen, scrambling to snatch it off the counter.

> **COLIN (1:03 P.M.):** I wasn't offended.

> **COLIN (1:04 P.M.):** For what it's worth, maybe you should cut loose more often.

Oh sure, because tipsy Truly was a riot.

> **TRULY (1:06 P.M.):** Just do me a favor and don't let it go to your head, McCrory.

A half an hour later, just as she was about to hop on a call with her agent, Colin finally responded.

> **COLIN (1:41 P.M.):** Wouldn't dream of it, St. James.

FOR SOME REASON, he kept texting her.

Wednesday it was a recipe for cow cod soup, which, lo and behold, contained, to her immense disgust, bull pizzle.

> **COLIN (11:31 A.M.):** Cow cod and bananas and Scotch bonnet peppers cooked in

a white rum sauce. Apparently, it's a rural delicacy in Jamaica. Who knew?

TRULY (11:34 A.M.): Good for them! I'll pass. 😔

COLIN (11:37 A.M.): Pizzle is low in cholesterol and high in protein, calcium, and magnesium. It's thought to boost stamina.

Why that brought a fond smile to her face would forever remain a mystery.

TRULY (11:38 A.M.): Are you seriously looking up facts on pizzle during your lunch break?

COLIN (11:40 A.M.): No, I'm texting you during my lunch break. I looked those up during a particularly lengthy call with a client that should've been an email.

TRULY (11:41 A.M.): Shame on you, McCrory. Not giving your clients your full, undivided attention? Tsk.

COLIN (11:42 A.M.): I'm great at multitasking.

COLIN (11:43 A.M.): Apparently cow cod soup is thought to be an aphrodisiac.

TRULY (11:45 A.M.): hahahahah no.

TRULY (11:46 A.M.): Also, your pickup lines need work.

COLIN (11:49 A.M.): Not a pickup line. If I was using a pickup line on you, you'd know it.

COLIN (11:50 A.M.): But also, noted.

Thursday morning it was a picture of an extra-large to-go cup of coffee, a rain-soaked sidewalk out of focus in the background. No actual text message, just Colin's big hand wrapped around the cup, fingers long, and his knuckles thick.

Truly zoomed in on the side of the cup and laughed—caramel macchiato with an extra pump of vanilla syrup, two pumps dark caramel sauce, and mocha drizzle. And he'd given Caitlin grief for her coffee order.

TRULY (9:27 A.M.): Looks like someone has a secret sweet tooth.

COLIN (9:35 A.M.): It's your fault.

Her brows rose. She couldn't wait to hear how he was going to spin this.

COLIN (9:36 A.M.): I was up until two finishing your book.

COLIN (9:37 A.M.): Never really understood what all the fuss was when people talked about having a book hangover.

COLIN (9:37 A.M.): Now I get it. Thanks to you.

COLIN (9:38 A.M.): You're so good at what you do, Truly.

When the *New York Times* called her debut *compulsively readable*, Truly had felt like she'd chugged a bottle of champagne—restlessly giddy and a little sick to her stomach because what if this was *it*? What if this was as good as it gets? What if she couldn't live up to everyone's expectations? What if her next book left something to be desired? What if she was a one-hit wonder? What if this moment right here was the pinnacle of her career? What if everything else was downhill?

Colin's praise was like swallowing the sun. It left her hot all over, flushed not just in the face but from her hairline down to her feet, damp in the creases of her elbows and her knees, uncomfortably sweaty all over. It was too much, but she'd be damned if she didn't want to bask in it, if she wasn't greedy for more.

COLIN (9:39 A.M.): I don't mean to sound surprised. I knew you were talented.

COLIN (9:40 A.M.): But it's something else, I guess, losing sleep over someone's words because they're that fucking talented. Because you just can't get enough.

She wasn't sure how her hands managed to be so steady as she typed when her stomach felt like a washing machine set to spin.

> **TRULY (9:41 A.M.):** Book hangover, hm?

> **TRULY (9:42 A.M.):** Just a thought, but have you considered trying pizzle?

She bit back a smile, staring at her screen, waiting for a reply.

> **COLIN (9:44 A.M.):** Ha freaking ha.

> **COLIN (9:45 A.M.):** Bet you think you're real cute, huh?

How had he put it?

> **TRULY (9:46 A.M.):** You happen to look in a mirror lately, sweetheart?

Never let anyone say Truly couldn't give as good as she got.

> **COLIN (9:49 A.M.):** Well played, St. James. Well played.

Her thumbs felt sloppy as she tapped at her phone's screen.

> **TRULY (9:50 A.M.):** Thank you. I'm glad you liked my book.

A strange way of saying *thank you for liking my weird brain and the stories it birthed*. Because everything she wrote had a teeny-tiny piece of her embedded in it. If Colin liked her books, he had to like her, right?

She snorted. Stupid question. It didn't matter whether he liked her. She didn't *care*.

Colin was just some guy she worked—consulted?—with. It didn't matter that he had thighs she wanted to bite or beauty marks she wanted to play connect-the-dots with using her tongue or that she'd been waiting with bated breath to know whether he liked her books since the moment he'd texted her that picture of his Kindle.

She didn't care.

She *didn't*.

FRIDAY, HE SENT a screenshot of his email inbox showing 122 unread messages along with a string of upside-down emojis. She sent back a screenshot of her word processor's stats window showing her target word count for the day along with several skull emojis. She'd written a measly four hundred words and had two thousand more to go. He replied with—

She fumbled her phone.

Jesus Christ.

It was a selfie.

No.

It was soft-core pornography.

Colin's pale pink button-down stretched tight across his broad shoulders, a triangle of chest hair peeking out from where he'd left the top two buttons undone. His sleeves—*mercy*—were rolled to his elbows, one forearm corded with muscle and dusted with dark hair visible in the shot as he held up a thumb and smiled at the camera, silver wire-rimmed glasses sliding down the bridge of his nose.

COLIN (3:13 P.M.): You've got this.

She wasn't entirely convinced this guy wasn't put on this planet for the sole purpose of driving her insane.

TRULY (3:15 P.M.): I didn't know you wore glasses.

COLIN (3:17 P.M.): I'm just a little far-sighted. I can usually get by without them.

TRULY (3:19 P.M.): You look good.

Wait. No, that wasn't what she wanted to—
The message went from *sending* to *sent*. Shit.

TRULY (3:19 P.M.): I mean, you look good wearing them.

TRULY (3:20 P.M.): They look good, is all I'm saying. They suit your face.

She set her phone down before she could dig the hole any further.

COLIN (3:22 P.M.): Careful. Don't hurt yourself.

Oh, sure. Make fun of her.

TRULY (3:23 P.M.): Don't be a dick about it.

COLIN (3:24 P.M.): Wow. You were right, I guess.

TRULY (3:25 P.M.): About?

COLIN (3:26 P.M.): Me being so pretty it pisses you off.

Blood rushed to her face and her insides twisted unpleasantly.

TRULY (3:28 P.M.): I thought we agreed to forget I sent that.

COLIN (3:29 P.M.): Technically, I never agreed to anything.

Technically, her ass. It was implied.

COLIN (3:30 P.M.): Come on, Truly. It's not a big deal. Nothing to be embarrassed about.

TRULY (3:31 P.M.): Bold of you to assume I'm embarrassed.

She wasn't embarrassed. She was mortified.

COLIN (3:33 P.M.): . . . so, are we going to talk about it?

Talk about it? Really? What was there to say that hadn't already been said? Or heavily implied.

TRULY (3:37 P.M.): There's nothing to talk about.

COLIN (3:45 P.M.): If you say so.

She did say so. She said so emphatically, in fact. With her whole chest, metaphorically speaking.

She typed that out, felt weirdly *doth protest too much* about it, and deleted the whole thing, letting her silence speak.

She thought he was gorgeous, and he knew it, and that was all there was to it.

It didn't have to mean more than that. She didn't know if she wanted it to mean more than that. But she had a feeling she was going to need to figure it out.

Soon.

SATURDAY MORNING PASSED without a text from Colin.

Which was perfectly fine. For the best, even. He was a distraction she didn't need, definitely not when she had four pesky chapters left to write, a list of admin tasks the length of her forearm to knock out, and some planning to do if this trip to Chelan was going to go off without a hitch.

Not that she was going to get any of it done if she kept glancing at her phone every five minutes waiting for a text that might never come because damn it, Colin was a distraction whether he was texting her or not.

Truly pressed the heel of her hand to her forehead, checking for a fever, something, anything that would explain away this preoccupation, the persistent fluttering in her gut. Occam's razor stated that the simplest explanation, the one that made the fewest assumptions, was preferable to those that were more complex, but there was nothing preferable about having a dumb crush.

And God, was it dumb.

So what if she liked Colin's stupidly gorgeous face and wanted to run her fingers through his Pantene-commercial hair and trace a new constellation out of his beauty marks using her tongue and sink her teeth into his big, dumb biceps that no goddamn lawyer had any right to have? So what if he made her laugh and wasn't too proud to say sorry? He was also argumentative and annoying and got a sick thrill from pushing her buttons and he made it hard for her to focus. And that? That was something she could not abide.

Not now, with Mom and Dad's marriage on the brink of collapse and Truly the only person who gave enough of a damn to fix what was wrong.

A shadow fell across her table and her gaze left her screen, flickering to the half inch of watery coffee and melting ice left in her cup, her hand covering the plastic lid protectively, not ready for a bored barista to clear the table and boot her out when she'd accomplished squat despite the change of scenery.

"So this is where the magic happens."

Her head snapped up.

Colin stood beside the table, coffee in his hand. His dark hair was damp from the rain, curling in front of his ears, his thin white tank cut under the arms to nearly his waist, so damp it was practically see-through. All she could think about was that stupid picture she'd screenshotted on his IG. The one of him wearing those obscene swim trunks, rivulets of lake water clinging to his chest.

Her breath caught, voice clogging in her throat.

Inexplicably, Colin's face fell. "Sorry. I didn't mean to bother you, I just wanted to say—"

"No!" She gestured to the chair across from her. "Hi. Sorry, I'm a space cadet. Did you, um—" It would be weird to ask him if he wanted to sit, right? Wait. "Hold on. You live across town. What are you doing here?"

In her coffee shop. The one just two blocks from her apartment.

"Before you ask—because I know you're going to—no, I'm not stalking you." Until now, she didn't know it was possible for an eye roll to look fond. "I was in the area."

Truly leaned back in her chair and crossed her arms. Did she honestly believe he was stalking her? No. Could she help but give him a little grief? Also no. "In the area, hm? You don't say."

Colin tipped his head back, mouthing a silent prayer up at the ceiling. For patience, probably. If she happened to get a thrill at the way the move bared his throat, putting his Adam's apple and his moles on display? That was between her and God. "I coach Little League, okay? We've been dealing with some scheduling issues at our usual park, and uh, Kinnear doesn't have a diamond but it's big enough so . . ." Rambling had never been so infuriatingly adorable. "Anyway, I was in the neighborhood."

"Because you coach Little League." Jesus. "Do you rescue kittens from trees in your downtime, too?"

A smile ghosted across his face, the corners of his eyes crinkling and his lips twitching. "Your ability to make any compliment sound like an insult is *truly* a gift, you know that?"

Ha freaking ha. "Maybe I'm just waiting for the skeletons to come tumbling out of your closet. I mean, you take on adoption cases pro bono, you're Mr. Emerald City Family Defense Fund Volunteer of the Year, and now you coach Little League? There's got to be something to balance it all out. Road rage or maybe you've got a secret porn addiction or—"

Colin choked. "A porn addiction? Yeah, *no*."

She clicked her tongue against the back of her teeth and tried not to smile. "It's nothing to be ashamed of, McCrory. We all have our weaknesses."

A sly smile graced his face. "Someone sounds awfully curious about my masturbatory habits."

Her cheeks warmed.

Like she said. They all had their weaknesses.

"It was an example. Don't—" She cleared her throat to disguise the way her voice nearly broke. "Don't read into it."

Colin *hmmed* and leaned in, forearm resting on the back of the chair across from her. "Like I probably shouldn't read into how you somehow knew I was named ECFDF's Volunteer of the Year?"

"Exactly." Wait. "No, that's not—" *Fuck*. She huffed and damn it if Colin didn't smile. Damn it if his smile didn't whip the flock of butterflies inside her stomach into a frenzy. "Why can't you just ignore my blunders like any other perfectly polite person?"

Colin cocked his head, a thoughtful if not feigned frown puckering his brow. "You know what? Maybe that's my flaw. Maybe I'm not perfectly polite. Maybe I like giving you grief. Ever think about that?"

Only nonstop for the last three weeks. "Colin McCrory admitting to having a flaw? Alert the presses."

He snorted. "Truly St. James giving me the Heisman? Must be a day ending in *y*."

"Sorry," she said, reaching for her drink. "I don't speak sportsball."

"Don't play dumb. You know what I mean."

She wrapped her lips around her straw and took a measured sip, heart racing. "I thought we agreed not to talk about that."

"Once again, I'll remind you I never agreed to anything of the sort."

The man was a menace.

"Well?" She looked pointedly between Colin and the chair he was gripping. "Are you planning on standing there all day and giving me grief, or are you going to sit?"

The cutest wrinkle formed along the bridge of Colin's nose. "That was without a doubt the world's *worst* invitation I've ever heard. Award-worthy awful."

"Bold of you to assume it was a request." In a move she'd probably brag about later, Truly managed to hook her ankle around the chair and kick it out. *Ta-da.* "*Sit.*"

Colin hesitated before lowering himself into the seat across from her with a smile. "Don't let me disturb you."

"You aren't. Disturbing me. I've been here an hour and I've written . . ." She peeked at her screen. "Three sentences. And they're not very good sentences at that. So, if I'm disturbed, it's not because of you."

His lips folded in, the corners of his eyes crinkling like he was trying not to laugh.

If I'm disturbed—Jesus. She shut her eyes. "You know what I mean."

Since the moment she met him, it felt like her center of gravity was off-kilter *just* enough that she had to work a little harder to maintain her balance.

"If you're disturbed, I'm free from any and all responsibility. Got it." He lifted a hand to his chest. "It's quite the relief. I was losing sleep wondering if the problem was me."

"Ass," she said, fond.

"Careful." Colin grinned. "That time it almost sounded like a compliment."

"Maybe you're the one who's disturbed if you think *ass* is a compliment."

"Whether I was disturbed was never a question." Colin gestured to her computer. "Three sentences, huh? New book?"

"Interview, actually. For my alma mater."

"Alma mater?" His eyes narrowed. "Hm. Let me guess, UW?"

"Why, did you go to WSU or something?"

He made a face. "God, no. Stanford."

She wrinkled her nose and he laughed.

"You got a problem with that, St. James?"

There he went again, saying her name. *Saint* James.

"Your mascot is a tree, *McCrory*."

Colin scoffed. "Unofficially. Officially, we're the Stanford Cardinal. Not that there's anything wrong with trees. They're, uh, sturdy."

She snorted. "Oh, that's right. A color. So intimidating."

His tongue pressed against the inside of his cheek, lashes lowering as he cut his eyes. "Don't tell me you went to USC."

"No, you had it right the first time. I did go to UW. I just didn't graduate. The interview's for my high school alma mater."

At nineteen, she hadn't a clue what she wanted to major in, let alone what she wanted to do with the rest of her life. Rather than waste a bunch of money on classes trying to figure it out, she'd taken a gap year and worked at the box office at the Emerald City Repertory Theatre to make a little money, a job that gave her plenty of downtime to read.

And that was around the time she'd started writing.

Part of her expected him, successful attorney that he was, to balk at her not having a degree. But leave it to Colin McCrory to defy her expectations. "Shouldn't they have awarded you an honorary degree by now?"

A laugh escaped her. "What?"

"For all those times you hit the *New York Times* bestseller list. I mean, doesn't Taylor Swift have an honorary doctorate from NYU?"

She snorted. "While I'm flattered you just compared me to *the* Taylor Swift"—and weirdly turned on that he even knew that about NYU—"you're delusional. She's *Taylor Swift*."

Colin shrugged. "And you're Truly St. James."

She stopped laughing. Be still her fucking heart.

She cleared her throat. "Well, no. No honorary degrees for me."

"Not yet."

She rolled her eyes, suppressing a smile. Ridiculous.

"So this interview—is it about your books?"

Truly ran her thumbnail along the edge of a peeling sticker on her laptop. "Kind of? The school paper is running a series of alum interviews, so most of the questions are pretty standard, but the Gender and Sexuality Alliance asked if I'd be willing to answer a few more specific questions on bi-erasure and biphobia in media. Those are the questions that are tripping me up."

She wrote queer romance novels. She'd typed the word *bisexual* at least a hundred, two hundred times, but she'd said it out loud a total of fifteen? Twenty times? The number of people she'd come out to in person was even smaller: her parents, Justin, Lulu . . .

She'd been in a serious, monogamous relationship with a guy for the last six years, during which time she'd worked out that her appreciation of women transcended mere admiration and fell firmly into the camp of attraction. That straight girls didn't look at each other and *feel* the things Truly felt. They didn't zone out thinking about how soft another girl's skin was or get a jumpy thrill in their stomach when they shared lip gloss or sipped from the same can of soda because *holy shit it was like their lips had touched*. They didn't eagerly agree to play spin the bottle on the off chance they might land on their best friend the way she had in eighth grade. They didn't drink too much vodka as an excuse to make out with each other the way she had in high school. They *definitely* didn't feel sick to their stomach the next day when everyone laughed it off because *no harm, no foul, guys got off on watching girls do that sort of thing*.

By the time she'd discovered this part of herself, put a name to it, she was two years into dating Justin and being bi was just an ancillary part of who she was. She wasn't about to break up with him just so she could—what? Explore that part of herself? She didn't feel the need to explore something she already felt sure in.

But it made coming out kind of weird. Unnecessary? She was in a serious relationship with a man; did anyone really *need* to know? She didn't have a problem saying it; the words themselves came easy. If she was doing a book event and someone asked—as people often did, curious about what had drawn her to queer fiction—she'd answer. But in her day-to-day life? She could probably count on one hand the number of people she'd come out to.

She'd hardly had any practice, not that practice mattered when each time felt brand-new.

She stole a glance at Colin from beneath her lashes.

He didn't look weirded out, not even confused the way Justin had when she'd told him she was bi. He just looked curious, a wrinkle forming between his brows she'd feel tempted to give him shit about under any circumstance other than this.

"What's tripping you up about it?"

"I guess I don't feel the most . . . qualified," she admitted. "I feel like there's got to be someone out there who'd be better suited to answer these questions than me."

His dark brows slanted low over his eyes. "I'm not sure I follow."

"I mean, I like girls, I like guys, I like *people*. But I've never dated a girl. I've never walked down the street holding another girl's hand before. I was with Justin for two years before I had my big *Aha!* moment." Which was less one moment and more many realizations that had occurred over the course of several months, culminating in her getting wine-drunk with Mom and telling her everything through snotty tears. Because even though her parents were the kindest, most open-minded people she knew, there was still this awful, insidious voice in the back of her mind that had whispered *what if.* What if everything was different when it was their daughter? "I don't know if I'm saying any of this right. I guess it just feels like . . . you know when someone asks if you've been somewhere, and you've only ever been to the airport? So, geographically the answer is yes, technically, but you feel like a fraud for saying so because you haven't *really* been there?"

That's what it felt like whenever anyone asked her about being bisexual. Like she was Bi Lite.

She chanced another glance at Colin, praying her metaphor had made some modicum of sense, steeling herself for whatever expression she'd find.

Colin's soft smile nearly bowled her over. "For what it's worth, speaking as someone who spent *a lot* of time hanging out in the airport before ever actually exploring the, uh, surrounding scenery? It counts, Truly. And anyone who says it doesn't?" His lips parted just enough for her to get a glimpse of his tongue tracing the edges of his front teeth. "They can go fuck themselves."

Her brain glitched, a distant memory of an old computer making an ancient dial-up noise filling her head like static. There was something absurdly hot about Colin saying *fuck* with his whole chest, so hot she was pretty sure her system had just undergone a hard reboot because of it.

She cleared her throat. "So, you're, um . . ."

The airport metaphor was vague and she didn't want to assume.

"Bisexual?" He filled in the blank for her. "Yeah, I am." For the first time since he'd sat down, Colin looked distinctly uncomfortable, eyes darting away. "Do you have a problem with that?"

She reared back so fast her chair legs scraped earsplittingly shrill against the tile floor. "I literally just told you I was bi. Why would I have a problem with you being queer if I'm queer?"

The math wasn't mathing.

One side of Colin's mouth quirked, but he still had yet to look her in the eye. "People have double standards about all sorts of shit."

People were hypocrites, sure, but she wasn't.

"People suck." Perhaps it wasn't the most eloquent, but it was honest.

Colin laughed and pressure she didn't even realize she was

holding inside her chest eased. "Yeah. Yeah, they really do." He stole a glance at her from beneath his lashes. "My ex-girlfriend seemed really chill, you know? Put the *A* in ally, even had a rainbow bumper sticker on her Beemer. Until I say it's bullshit queer men can't donate blood unless they've abstained from sex with other men for three months and she shrugs and says *well, statistically . . .*" He scoffed. "Talk about a red flag. But I was stupid, and, you know, at that point living in the airport lounge, if we're still working off that metaphor."

Justin's foot had practically lived in his mouth during their relationship, but he'd never said anything that offensive. Nothing that had ever gotten her blood boiling quite the way it was now.

"Your ex-girlfriend sounds like a cunt." She slammed her computer shut and slid it to the side so she could rest her elbows on the table. "Good riddance."

A flabbergasted laugh escaped his lips. "Yeah." He nodded, pink-cheeked and grinning. "I guess she does, doesn't she?"

Truly smiled around the straw of her coffee, inordinately pleased and buzzing because of it. "She *totally* does."

Colin nudged his coffee cup farther to the side so he could mirror her, elbows on the table, leaning in, his gaze steady. "My point, before I got off on a personal tangent, was that there's no such thing as being queer *enough*. Action and attraction are two different things. You could go the rest of your life never dating a woman and it wouldn't change a thing. If anything, I think you're the perfect person to talk about bi-erasure in media *because* you spent the last six years in a straight-presenting relationship that was queer because *you're* queer. And the gender of your partner? Doesn't change that."

The heat inside her chest unfurled, settling into a syrupy

warmth that made her swallow hard, like she wasn't so much breathing oxygen but something thicker and sweeter.

"That's—" Words were her bread and butter and yet she couldn't find the right ones to do her appreciation justice. "Thank you."

Colin did the unexpected, frowning.

She frowned back at him. "What's with the face?"

"You're thanking me? For what?"

For saying the right thing. For saying what she hadn't realized she'd needed to hear until he'd said it. For seeing her.

"For, you know"—she waved her hand in the air—"saying what you said. It was . . . nice."

"*Nice*," Colin repeated, brow still furrowed. "Why do I feel like you meant to add a *surprisingly* in there?"

Her chest constricted. She'd bust his balls about plenty, but not this. This wasn't a laughing matter.

"No. No qualifiers necessary." She ignored the urge to cross her arms and curled her fingers around her coffee instead, grip so tight the cup crunched under her fingers, plastic lid nearly popping off. "You said what I needed to hear. So, this is me saying thank you."

"Careful, St. James. That *really* sounded like a compliment."

Without permission, outside of her volition, her hand crept across the table, stopping just shy of Colin's. Close enough that a single twitch of her pinky would cause their skin to brush. "It was. A compliment."

A small, almost disbelieving smile crept across Colin's face. "Oh. Well." He ducked his chin, smile growing as he stared down at the table at where their hands almost touched. "You don't have to thank me for being honest."

"Christ, McCrory, can you just take the damn compliment?"

His fingers ghosted across the back of her hand, so soft, so brief she wasn't sure whether it was an absentminded gesture or deliberate. Either way, her stomach fluttered. "It was nothing, Truly."

It wasn't nothing. It was something. Something she didn't have the words for.

Not yet.

"Bullshit. You were *not*."

"Hand to God, I swear." Colin dug his fork into the slice of red velvet loaf cake between them. "Just ask Caitlin. She's got pictures. Dig back through *her* Instagram and you might even find one."

She steadfastly ignored the way her cheeks heated at the jibe. "No wonder you were so defensive of the tree. You *were* the tree."

He wasn't more than a few years older than her. She racked her brain, thinking back on the football games she'd gone to her freshman year. The idea that their paths might have inadvertently crossed, even at a distance across a football stadium, while Colin was dressed up like an evergreen tree, was too funny.

"Put some respect on the name, St. James." He set his fork down. "I was *The* Tree, representative of El Palo Alto, a 1,083-year-old coast redwood and the namesake of the city."

"My sincerest apologies." She held up her hands in supplication. "Those must have been some big shoes—sorry, roots?—to fill."

"Ha fucking ha." He rolled his eyes. "I auditioned on a dare, okay? My cousin Cillian—he's my best friend—he didn't think I'd do it and I—" He cringed. "Ah, shit. There's no way to confess this without sounding like a douche."

"Is that new for you?" She grinned. "Go on. Stop stalling. Spit it out."

Colin heaved a sigh. "Fine. Disclaimer, I was eighteen—"

"You were stupid. Got it."

Colin scoffed. "Not every eighteen-year-old is stupid."

"True, but everyone who uses *I was eighteen* as a disclaimer either did something stupid or hormonally driven. If there were a Venn diagram, it might even be a circle."

"Maybe I was a little stupid."

She hummed the *Jeopardy!* tune.

Colin looked up, stone-faced, unamused save for the persistent and undeniable twitching of his left brow. "Fine. I heard the mascot got to, you know"—he made a frazzled, senseless gesture before raking both hands through his unfairly luscious hair—"hang out with the cheerleaders."

"You decided dressing up like a tree and learning to dance to an eight-count beat was preferable to, I don't know, asking someone on a date like a normal person?" She reached for her drink. "Weird flex."

Colin smirked. "You haven't seen me do yoga."

Wrong time to take a sip. A vivid image of Colin bent over in downward dog flashed through her brain, making her sputter, little drops of her iced latte splattering across the table and, naturally, the back of Colin's hand.

Rather than reach for a napkin, Colin wiped her spittle off with his thumb. She was really glad she was sitting down.

"At least tell me your ploy paid off."

His brows rose. "You're asking me if I got laid? You what—you want to hear about my college exploits? Are you serious?"

"Exploits? Ew." She tossed her napkin at him, which he dodged, and nudged him harder, nearly a kick. Her foot slipped and her ankle hooked around his under the table and her heart lurched. "I'm not asking for the details. I just want to know whether the whole mascot idea was worth it."

"In the sense that I was offered the position and I saw what a Division I athletic scholarship looked like?" He laughed. "It started as a dare, but considering I probably wouldn't have been able to afford law school otherwise, yeah, I'd say my humiliation paid off."

Oh. Shit. Now she felt like an asshole. "Sorry, I—"

"Don't. My parents could've afforded it. They just didn't want me to go to Stanford. *Stay in state, Colin. Go to WSU, Colin. Join the family business, Colin.*" He rolled his eyes.

"Family business?"

"McCrory and Sons Contracting." There was a bitter edge to his laugh that made her chest squeeze. "Well, McCrory and *Son* Contracting. My dad officially changed the name the day I passed the bar."

Jesus Christ.

Both her parents were in show business and not once had either pressured her to follow in their footsteps. They'd only ever wanted her to follow her dreams, pursue her own passions no matter how wild or outlandish or even mundane they were. Because they loved her. Because they wanted what was best for *her* and not some version of her they had cooked up inside their heads.

Mom and Dad had always given her the space to reach for the stars and provided her with the comfort of a safety net should she fall. She'd never taken it for granted and yet someone claiming to love their child and yet giving them hoops to jump through to attain that supposedly unconditional love was unfathomable.

"Contracting? So your father's a what? Builder? Architect?"

They'd already covered that he was an ass.

He nodded. "Technically, my first job was hauling four-by-fours and H-beams on weekends. But I never got paid, so I'm not sure it counts."

Four-by-fours and H-beams? That explained the arms.

"Truly?"

She tore her gaze from where it had landed and lingered on the long line of his shoulders that led to the swell of his biceps. "Sorry?"

Amusement sparkled in his eyes, making it painfully obvious she'd been caught staring. At least he was polite enough not to point it out. Instead he nudged the plate of pound cake toward her, wordlessly offering her the last bite. "I asked what your first job was. Fair is fair, after all."

"Nothing as exciting as being a sanctioned furry."

Colin rolled his eyes, a smile still playing at the edges of his lips. "You're hilarious."

"I'd say I try, but that would be a lie. It comes naturally." Truly split what should've been the last reasonably sized piece of pound cake in half. "I worked as an usher back before my mom retired, when both of my parents were still with the theater. That was my first job. Not the most exciting, but I did get paid minimum wage and I got comped tickets for my friends."

She pushed the plate across the table only for Colin to push it right back.

"That's yours," he said.

"I split it in half."

"That's not even a bite, that's a crumb."

"Just eat it, McCrory."

"*You* eat it, St.—"

Her name died on his lips as a shadow fell across the table.

"Can I clear that for you?" a barista with a strained smile asked, hand already halfway to the plate.

Truly looked at Colin. "Um, we weren't quite finished yet, but—"

"We closed five minutes ago."

But they didn't close until—the clock mounted over the door read *8:05*. Oh, shit. Already?

"Sorry." Colin handed the crumb-covered plate to the barista with a contrite smile. "We'll get out of your hair."

The barista took the plate and walked away.

Wordlessly, Truly gathered up her things, tucking her laptop inside her bag even though she hadn't so much as looked at it once in the *four* hours since Colin sat down. She had sprawled, pens strewn across the table, two dog-eared notebooks splayed open beside what remained of her third latte and trusty bottle of water she never left the house without.

It took her twice the time it took Colin to grab his belongings, but he waited, the bell chiming above the door as he held it open for her on the way out.

Had Justin ever held the door open for her?

Maybe? No? She couldn't care less about doors and who held

them open, but . . . it was emblematic of how Justin had never cared, how he'd always assumed Truly would be there, one step behind him, her hand on the small of *his* back.

"Is your car—"

"I live around the corner," she said, jerking her thumb over her shoulder in the approximate direction of her apartment. "I walked."

"Ah." Colin pressed a button on his keys and the headlights on the silver Honda Civic three spaces down flashed. "That's me."

"This was . . ." She searched for the right word. "Fun?"

Colin spun his key ring around his finger and laughed. "Are you asking me or telling me?"

"Well, now I'm rethinking my answer altogether."

He grinned. "Bullshit."

"Shut up," she said without heat.

His teeth sank into his plush bottom lip and his gaze dropped to the pavement. After a moment he looked up at her through his stupidly long lashes. "What do you say about doing this again?"

She frowned. Doing what? "Running into each other at a coffee shop?"

He laughed, one tooth still snagged on his bottom lip, his smile charmingly lopsided. "I was hoping we might do it intentionally next time. I could even text you ahead of time."

Her heart hurled itself against her chest. "You mean . . . like, a date?"

Saying the word out loud made her palms sweat.

Another laugh escaped his lips. "Yeah, Truly. Exactly like a date."

"*Why?*" she blurted.

Colin smiled patiently. "Because I like you. Because I like spending time with you. Because I'd like to spend more time with you."

This wasn't supposed to happen. Not now. Not like this. It was too soon. She wasn't ready. "That's not a good idea, Colin."

His smile fell and even though she had to do it, even though the words had to be said, her throat ached with the near over-whelming urge to take the words back.

"Ah." He scratched his jaw and looked away. "I—look, I know we're not talking about it, and I know attraction doesn't always equal interest, but . . . did I read this wrong?"

Colin pointed between them, like it wasn't already clear what he was asking.

"No. You read it right," she conceded with no small amount of reluctance.

His being right was worse because it meant she'd unfairly made him party to her confusion.

"*Okay.*" He dragged out the word, staring at her from beneath lowered brows, looking at her like she was a puzzle he intended to solve.

She crossed her arms and averted her gaze, pulse pounding painfully in her throat. "I just got out of a relationship and every-thing with my parents is so messed up that I'm not—I'm not in the right headspace for . . . that."

"Those sound like excuses to me," he said, not unkindly.

He sounded like Lulu. "If I didn't want to go out with you, I'd have no problem telling you that. Trust me."

Colin laughed and some of the tightness in her chest eased. "Somehow, I don't have trouble believing that." His smile faded, his stare softening, less like he was trying to solve her like a puzzle and more like he hoped she'd hand the pieces over. "What *do* you want, Truly?"

If that wasn't the million-dollar question, she didn't know what was.

"I don't know," she admitted.

He nodded to himself, taking the answer in stride. "Let me know when you find out."

Chapter Nine

Three days passed without a text from Colin, and she'd be lying if she said she didn't miss the little *ping* her phone made, softly vibrating against whatever surface she'd set it on each time he messaged.

She'd be lying if she said she didn't miss *him*.

So maybe it wasn't the wisest decision, but Truly opened Instagram to treat herself to a private dose of Colin McCrory. She could drool over his abs and his arms and his smile from the safety of a screen and as long as she didn't screw up and text him any screenshots, he'd remain none the wiser that she *maybe* knew what she wanted more than she was letting on.

In the most abstract sense of the word. The lustiest sense, at least.

Five minutes. She'd peruse his profile for five minutes and put her phone away, get back to work.

Thirty minutes later, somehow, she was 158 weeks deep in Colin's past, heart squeezing sweetly as she stared at a picture of a girl who couldn't be older than five perched on Colin's knee. Her lopsided pigtails brushed his chin as she painted his nails pink, more polish on his skin than on his nails, but Colin smiled soppily, looking for all the world like there was nowhere else he'd rather be than getting a messy manicure from a preschooler whose face was concealed with a giant heart emoji.

The caption simply read, *quality time with my best girl.*

When she imagined her future, kids were definitely something she wanted. Five years from now, maybe ten, the timeline dependent on if and when she met someone she wanted to have kids with and, to be honest, if said person had good health insurance because, face it, health care in this country sucked.

She was only twenty-seven, in no big hurry to rush into that chapter of her life, but she'd be lying if she said the sight of Colin smiling fondly at that little girl didn't do *something* to her ovaries. Metaphorically.

The way her heart simultaneously squeezed and swelled was a lot harder to ignore and even more complicated to unpack. Which was why it took a second to realize the bright red heart staring back at her from beneath Colin's picture wasn't a figment of her imagination.

She'd accidentally liked the photo.

The photo from 158 weeks ago.

Shit.

As fast as she could, she clicked that heart again, tension melting from her shoulders as it shifted back to black in the blink of an eye. Oh thank God. Her head flopped against the back of her couch and she covered her face with both hands, muffling her frazzled laugh.

Okay, that was it. Officially no more Insta-stalking for her. The universe need not deliver any more signs. She had *more* than learned her—

Her phone buzzed against her stomach and her heart, still beating too fast, stuttered and stalled before sinking.

COLIN (11:09 P.M.): I saw that.

She whimpered.

Stupid technology. Even stupider lusty thoughts. Stupid *her* for playing with fire when she knew better.

TRULY (11:10 P.M.): Saw what?

Even as she hit *send*, she cringed.

COLIN (11:11 P.M.): Really? That's how we're playing it?

How many times could she claim she'd drunk texted him within the span of two weeks before it started to look like she had a drinking problem? She cringed. If she had to ask . . .

TRULY (11:12 P.M.): I was just scrolling my feed.

COLIN (11:13 P.M.): A picture of me with my goddaughter from three years ago just happened to appear on your feed?

Colin followed that jibe up with a GIF of Marcia Brady quipping, *sure, Jan.*

She scoffed loudly into her silent apartment. That sassy son of a bitch was lucky that she, for some reason that was utterly beyond her at the moment, liked him. Otherwise a comment like that might've earned him a solid ghosting.

> **TRULY (11:15 P.M.):** It was an accident, you ass.

> **COLIN (11:15 P.M.):** You accidentally scrolled through three years of my photos? Or you accidentally liked the picture?

> **COLIN (11:15 P.M.):** I just think it's important we're on the same page.

Her lips twitched. Clearly, she was beyond hope if a smart-ass remark like that made her smile.

> **TRULY (11:16 P.M.):** Screw you, McCrory.

> **COLIN (11:16 P.M.):** Promises, promises.

The heat that had collected in her cheeks spread down, down, *down*, her toes curling in the fluffy pile of her bright blue area rug.

When, *when*, was she going to learn not to bite off more than she could chew?

She backed out of her convo with Colin and tapped on the one just beneath, tapping out a quick text to Lulu.

> **TRULY (11:17 P.M.):** Having a crush as an adult is so embarrassing.

Calling it a crush felt wrong, the word too tiny. But anything else felt just as ill-fitting, romance too big, infatuation too airy, desire too . . . hot, even if it was a little closer to the truth.

Lulu, bless her, responded almost instantly.

> **LULU (11:17 P.M.):** what did you do??

Truly huffed.

> **TRULY (11:17 P.M.):** Why are you assuming I did something?

> **LULU (11:18 P.M.):** oh sorry were you texting me after 11 on a school night for a non-emergency?

> **LULU (11:18 P.M.):** ah shit, I just called a weeknight a school night. i'm old 🧛

Lulu sent a GIF of Jamie Lee Curtis in *Freaky Friday* bemoaning that she was like the crypt keeper.

> **TRULY (11:19 P.M.):** I love you but shut up and have your age-related crisis later. I DID SOMETHING BAD.

> **LULU (11:20 P.M.):** at least tell me it felt so good

> **LULU (11:21 P.M.):** can you feel the flames on your skin?

LULU (11:21 P.M.): was it the most fun you ever had?

LULU (11:21 P.M.): could you do it over and over and over again?

TRULY (11:22 P.M.): Stop it. This is serious.

LULU (11:22 P.M.): and so is my adoration for the one and only Taylor Alison Swift

TRULY (11:22 P.M.): Amazing how you chose to capitalize that and nothing else.

LULU (11:23 P.M.): i believe in putting proper respect on the name. now tell momma Lulu what you did

TRULY (11:23 P.M.): I liked one of Colin McCrory's photos on IG from 158 weeks back and he saw it and called me out 😬

LULU (11:24 P.M.):BAHAHAHAHAHAHA HAHAHAHAHAHAHAHAHAHAH

LULU (11:24 P.M.): OMG YOU DUMB BITCH I LOVE YOUR STUPID ASS SO MUCH

Truly rolled her eyes.

TRULY (11:25 P.M.): Haha so funny! Truly made an ass of herself! So hilarious! LOL. What a knee slapper.

LULU (11:26 P.M.): 1) we can tone down the sarcasm and 2) who the fuck says knee slapper??? gen-z grandma

LULU (11:26 P.M.): also for the record it's so cute how you say his whole name as if i know another colin

Even as Truly rolled her eyes, her cheeks burned.

TRULY (11:27 P.M.): I asked for help, not to be razzed within an inch of my life.

LULU (11:28 P.M.): bold of you to assume i can't do both

LULU (11:28 P.M.): i just don't understand what you're waiting for

LULU (11:28 P.M.): clearly you like the guy

LULU (11:29 P.M.): clearly he likes you

TRULY (11:29 P.M.): It's more complicated than that.

LULU (11:30 P.M.): bullshit. it's only as complicated as you make it and babe i don't understand but you seem bound and determined to make this more complicated than it needs to be

LULU (11:30 P.M.): you had a good time the other day right? you'd probably have a good time if you grabbed coffee with him again right?

TRULY (11:31 P.M.): I suppose.

She could concede that much.

LULU (11:32 P.M.): now pretend the podcast isn't a thing. you're done recording. you have zero professional obligation to see him ever again. you walk out the door and that's it. never again will colin mccrory darken your proverbial door. how do you feel?

Even though it was strictly hypothetical, her heart shrank.

TRULY (11:33 P.M.): Okay. I get it.

LULU (11:34 P.M.): no one regrets the chances they took

LULU (11:34 P.M.): people regret the chances they didn't take

She snorted. Now *that* was an utter crock of shit.

TRULY (11:35 P.M.): Okay, Wayne Gretzky. If I went bungee jumping and broke both my legs, I can safely say I'd regret it.

LULU (11:37 P.M.): you asked for my opinion so here it is

LULU (11:39 P.M.): i think you do know what you want and it scares you so you're looking for an excuse not to take the flying leap of faith we both know you want to. the one the truly six years ago would've taken in a heartbeat, without question

Lulu was right; six years ago, Truly would have gone after what she wanted, consequences be damned. But that girl had unwavering faith in happily ever afters.

LULU (11:40 P.M.): take my advice or don't, but i'm not going to be the one to tell you not to take a chance just because that's what you want to hear

LULU (11:41 P.M.): go out with him or don't. take it slow or go full throttle pedal to the metal

LULU (11:41 P.M.): do what you need to do

LULU (11:42 P.M.): i'd just hate to see you let what could be an amazing opportunity pass you by because you're scared

She wasn't scared. She was . . . discerning. She had self-preservation.

She cringed.

She had self-preservation except for when it came to Colin McCrory and Instagram.

TRULY (11:43 P.M.): You've given me a lot to think about. Thank you.

LULU (11:43 P.M.): ugh code for you're gonna ignore me

LULU (11:44 P.M.): whatever let the record show i tried

LULU (11:44 P.M.): you're lucky i love your stubborn ass 💟

TRULY (11:44 P.M.): Love you, too. Even though the way you text makes me want to strangle you 😇

LULU (11:45 P.M.): ✋😵

Truly flipped back to her conversation with Colin, frowning at the wall of unread texts that awaited her.

COLIN (11:32 P.M.): I'm sorry if my last text crossed a line.

COLIN (11:33 P.M.): See, the problem is, I'm not really sure where the line is?

COLIN (11:33 P.M.): I'm hoping you'll tell me.

COLIN (11:34 P.M.): But if you'd rather this whole conversation be another one of those things we pretend didn't happen, that's okay, too.

COLIN (11:35 P.M.): Cards on the table, I'd rather it not be something we pretend didn't happen.

COLIN (11:36 P.M.): But I'm following your lead.

COLIN (11:42 P.M.): Sorry for the sexiest text.

COLIN (11:43 P.M.): That was supposed to say sextuple, not sexiest. Fucking autocorrect. You know what? To keep what remains of my dignity intact, I'm going to say goodnight. So, goodnight.

She frowned. Apparently, she didn't have the market cornered on overthinking.

> TRULY (11:46 P.M.): You're fine. No lines crossed.

> TRULY (11:47 P.M.): And let's not discuss dignity when I'm the one who liked a photo from 158 weeks ago.

Three dots danced across her screen, stopping and starting as Colin typed, either writing the world's lengthiest text or deleting what he'd already written. Finally, her phone vibrated, a new message appearing on the screen.

> COLIN (11:52 P.M.): So, I take it we're not pretending it didn't happen?

What was the use when they both knew otherwise?

> TRULY (11:53 P.M.): I think at this point, pretending would be silly.

> COLIN (11:55 P.M.): It was already silly.

She rolled her eyes. He sounded like Lulu.

Who, Truly could begrudgingly admit, had a point. Not that she was ready to take that flying leap of faith Lulu talked about, but Truly could take a baby step.

A teeny-tiny one.

> **TRULY (11:56 P.M.):** Look, I'm still figuring some stuff out, but if you want to send me bizarre facts about bull penises, I wouldn't be entirely opposed.

She read back the text twice before hitting *send*.

> **COLIN (11:58 P.M.):** Are you asking me to text you bizarre facts about bull penises?

She huffed, unsure whether he was being difficult or legitimately asking for clarification. She couldn't tell over text, not the way she'd be able to if Colin was standing in front of her and they were having this conversation face-to-face.

> **TRULY (11:59 P.M.):** No. I'm saying you don't have to go totally radio silent just because of what I said the other day.

If her last text wasn't clear, she prayed this one would be.

> **COLIN (12:00 A.M.):** Do you want me to text you?

> **TRULY (12:01 A.M.):** If you want.

> **COLIN (12:03 A.M.):** I'm asking what you want, Truly.

Her stomach twisted, Colin's question nudging her a little too close to taking that *flying leap of faith* for comfort.

She hesitated, thumb hovering over the screen. It would be so easy to put her phone on *do not disturb*, so easy to simply not respond. But that would only be delaying the inevitable. In three days, they'd be back in the studio and her gut told her Colin wasn't going to let this go. Not unless she asked.

She didn't want to, and she didn't want this conversation to end just because she was too afraid to be honest. With Colin or with herself.

> **TRULY (12:06 A.M.):** Yeah, I guess I do.

As soon as her phone buzzed, Truly let out a breath she was very well aware she'd been holding.

> **COLIN (12:08 A.M.):** Did you know pizzle is the Middle English word for penis?

A laugh burst from her lips, taking her by surprise and leaving her breathless as she sank back into the couch, tension bleeding from her muscles, leaving her loose and lax and lighter than she'd felt in weeks.

> **TRULY (12:09 A.M.):** You were just dying to whip that out, weren't you?

> **COLIN (12:10 A.M.):** Was that a pizzle pun?

> **TRULY (12:11 A.M.):** You're a little odd, McCrory.

COLIN (12:12 A.M.): Right back at you, St. James.

That night, she fell asleep with a smile on her face.

CAITLIN GREETED HER in the hall outside the studio with an exuberant hug and an air-kiss administered against both cheeks. "You're here! Thank God."

"I'm not late, am I? We said five, right?"

"God no. You're fine." Caitlin waved off her concern and wrapped a hand around Truly's wrist, tugging her toward the door at a faster clip than Truly's shorter legs could comfortably keep up with. "Colin's just been driving me insane. He got here forty minutes early and he won't stop talking. The last time he was like this was when he was—" Caitlin's mouth shut with an audible snap as she clammed up out of nowhere. "Can you forget I said that?"

"Said what?"

"Thank you," she breathed, mistaking Truly's confusion for acceptance. "Anyway, I'm so glad you're here. Maybe now he'll calm down."

Truly tried not to read into that and instantly failed. "Why would, um, why would that matter? Me being here?"

"Because." Caitlin made it sound like the answer was obvious, and maybe it was, but it was sure eluding Truly. "He promised me weeks ago—after the first debacle of a recording—he'd be on his best behavior around you."

She couldn't help but laugh. "If this is his best behavior, do I even want to know what his worst looks like?"

Caitlin shot Truly an appraising look over her shoulder. "I don't know. Do you?"

Before she could unpack *that*, her phone vibrated from inside the back pocket of her jeans. "Sorry, one sec."

She tugged her phone free and unlocked the screen.

COLIN (4:56 P.M.): How many covert pizzle jokes do you think we can make today before my sister catches on?

COLIN (4:56 P.M.): Also, where are you? Caitie's getting on my last nerve.

"*Oooh*, that's a big smile. Special someone?"

"Um. Maybe?" Truly pocketed her phone. "I'm not sure yet."

"Ah, gotta love a *maybe*. Maybe you'll get married! Maybe they'll break your heart, crush your soul, and send you back to therapy! Who the hell knows?" Caitlin grinned and opened the door to the studio, gesturing her through with an exaggerated wave. "After you, my dear."

Truly slipped inside the room and—that was unfair.

In the center of Caitlin's ostentatious yellow sectional, Colin sat, long legs spread, bent elbows resting on his knees, phone cradled in his hands, the sleeves of his baby-blue button-down rucked up, revealing a swath of beauty-marked skin she wanted to put her mouth all over.

Taste, trace, *mark*.

Want, take, *have*.

She must've made a noise, a soft utterance of desire escaping her lips, because Colin looked up, brown eyes catching hers from across the room. Their gazes met, locked, her breath stalling, a quiet but not inaudible catch in her throat.

"St. James." Colin set his phone aside. "Long time no see."

Something inside her stomach fluttered. "Miss me, McCrory?"

He laughed and the butterflies trapped inside her chest fluttered frantically. "Don't let it go to your head."

She wouldn't dream of it.

Chapter Ten

And that's all the time we have today, folks. Thank you ever so much for listening and we all hope you enjoyed this extra special episode of *Unhinged* wherein we discussed what to do when you accidentally find an engagement ring in your significant other's sock drawer and you *really* don't want to marry them, along with how to cope after running into your parents on—gasp—a swingers' cruise. Join me, your host, Caitlin McCrory, this Thursday for our regularly scheduled episode wherein I'll be chatting with local sexpert McKenna Manansala about everything from upgrading your orgasm with toys to how to remove come stains from cashmere because, hey-o, we've all been there, haven't we?"

Colin's expression went pained and he muttered something that sounded an awful lot like *please shoot me*, under his breath.

Caitlin waggled her fingers at the camera. "As always, a gentle reminder to subscribe and leave a glowing review because my rent un-fucking-fortunately does not pay itself. And if you want to tell your friends and the most open-minded members of your family to check me out, who the hell am I to say no? Until next time, *Unhinged* fam."

Caitlin pointed finger guns at the camera and winked before reaching for the remote.

"Another episode for the books." Caitlin stretched her arms over her head, back cracking. "Any fun plans tonight, Truly?"

"If by fun plans, you mean a hot date with a box of Kraft mac 'n' cheese eaten in front of my computer while I revise, then yeah, totally."

"Wow, not to be a bitch, but that sounds tragic." Caitlin stood. "Back me up, Colin."

"It does. Neon-orange powder should not be allowed to call itself cheese. That's—that's dairy sacrilege."

"Dairy sacrilege? Who are you, the pope of pasteurized milk?" Truly laughed. "It's cheese *product*, McCrory. It comes out of a box. I think you overestimate my standards while I'm on deadline. My diet mostly consists of mac 'n' cheese, frozen pizza, and Chinese takeout."

Colin full-body cringed.

"Ignore him." Caitlin laughed. "He's a food snob. But it's Saturday and those are some of the worst weekend plans I've ever heard. Let me buy you a drink."

"And a real meal," Colin muttered.

"You, shut up," she said to Colin before turning to Caitlin. "That's sweet of you, but—"

"I am far from sweet. I want to." Caitlin jutted out her bottom lip. "Please? You've been such a doll, putting up with me and Colin these last few weeks. Not to mention, I have you to thank for my frankly phenomenal new deal with Spotify. Colin and I already have plans to check out this new bar over on Lenora. Come with us. We'll have so much fun."

Lenora was only a street over from her apartment, but Truly

had a long Sunday ahead of her. The drive to the lake house in Chelan was five hours and she still had to pack and she'd really love it if she could make a little headway on her revisions. Because as soon as she got to Chelan? Her number one priority was her parents. She had no clue when she'd have the time or energy to work on her book when she had a real-life happily ever after to help orchestrate. "I don't know."

"Pretty please?" Caitlin batted her lashes. "Come on! First round's on Colin."

He huffed. "Says the girl who just got paid an absurd amount of money to talk about how to get come out of cashmere."

Caitlin punched him in the arm. "Don't act like you aren't proud of me."

Colin wrinkled his nose, but dragged her in, kissing her forehead and no, Truly did not melt a little.

"I really wouldn't want to impose."

"Don't be ridiculous," Caitlin chastised. "Colin, tell Truly she wouldn't be imposing."

He smiled, a flash of white teeth against pink lips stretched wide. If her heart happened to skip a beat? No, it didn't. "If anything, you'd be doing me a favor."

Caitlin grumbled under her breath, too quiet to make out the words. Not that Truly was trying particularly hard, still snared by Colin's stare and the brightness of his smile, the quirk of his lips and the lift of his brows all but screaming, *what do you say, St. James?* without him having to open his mouth.

And God, what a mouth it was. Lips like those should be illegal. In the right light, they didn't even look pink, they looked red. A color she'd have to reach for a tube of lipstick to achieve. *Kiss bitten.* Wind chapped, probably, but the thought of someone else, someone who wasn't her, scraping their teeth against the swell of Colin's bottom lip until it plumped, until it turned tender and swollen, made her blood boil.

Just because she had no business kissing Colin didn't mean she relished the thought of someone else kissing him instead.

Lips like those were practically begging to be kissed. Plenty of people would agree, people who would be out at a bar on a Saturday night, looking for someone like Colin to kiss.

What harm could come from one little drink? A chaperoned one at that. Baby steps.

"Text me the address," she said. "As long as we're not drinking tequila, I'm in."

"Okay, picture like forty-some-odd McCrory relatives crammed into our parents' house. Distant cousins and—hell, even our great-grandmother from County Sligo flew all the way across the pond. It's a big thing." Caitlin slammed back a shot of whiskey like a goddamn champ because she had no compunctions about indulging even if Truly did. "There's, like, eggnog and cider and a dozen different kinds of cookies and Mariah Carey's crooning about how all she wants for Christmas is you, ya know?"

Truly took a delicate sip of a Dirty Shirley, pacing herself. "I follow."

"Perfect. So, now imagine—oh hell yes." Caitlin wiggled excitedly on her barstool. "I'm *starving*."

"Good. I think I ordered enough food for a small army," Colin said, back from ordering at the bar. He placed a bowl of roasted brussels sprouts in front of Truly before setting a basket of parmesan truffle fries that smelled like salty deep-fried heaven in the center of the table, along with some sort of fancy beet salad, and a plate of wings smothered in buffalo sauce. "Dig in."

"Don't mind if I do," Truly said, reaching past the bowl of brussels sprouts for a fry covered in cheesy, garlicky goodness.

With a put-upon sigh, Colin pointedly nudged the bowl of brussels sprouts closer. "Eat something green, please."

"Let the woman eat her fries in peace, *Dad*." Caitlin snorted. "You know very well our father has never once willingly eaten a salad that didn't have Caesar in the name. Or that wasn't smothered in blue cheese dressing and bacon bits."

"It was Dad energy," Caitlin said.

It was, and Truly would be lying if she said it wasn't kind of hot in a weird, *let's unpack that later during sex-positive therapy* kind of way. Right now she just wanted to stuff her face and hear Caitlin finish her story.

"I'm not anti-vegetable. I understand the value of dietary fiber. I just happen to prefer my veggies covered in cheese and deep-fried. That's my choice." She popped another fry in her mouth and moaned at the flavor explosion. Those truffles were fucking magical.

"A perfectly valid choice at that." Caitlin tapped her own fry against Truly's.

Colin shook his head and speared a golden beet on his fork. "There's goat cheese on these, if that persuades you to eat something *not* deep-fried."

"Now you're speaking my language." Truly scooped a beet with goat cheese onto her plate. "Caitlin? You were telling me about . . . I don't remember actually. Something about Christmas and County Sligo?"

Colin groaned. "Caitie, no."

"Caitie, yes." Caitlin grinned. "Okay, imagine that the holiday music is running through the Bluetooth speaker system in our house."

Colin tipped his head back and groaned. "Caitie—"

"Shut the fuck up." She shoved him. "This is my story. As I was saying . . . wait, where was I?"

His ears had gone pink, and the front of his throat was splotched red. "You were about to shut up and eat your goddamn vegetables."

"Bluetooth speakers?" Truly said, grinning as Colin glared.

Caitlin snapped her fingers. "Bluetooth speakers! Right. Colin mumbles something about grabbing *something* from his room and disappears upstairs. A few minutes later the music cuts off and none of us can figure out why." Caitlin's gaze slid over to Colin. "And that's when the unmistakable sound of porn starts playing through the speakers."

Truly gasped. "No!"

Colin slunk down in his chair, looking like he wished he could slide under the table. Maybe sink straight through the floor. His blush had deepened, surpassing scarlet and leveling up to burgundy, the splatter of freckles across the bridge of his nose disappearing entirely as he chewed grumpily on his roasted brussels.

"Yes!" Caitlin cackled. "And it wasn't just a little light moaning, either. I'm talking skin slapping, *ooooh yes, fuck me harder! Need your come! Need you to fill me up! Want it dripping out my ass!*"

"Fucking A, Caitie!" From the way he jerked, and Caitlin immediately yelped, he'd kicked his sister under the table. "Truly doesn't need a play-by-play and I don't need to hear you make those noises ever again."

Colin scrubbed a hand over his flushed face; it was a wonder his moles didn't streak across his skin like little melted chocolate chips.

Caitlin snickered, unrepentant, and grabbed another fingerful of fries. "My point is, there was X-rated filth pouring through the speakers for everyone in our family to hear."

Truly pressed a hand to her cheek, her own skin feverish beneath her fingertips. She could only imagine how mortifying that must've been. "What happened?"

"I died," Colin deadpanned, staring down at the table with haunted eyes, expression vacant.

"He *wished* he died." Caitlin leaned over and punched him in the shoulder. "What happened was, Mom goes flying up the stairs to Colin's room, since you know, he disappeared from the party ten minutes before and she's got two teenage sons, so she's not an idiot. And because our family is full of nosy fuckers, the entire McCrory clan follows, hot on her heels."

Truly turned to Colin, horrified. "No."

He cringed. "Yes."

"Mom's face is bright red, and her ears look like two little turkey timers about to pop. She's clearly desperate to put a stop to the soundtrack of some girl getting her brains fucked out by some dude's—apparently—massive cock, so she doesn't even knock. She just throws open the door to Colin's room and Colin lets out the loudest, shrillest scream I've ever heard before falling off his bed, dick out, and get this—*breaking his wrist*."

She wheezed. No way could that much misfortune befall one person in a night. "You're lying."

Caitlin held out her pinky. "God's honest truth. I am a great many things, but a liar isn't one of them. Tell her, Colin."

Colin brought his beer bottle to his lips and sighed. "It's true. Every last horrifying detail."

A giggle sneaked through the tight press of her lips. She didn't mean to laugh, but the mental image was so *vivid*, so mortifying, the sort of scenario that if it happened in a movie would have her diving behind her sofa or hiding in the bathroom until it was over. Once that one giggle slipped out it was as if the floodgates had been opened and she couldn't stop.

"Sorry!" she said between gasping laughs. "It's not funny, it's just—"

"Oh, it's hilarious." Caitlin grinned. "Trust me, I was there."

Truly clapped a hand over her mouth, which did shit to stifle her laughter. If anything, it just emphasized the shaking of her shoulders and made the ice click against the sides of her cocktail glass.

"Laugh it up, St. James." Colin ran his thumb along his mouth, wiping up foam left behind by his beer in a move that made the laughter die right on her lips. *R-I-fucking-P.* Her thighs clenched, and even though there was no way Colin could've possibly known, the sly smile that stretched across his face sure as hell made it seem like he knew the effect he had on her. "Fair's fair. Your turn."

"My turn to—oh. No, no, that's not happening. This was not a tit-for-tat deal."

In a move that was far from fair, Colin's tongue sneaked out, wetting his bottom lip. "Come on. Fess up."

"She doesn't have to if she doesn't want to," Caitlin rushed to her defense. "That being said, if the spirit moves you to share . . ."

Colin's beer bottle hit the table with a thud. "*If the spirit moves you?*" He laughed, slumping back in his chair, shoulders loose, so much more relaxed than he'd been minutes before. "That's a new one."

Caitlin's curtain bangs parted with the ferocity of her sigh. "I was trying not to be overeager and scare her away."

"Sure." He smiled, knee bumping Truly's beneath the table. "If Truly's scared, she doesn't have to share."

A flush of disbelief tangled up with delight raced through her veins. "Was that a *dare?*"

Colin leaned back in his seat, legs sliding farther beneath the table so that it wasn't just his knee pressed against hers, it was his whole damn thigh. The denim of his jeans rasped against her bare skin, and yeah, those were definite goose bumps rising along the backs of her arms.

"I don't know." He shrugged. "Was it?"

"I'd be more than happy to rise to the occasion"—yeah, she absolutely let her eyes dip to where his lap was hidden behind the table—"but embarrassment implies shame and me?" She shrugged. "I don't really *do* shame."

His brows rose as if to say *oh, really?* "I didn't peg you as a coward, St. James."

"I don't remember you pegging me at all, *McCrory*," she fired back, mouth moving faster than her brain.

She bit down on the straw of her drink, heartbeat quickening to an outright sprint as the implication of her words caught up with her.

Colin went delightfully pink, and her relief mingled with the bone-deep satisfaction of making him blush.

"You two do realize I'm still here, right?" Caitlin asked, voice dry.

Truly forced a laugh. "Truth is, Colin's had a courtside seat to enough of my humiliating moments. He doesn't need to know more."

Caitlin held up a hand. "Hold the phone. What are these humiliating moments and how does my brother know about them?"

She looked at Colin in alarm. That was a can of worms Truly did *not* want touched. "Um—"

"Caitlin shit her pants on a date once and called me crying, trapped inside the bathroom of the Cheesecake Factory. I had to bring her a change of clothes."

Caitlin pelted him with a beet, leaving a scarlet streak across his cheek. "You pinky promised you'd take what happened that night to your grave."

"That was before you blabbed about the Bluetooth." He reached for his napkin and met Truly's eye across the table, eyes twinkling in the dim amber-hued light of the bar. "All bets are off now."

"You know what? The next round is on you, dickwad." Caitlin manhandled Colin out of his chair.

"Caitie, do *not* stick your—"

Caitlin shoved her hand into Colin's back pocket and gave a crow of delight as she managed to slip his wallet free. "Ha!"

"I said one round. *One.*"

"All bets are off, remember?"

Truly laughed. "She's got you there."

"Another?" Caitlin asked, nodding to the nearly empty highball glass in front of her.

She shouldn't. There were a dozen reasons to say no, right on the tip of her tongue ready to be rattled off one after the other, but she didn't want to. She wanted to stay and have another drink and revel in Colin's thigh pressed with intention against hers, a solid line of heat spanning from her knee to her hip.

Truly only felt a passing pang of guilt for wishing she and Colin were alone, a pang she quickly shoved down. She couldn't help how she felt any more than she could help what she wanted.

And right now, she wanted that drink.

"Yes, please."

With a jaunty salute, Caitlin skipped off to the bar, Colin's credit card in hand.

"Thanks for the save," she said, now that they were alone. "I wasn't looking forward to reliving my humiliation in front of your sister."

That look had returned to Colin's face, the one where he stared at her like she was the Sunday crossword. "Humiliation would be if the attraction weren't mutual." Hearing it put so plainly put a funny but not altogether unpleasant knot in her stomach. "Humiliation would've been if I had gotten that screenshot and said something along the lines of, *Gosh, Truly, I'm flattered*."

Hypothetical or not, she cringed.

Colin laughed. "See? Not humiliating." He slid the beet salad toward her. "Eat up before my sister lodges another vegetable at my head."

"You kind of deserved it." She popped a quartered beet in her mouth before reaching past Colin for a buffalo wing. "That story you blabbed? Now *that* was mortifying."

"Eh, it was you or her. Sacrifices had to be made."

"And you chose me? Shucks, I'd tell you I'm flattered but we've already established that phrasing sucks."

Colin smiled, eyes dropping to her plate. "Did you know the history of the chicken wing is disputed?"

The question took her off guard enough that she laughed. "Random, but all right, I'll bite. Disputed how?"

Colin had a perfectly good plate of wings sitting beside him and yet he chose to steal the wing off her plate. That would've gotten under her skin a month ago, but now she just felt weirdly fond that he wanted *her* wing. The one she'd touched. "Okay, so there are two general theories. One's that Anchor Bar in Buffalo—sorry, is this boring? This is probably boring. We can talk about something else. Do you want to talk about something else?"

There was an odd note in his voice she desperately wanted to dispel, a twist to his lips she wanted to smooth away. She reached for another wing and kept her hands to herself. *Please remain seated and keep arms and legs inside at all times.* "Anchor Bar in Buffalo . . . what's the 411? What's the hot gos, McCrory? Tell me everything. Don't leave me hanging."

Colin laughed and something inside her eased. "Settle down. The year was 1964."

"1964." She nodded as if she knew a damn thing about the '60s other than civil rights, counterculture, the Beatles, Bob Dylan, and Twiggy. "A good year."

"Even better when you learn that the Bellissimo family of Buffalo claim that to be the year they invented the buffalo wing. Now, there are several conflicting stories circulated by the family and others about how exactly the buffalo wing, as we know it, was born, but what's more interesting is that John Young, a guy who moved from Alabama to Buffalo in 1948, began selling wings fried and served in a tomato-based Mumbo sauce in 1961. He claimed the Bellissimo family didn't start selling wings as a regular menu item until, get this, *1974.*"

"Hot gossip indeed."

Colin stole a celery stick and tore it down the middle, dipping one half in ranch and the other in blue cheese. "Just wait. Young also claimed in an interview that Frank Bellissimo used to come to his restaurant and eat wings. Even though Anchor Bar still claims to be the home of the original chicken wing, history's not on their side."

"Juicy," she said. "And you know all of this, how?"

Colin reached for his beer. "Uh, too much time spent on Wikipedia?" he admitted, bringing his pint glass to his lips. "And I have trouble sleeping. Side effect of Adderall. I have a bad habit of forgetting to take it and then taking it too late." He set his glass down. "I have a tendency to latch onto a topic and—"

"Obsess?"

Colin thumbed away the foam from his upper lip. "I was going to say *hyperfixate*, but sure, that works."

"So, this week it's buffalo wings?"

"Technically, I started researching pizzle, which naturally led to bulls, which led to buffalo, and that led to buffalo wings."

"Naturally." She nodded. "So, what else does Colin McCrory research in his spare time?"

Colin paused, staring at her like he was weighing his next words against the look on her face. Whatever he was searching for, he must've found because he asked, "Still don't know what you want?"

And *that* sudden segue warranted a drink. Truly reached for her glass and—awesome. Empty. "I don't know."

Screw it. She stole Colin's pint glass, erasing the bitter aftertaste the lie had left behind with a mouthful of equally bitter beer. *Blegh.*

Colin's lips twitched, not even trying to hide his amusement as she wrinkled her nose and pushed his glass away. *Far* away. "You don't know what you want, or you don't know whether you don't know what you want?"

"I—hold on." She kicked Colin right in the shin. "You didn't answer my question."

"I was getting to it." He locked both his ankles around hers, effectively trapping her leg against his. "Nice deflection, by the way. But I'll let it slide. This time."

"How gracious of you," she muttered, cheeks burning as Colin's foot trailed up the back of her bare calf.

He smiled and—how was he so calm? How was he not practically vibrating out of his skin like she was? Did he even realize he was playing footsie with her? No one could possibly be that oblivious.

"See, I thought that might be the case. You not knowing or not knowing about not knowing," he teased. "So, in addition to pizzle and buffalo wings, I've also been researching non-date dates."

"Non-date dates," she repeated. "What does that even mean?"

"Well, I like you, is the thing. And I enjoy spending time with you. I'd like to spend more time with you, and at some point, in the—hopefully—near future, I'd love nothing more than to take you on a date. A real one. But I also respect that right now, you're not ready for that." He raised his glass, his mouth pressed to the same side of the glass her lips had touched, and she had to fight a shiver at how close to being a facsimile of a kiss it was. How much she'd rather he press his mouth to hers directly instead. "But I'm not a quitter. So, I was thinking we could go on a few . . . test runs. Unconventional outings. No dinner and a movie, I promise. I won't even bring you flowers."

"A test run." She couldn't stop repeating what he'd said, but she felt like she should be afforded a little grace. He'd thrown a lot at her.

"Get you used to the idea. Or, if you wind up hating spending time with me, that can be that and I can at least say I tried."

"You could end up hating spending time with me."

"Doubtful."

She shivered under the warmth of Colin's gaze.

"Tell me about these non-date dates," she said, aiming for nonchalant and missing by a mile, eager and painfully obvious. "I should know what I'm getting myself into before I actually agree to anything."

"Okay, let's see . . . Ikea."

Her jaw dropped. "You want us to go to Ikea? The place that's known for testing relationships?"

"Ah, ah, but that's the brilliance of it. We aren't in a relationship." He grinned and she'd swear she could hear the unvoiced *yet*. "And I really need a new bookshelf."

Against all odds, she was charmed. "You want to drag me on an errand. So you can buy yourself a bookshelf."

"Could be fun."

"So could sitting and watching paint dry." With Colin, it just might.

"I'll add it to list," he joked.

"What else you got, McCrory? You want me to drive you to the dentist? Take you to get your tires rotated, maybe?"

"Bowling," he said, leaning across the table. She held still, heart pounding and stomach dipping as Colin thumbed away a streak of sauce at the corner of her lip.

Telltale heat gathered between her thighs as he popped his finger in his mouth and sucked the sauce off.

"Bowling?" she echoed faintly, breathless. "I'm, um, I'm pretty sure bowling is a traditional date activity."

"But what you don't know is that I suck at bowling," he said, nudging aside the plate of wings so he could rest his elbows on the table. "Planning an activity in which you suck doesn't scream first date to me. Bonus, you'll get to watch me make a fool of myself."

"Sweeten the deal, why don't you," she teased, trying to regain her footing after finding herself on less than solid ground. "You've really put a lot of thought into this, haven't you?"

A lot of thought into *her.*

"Hyperfixation," he joked, a delicate pink flush creeping up his throat. "Curling is another option. There's nothing sexy about curling. Or we could take a hot yoga class together and work up a sweat in a decidedly platonic fashion."

She could perfectly picture how the sweat would bead at his hairline and drip off his stubbled jawline, slide down his throat, gather in the shallow bowl formed by his collarbone. The same path she'd take with her mouth—if that was something she did. Something she allowed herself to do.

"Or boxing, maybe," he continued, none the wiser to her sordid thoughts. "Do a little sparring of the nonverbal variety. Or, if you don't feel like going out, we could always watch Netflix and—"

"What?" She snorted. *"Chill?"*

Colin threw his head back, his laugh coming from deep inside his chest, the sound sending another shiver down her spine. "Only in the literalist sense. I was honestly going to suggest we watch *Bizarre Foods with Andrew Zimmern.* He travels the world eating regional foods that are generally perceived as gross. You know, like cow cod soup." He smirked. "But good to know where your mind is at."

She gathered the hair up off the nape of her neck, skin feverishly hot. "Shut up."

"Not even going to deny it?" he asked, brows rising, unmistakable surprise splashed across his face.

"What would be the point?" She was a terrible liar; he'd see right through any lie she told, and it would just become one more item added to the list of things she knew he knew that they weren't talking about.

All of this pretending was exhausting.

His mouth opened, but nothing came out except for a stuttered exhale. He scrubbed a hand over the lower half of his face, fingers rasping against his stubble, his narrowed eyes sweeping her face, a fiery flush following in their wake. "What exactly are you saying?"

"I'm saying—" Screw it. "I'm saying I like flowers, okay?"

He blinked rapidly. "You—you like flowers. Okay."

"Don't be obtuse, McCrory." She crossed her arms. "I'm telling you I like flowers. I like flowers, and I'll go help you pick out your stupid bookshelf from Swedish hell if you promise to buy me meatballs and—and I don't know what the fuck curling even is. And if I'm going to work up a sweat with you, it's sure as hell not going to be doing yoga, hot or otherwise. *That's* what I'm saying."

His forehead smoothed, his eyes darkening, his lips parting, and she wanted to kiss him, wanted it more than she'd ever wanted to kiss anyone. She wanted to draw that plump bottom lip between hers and bite down. Hear what noise he'd make when she did. "Are you saying—"

"Yeah," she breathed. "I'm saying I want to—"

"*Holy shit.*" Caitlin appeared, weaving her way through the crowd. She set a fresh pint in front of Colin and a new cocktail in front of Truly. "That line was insane."

Colin gathered his wits before she could. "I don't see a drink in your hand?"

"Well spotted." She grinned. "This is Rochelle." She jerked her chin toward the stunning dark-skinned Black woman standing behind her. "There's a 24-hour donut shop across the street from her place. We're gonna check it out. Think you can make it home on your own?"

"Sure," Colin said. "Be safe."

"Always am." Caitlin blew a kiss at them, already backing away. "Have fun, you two! Don't do anything I wouldn't do."

"That sure limits things. *Not*," he said, stealing the thought right out of her head.

Truly sipped her drink and tried to ignore the ferocious fluttering inside her stomach, like the butterflies inside her had gone feral.

"I should probably be getting home," she said. "Long day tomorrow and all that."

Colin stood, leaving his beer untouched. "I'll head out with you."

Truly stepped out onto the sidewalk and into a wall of rare humidity. The weather was unseasonably warm for this time of year and the earlier rain shower had left the air heavy and her skin sticky damp. Good thing she lived right around the corner.

"Where'd you park?" Colin asked, stepping out of the bar after her with his hands tucked inside the pockets of his dark jeans, snug fabric drawn obscenely around his slim hips, thighs filling out the denim like the pants were made specifically for him.

Truly jerked a thumb over her shoulder. "I actually live a couple blocks that way on Bell."

After Caitlin had named the bar, Truly had decided that hunting for parking on Saturday sounded like an unnecessary hassle.

She'd saved herself the headache and parked at her place, walking over instead.

He frowned. "Bell and what?"

"Bell and Elliott."

At that, his frown deepened. "I think you and I have a different definition of *a couple of blocks*."

"It's only four."

Colin looked up at the sky, too much ambient lighting from streetlights and stoplights and buildings for there to be any stars. But the moles on his face and neck could easily be traced into constellations. "Not that I don't think you can take care of yourself, but can I walk with you?" He lifted his head, and she was too slow, her reflexes far from finely honed enough to look away before his eyes met hers, his gaze trapping her, making it impossible for her to look anywhere but at him. "I'd sleep better knowing you made it home safely."

Maybe it was a line, but she didn't care.

"Sure." Her heart raced. "I'd like that."

Chapter Eleven

" —**a**nd it was a great book, don't get me wrong, but now I can't step foot in an Ikea without being consumed by the thought that some seriously shady shit probably goes down after dark, you know? Closed big-box stores are, like, the mother of all liminal spaces. At the very least, unauthorized employee sleepovers must be happening. I mean, all those beds? And honestly? Why haven't they turned Ikea into a hostel? Or housing for those who need it? The beds just sit empty night after night and—"

Colin's fingers circled her wrist, grip gentle but firm. "Truly?"

She stopped walking, only a few steps shy of the vine-covered gate that kept her building mostly obscured from the street. She held her breath, pulse racing beneath his fingers. "Hm?"

"I'm not making you nervous, am I?"

Nervous? Her? Ha.

Yes.

The thumb resting over her pulse smoothed over her skin and she shivered, gulping quietly. "Why would I be nervous?"

"Maybe because you haven't stopped talking since we started walking?" The corner of his mouth curled up. "Not that I didn't find your take on the secret evil goings-on inside Ikea fascinating."

"Well, I'm not." Her heart sped and there wasn't a doubt in her mind that he could feel it, thumb pressed to her pulse like a human lie detector. "I'm fine. I'm—I'm peachy."

"You're peachy," he said, hand finally dropping to his side. It took an inordinate amount of self-control to not reach out and grab his hand, smack his open palm against her wrist like a slap band, and tell him not to let go. "So, you're not avoiding talking about what you said back at the bar?"

Her shoulders sagged. Was she that obvious? Or was Colin just that skilled at reading her?

She rubbed her wrist, her fingers a poor substitute for his. "We can talk about it. If you want. I'm just—" Terrified because this didn't feel like much of a baby step anymore. But she didn't want to take one step forward only to take two back. She wrapped her fingers between the rusted iron bars of the gate and pulled. "I don't know where to start."

Colin followed her into the dimly lit courtyard where weeds sprouted between cracks in the pavement and sweet-smelling clematis climbed the trellis outside her window. Her apartment complex was small—a single-story building comprised of six units, each with its own separate entrance off the shared courtyard, like town houses. A rarity on a street dominated by buildings five, six stories tall.

"We could get straight to the part where you confessed to wanting to work up a non-platonic sweat with me."

She fumbled her keys.

"Or we could talk about flowers."

The weak amber bulb above her door flickered as she shoved her key in the lock and turned, facing Colin. "I like amaryllis and camellias. Cornflowers and dahlias. Dogwood and edelweiss. Hawthorn and lily of the valley are nice, too."

"You're killing me," Colin croaked. "You know that?"

She slumped back against her door. "*I'm* killing *you?*" She pressed the heels of her hands against her eyes until starbursts appeared behind her lids. "Flowers? Really, McCrory? You think I actually want to talk about—"

She pitched forward with a gasp, words dying on her lips as Colin yanked her against his chest, trapping her hand between them.

"What are you doing?" she whispered.

His fingers abandoned their hold on her wrist to tuck her hair behind her ear. The rasp of his fingertips against the soft, vulnerable skin of her throat made her dizzy. "Not talking about flowers."

His mouth came crashing down on hers, swallowing her gasp, capturing her lips in a kiss.

And dear God, what a *kiss*.

He tasted citrusy sweet and just a little tart, like the slice of orange that had come with his beer. She surged forward, rising on her toes, chasing the flavor, knees all but buckling when he nipped at her bottom lip, his tongue soothing the sting.

"*Jesus*, you taste like cherries." He mouthed at her throat, teeth scraping the juncture of where her jaw met her neck. "You know that, Truly?"

Her name sounded like a benediction, whispered against her skin. All she could do was pant.

His thumb traced the swell of her bottom lip, smearing what little was left of her lip gloss. "You drive me so fucking crazy, I—" He broke off with a chuckle, hiding his face against her shoulder. "*Fuck*. I can't say it."

"It's a little late to be getting shy on me." Hand still splayed against his chest, she let her fingers drift, finding and tweaking his nipple. Colin swore under his breath and something hot blossomed inside her when he jerked. "Tell me."

"Jesus. Okay." He dropped his forehead against hers. "You want to hear about how I haven't been able to stop thinking about you since the moment I met you? That I've stripped my cock raw for the last three weeks, obsessed with—with wondering what you taste like?" Words tumbled off his tongue. An avalanche of confessions. "Is that what you want to hear? That the first time I met you, you were wearing an engagement ring and I still wanted you? I wanted you the minute I saw you and—fuck, who wouldn't? You're so fucking gorgeous you broke my goddamn brain."

"More." She reached up, scraping her nails against his neck, watching enthralled as faint pink lines rose along his skin. Heat pulsed between her thighs. "Keep talking."

He panted against her neck, breath hot and sticky. "I left work last week and I—I couldn't even make it home." He laughed, ragged and frazzled. "I fucked my fist in the bathroom thinking about you. I fell to my knees on the floor of the public bathroom inside the courthouse." He huffed against her collarbone. "Do you know how desperate you've got to be to kneel on that floor? It's disgusting and I did it. I did it thinking about you." He mouthed at her throat, teeth scraping her skin over her pulse. "I spilled over my knuckles thinking about my tongue up your cunt, licking you out until you came all over my face. I thought about you dripping down my goddamn chin and—fuck if I didn't come so hard I saw stars behind my lids in a public courthouse bathroom." His teeth scraped against her jaw. "Is that what you wanted to hear?"

Holy shit.

The image of Colin hunched over, fist stripping his cock was so vivid inside her head it was like she was right there, watching it happen. She could practically hear the slap of skin against skin, and it made her drip, underwear drenched.

"More." She buried her fingers in his thick chestnut-colored hair and tugged. Colin choked on a noise that was half gasp, half groan, one hundred percent unreservedly filthy. His hands slapped against the door on either side of her, a groan spilling from his lips. "Tell me more."

He pressed her against her door, hands on her waist, damn near respectable until he ground against her. The rigid line of his cock pressed against her hip, unmistakably hard.

"I think it's obvious what I want." His hands migrated to her hips and then lower, palms cupping her ass. "I'm far more interested in—finally—hearing what you want."

Everything south of her navel was hot, panties ruined, thighs damp. Drenched and Colin hadn't even touched her underneath her clothes. "Isn't it obvious?"

He turned his head to the side, pressing his lips against the fragile skin of her wrist. "Maybe I want to hear you say it."

She trapped her lip between her teeth, trying not to smile. "Well, I haven't gotten myself off in any public restrooms while thinking about you, if that's what you're asking. My bedroom, on the other hand . . ."

"Jesus." He groaned. "Are you trying to kill me?"

She arched against him. "I'm kind of attached to coming before you die. What you do after is your business."

Colin laughed, low and broken. "What a fucking way to go out. Here lies Colin Beyn McCrory—"

"*Bean?*" She giggled. "Your middle name is *Bean?*"

"No, *Beyn*. It's a family name. Means *life* in Gaelic. Now hush, I'm eulogizing myself." He cleared his throat. "Here lies Colin Beyn McCrory, he died doing what he loved most—eating pussy."

Truly whacked him on the shoulder. "Shut up."

"Not classy enough for you?" Colin grinned. "Okay, how about . . . he suffocated between the thighs of the prettiest, smartest, funniest, *bitchiest* girl he ever had the pleasure of knowing."

Better. "Flattery will get you everywhere."

"Everywhere?" He reached down, fingers flirting with the hem of her dress. "Will it get me between your thighs?"

Her breath stuttered inside her chest. This was happening. It was really happening. She was going to have sex with Colin.

God, when was the last time she vacuumed? Dusted? God, she better not have left her laundry lying on the floor or she was going to kick her own ass into next week.

She rested her hand on the doorknob. "I mean, admission isn't exactly *free* but—"

One second Colin was standing, and the next he was on his knees in front of her, kneeling on the "I Knew You Were Trouble" doormat she'd purchased off Etsy.

Talk about providence. Because Colin McCrory? Was the definition of trouble.

And he looked damn good on his knees.

He smoothed his palms up the outside of her thighs, stopping at the hem of her dress. He trapped his bottom lip between his teeth, looking up at her through his lashes. "You have no idea, Truly. No fucking clue all the things I've thought about. Licking your pussy until you screamed. Until you fucking *creamed*." Colin bent forward and licked the stripe of bare skin above her knee. "Can I?" He pressed a kiss against the dimple at the top of her knee. "Please?"

No one had ever begged to—to *fuck*, eat her out before. Justin had done it, but only after she'd showered and he'd always expected a blowjob in return. Which, hey, Truly liked the weight of his cock against her tongue so it was hardly an imposition, but she'd never liked how . . . how transactional it felt. Justin had never gotten down on his knees and pleaded, never looked up at her with pupils blown. Never sounded like he was starving for it. For her.

"*Here?*" she squeaked. In the open, where anyone could see? "Outside?"

He mouthed at her thigh. "You got a problem with that, St. James?"

Okay, so her front door was tucked inside a deep alcove. No one walking past could see, not unless her front door was their destination. But the thought that someone could potentially stumble upon them, Colin on his knees and Truly with her dress hiked up around her hips?

"No," she breathed. "No problem at all."

Colin's thumbs sneaked beneath the hem of her dress, inching the fabric up her thighs. His fingers hooked around the sides of her panties and dragged them down her thighs, keeping her steady as she stepped free.

He held them up, bubblegum lace drenched dark pink.

"I'm keeping these," he said, pocketing her ruined panties with a grin.

Truly buried her face in her hands.

They weren't even her best panties, for Christ's sake. The elastic was all stretched out and she was pretty sure there was a rip in the lace.

"Don't be getting shy on me, St. James," Colin goaded. "Now, do me a favor and spread your legs."

She could feel his breath, hot and damp against her, the night air cool by contrast as he spread her open with his thumbs. He swore softly. "You're dripping down your thighs. This all for me?"

His tongue darted out, licking a hot stripe up her cunt, making her gasp.

"Harder." Truly rocked against him and mewled, pulling hard against his hair.

Colin curled an arm under her leg, wrapped his hand around her thigh, and hiked it up over his shoulder, spreading her open. He licked up her center, and if she weren't so delirious with desire, she might've been embarrassed at how wet she was. He didn't seem to mind; two of his fingers slid lower, circling her where she was dripping before slipping inside, thicker than her own and so good she could cry.

"*God*. I'm so—I'm so—*Colin*," she babbled, incoherent pleas tripping off her tongue as she shook, insides fluttering, stomach tensing, and knee trembling. She slammed a hand against the frame of the door and whimpered.

She was so close she could *taste* it.

He lifted his head and she bit the inside of her cheek, stifling a sob.

"You're close, aren't you?" He looked up at her from beneath his lashes, pupils swallowing up the brown of his eyes. His chin and the lower half of his face were slick, smeared with her up to his cheeks. "I can feel your cunt fluttering around my fingers. You gonna scream for me, Truly?"

"*Shutupshutupshutup.*" She yanked on his hair, trying to drag him back.

Colin nipped the inside of her thigh.

"Rude," he scolded, soothing the sting of his bite with a filthy kiss, painting her skin with her juices.

Her eyes slammed shut, desperation making her dizzy. If she didn't come soon she was pretty sure she'd do something mortifying like cry. Her bottom lip was already beginning to wobble. "I swear to God if you don't make me come, I'll show you rude, McCrory. I'll be so rude it'll make your head spin."

He moaned against her knee, low and broken, trailing off with a laugh that made her shiver. "Don't threaten me with a good time, baby."

There was no warning, just Colin sucking on her clit and his thick fingers curling inside her and—

Bright pinpricks of light exploded behind her lids as she fractured, pulsing hard around Colin's fingers, biting her lip to muffle her cry.

Colin gentled her through the aftershocks with kisses that eventually turned into him just breathing, panting against her pussy. She pried her eyes open, blinking dazedly up at the sky. Because *outside*. They were outside, for Christ's sake, and holy shit—she'd just come all over Colin McCrory's face outside. She giggled, quickly slapping a hand over her mouth.

"Something funny?" Colin kissed her hip bone. "Or are you just one of those people who laughs when you come?"

"Hush." She shoved him gently. Mostly because she felt as weak as a kitten and a little because she wasn't actually mad. Amused, to be honest, because *no*, she was not one of those people, but wouldn't it be funny if she were? If she snort-laughed through orgasms? *God*, she felt drunk. Drunk on Colin's fingers and his tongue, loose and lax and warm all over even though her dress was still hiked up around her waist, exposing her bare lower half to the cool Seattle night air. "You just made me come. *In public*."

She whispered, which was sort of hilarious because no one was around to hear her. Even if they were, if someone was scandalized to hear her say the words? They would've had a heart attack looking at her.

"I did." Colin grinned, one of those smiles that creased the corners of his eyes and made her heart thunder inside her chest. No one had any right to be that beautiful and he wanted her and *oh God*, he still had his fingers inside her. Life was a trip. "And I'm about to do it again."

What.

Colin leaned in and without breaking eye contact, licked her clit and it was a miracle she didn't perish on the spot.

Here lies Truly. She died with Colin McCrory's fingers buried up her cunt.

"You didn't think I was going to let you go with just one, did you?" He nuzzled into the damp thatch of neatly trimmed hair at the top of her mound, breathed deep, and—her cheeks prickled with heat that could give the sun a run for its money. "Truly, I'd *live* down here if you'd let me."

"I can't," she said and yet, for some ungodly reason, she fisted his hair between her fingers and dragged him closer. *"Colin."*

He rested his forehead against her hip, fingers working inside her, less a thrust than a relentless crooking against that bundle of nerves that made her breath hitch and her stomach clench. Little electric-like zaps of pleasure rippled up her spine, pressure bloom-ing inside her like a storm.

"One more," he panted, mouth open against her skin, breath hot and damp and—she was wrong. She'd been so sure the sight of Colin on his knees, staring up at her through his lashes, chin sticky with her come, was the hottest thing she'd ever seen. And maybe it had been. But this? Colin's hips working, making shaky, aborted little thrusts, the outline of his cock visible, straining against the denim of his jeans like he was so turned on by eating her out that he couldn't help himself? *Fuck*. "One more, baby. Please? Just give me one more and I swear to God I can die happy."

Truly whimpered, riding the edge of something so big it scared her. Because she wasn't just going to come, she was going to come *apart*, unravel at the seams. She knew it, with the level of cer-tainty she knew her name and knew that Colin McCrory was going to be the end of her.

"Don't stop." She tangled her fingers in his hair and dragged his mouth back where it belonged. The scent of her was heavy in the air, musk mingling with the sweet perfume of the clematis crawling up the building. "Don't or else I'll—"

There wasn't a threat on this earth that could properly capture let alone convey her sheer desperation. Not that it mattered. As soon as the words were out of her mouth, Colin's mouth was on her, lapping at her hungrily.

She was drenched, dripping down her thighs, the crack of her ass. A filthy slick sound filled the air, making her flush all the way to the roots of her hair as the pads of Colin's fingers pressed harder, quicker, expertly against that perfect, magical spot. Ev-erything inside her drew up tight, so tight, and then, all at once, snapped, pressure releasing rhythmically.

Distantly, she heard Colin swear. Just like she heard herself shout his name. He ignored her wail, kept going, curling his fingers hard against the front wall of her cunt, moaning against her when a sticky gush of fluid soaked the inside of her thighs.

She swatted the side of his face with limp fingers, oversensitive. Colin took the hint like a champ and left her clit alone, pressing messy kisses against her hip, the inside of her thigh, anywhere he could reach. He shuddered against her skin and her heart squeezed.

Down the block, a car alarm blared and Truly jumped. She giggled and leaned back against the knob, twisting her key in the lock with still-trembling fingers, punch-drunk and weak.

"Come inside?" she asked, the double entendre far from lost on her. "Not sure I want to press my luck out here and go for round three. That, and I'm pretty sure the condom in my purse is expired."

He let loose an awkward chuckle. "We, uh, might have to wait for round three."

She frowned.

Colin's eyes lowered pointedly to his lap, where a patch of denim had grown dark. *Wet.*

Her mouth went dry. "Oh. You—"

"Yeah." He cringed. "I did."

"But I—I didn't even touch you."

He scrubbed a hand over his face, avoiding her eyes. "Not my finest moment, I know. But seriously, Truly, give me thirty minutes and some Gatorade and I'll make it up to—"

"Shut up, oh my God."

Colin stared up at her, eyes wide and cheeks pink. "What?"

"Did you actually think I'd *care*?" That he'd wanted her that badly? That he'd gotten off on her taste and the sounds she'd made? In what universe was that *not* hot? "That's the hottest thing I've heard in my entire life."

He stared at her, disbelief giving way to relief even as his blush crept higher up his cheeks. "You're serious."

"You got off on making me feel good." She stepped over the threshold into her apartment, letting the door swing open behind her. "I might not have Gatorade, but I think that at least earns you rights to a glass of water and the use of my washing machine."

Colin stood, rising to his full height, cringing softly as he adjusted himself inside his jeans. "Lead the way."

Chapter Twelve

"How the hell have you made it this long without getting scurvy?"

Truly crossed her arms. "Um, maybe because I'm not a pirate during the seventeenth century, *Colin*."

"Scurvy still affects seven percent of the US population today, *Truly*," he said, studying the contents of her refrigerator with a scowl.

"Wikipedia spiral?"

"Don't change the subject," he chided, cheeks pink. "Your fridge is empty."

"It is not. I have cheese—"

"You have Velveeta. You have cheese *product*—"

"I have *cheese*, onions, and um—oh, hey! Look, I have Swiss cheese! Ha! Real cheese! Slices of it . . . four of 'em. *Ha*."

Colin checked the expiration date, lips wavering like he was trying hard not to smile. "Expires tomorrow."

"You know, you're sure acting awfully pretentious for a guy whose ass is hanging out of his borrowed apron."

He reached back, adjusting the bow tied over his bare butt.

You're delusional if you think I'm wearing your ex's sweats, he'd said.

It wasn't like she owned anything else that would fit him. Her Lululemon yoga leggings would've been obscene on him, and he'd have *definitely* hung out from her pair of Soffe shorts, a holdover from her days in high school cheer.

Cooking naked sounded like a recipe for disaster, so bare ass in an apron it was until his boxers finished their spin cycle.

And what an ass it was.

"When you said the contents of your fridge were lean, I wasn't expecting a *Chopped* situation." He shoved aside her oat milk and pickles, the wrinkle between his brows deepening.

She had bread and cheese and onions and—butter? She was pretty sure she had butter. And a drawer full of spices, and a freezer full of ice cream and frost-burned broccoli. It was hardly as dire as he was making it sound. "If you aren't up for the task—"

"Oh no, I'm up for the task," he said, reaching into her cabinet and pulling out a frying pan. "I just hate to think what you'd do without me here."

"Lucky for me, I guess I won't have to find out."

And *that* was a corny as hell thing to say. She'd written some cheeseball lines in her life that made her cringe when she reread them, but she'd never actually said anything that corny. Corny and presumptuous. She was diligently avoiding thinking about what this night meant—was this a hookup? One of those non-date dates Colin talked about? The beginning of something more? Insinuating that there was longevity here was too close to a conversation that she wasn't ready to have tonight.

Colin set the frying pan down with a clatter and stalked toward her in a way that should've been laughable—he was wearing a too-small, cream-colored apron with the words *baking, because murder is wrong*, emblazoned in hot pink, a gag gift from Lulu—

but there was nothing laughable about those quads or the soft look of single-minded focus on his face.

Her breath caught as his hands circled her waist, lifting her up and setting her down onto the counter without even a grunt. He framed her face with his hands, easy to do when they were that big, and tilted her chin, leaving her with no choice but to look directly at him. "If anyone's lucky, it's me."

It didn't sound corny coming out of *his* mouth.

She swallowed thickly and gave him a gentle push, her hand falling to her lap. "I don't know if you'll be saying that if you don't feed me soon."

Colin laughed. "Are you saying the way to your heart is through your stomach?"

"I'm saying I turn into a real bitch when I'm hungry."

"Hm." He opened the fridge. "And that's different than the rest of the time, how?"

"Hey!" She laughed and hurled the dish sponge at him. It sailed over his shoulder and into the vegetable drawer. "Rude."

"I didn't say it was a bad thing." He shut the fridge with his hip, his hands full. "I kind of like it when you get all bitchy." He threw a wolfish grin at her over his shoulder. "It's hot."

"You know how I called you a little odd? I was wrong. You're very odd."

"And you like me anyway." He dropped a kiss against her forehead as he passed on the way to the stove. Her heart squeezed at the domesticity of it all, how right it felt despite being new. "Think that says more about you than it does me."

She bit back a smile but didn't deny it. She did like him. And not just because he gave great head and could apparently cook. Though, that was a plus. "What are you making me?"

"Grilled cheese with caramelized onions. Sound okay?"

Her stomach rumbled. "Sounds amazing." Better than anything she would've whipped up with the abysmal contents of her refrigerator. "Can I help?"

"I don't know. *Can* you?"

"Ha ha." She hopped off the counter and padded across the kitchen on bare feet. "I *can* actually cook, you know."

Like five things and only half of them required an Instant Pot or air fryer.

"Hey, it's okay. There's got to be something you suck at. Keep the balance and all that."

"I almost sensed, like, half a compliment in that."

"I'll bite," he said. "What can you cook?"

"Okay, let's see . . . pasta—"

"You can boil water, congratulations."

"Ass. Okay, maybe I rely on a decent amount of takeout, but that's only because I tend to let my kitchen get a little lean while I'm on deadline."

"Uh-huh. And you're on deadline how many weeks out of the year?" he asked, managing to call bullshit without saying the word.

"A lot of them," she grumbled. "Look, maybe I'm no chef, but I'm perfectly capable of chopping vegetables and buttering bread."

His eyes raked over her, gaze hot, the way his teeth sank into his bottom lip even hotter. "Shame we don't have an apron for you."

It was a tiny galley kitchen, arguably too small for two adults to move around in comfortably, but they made it work. His hands settled on her hips, drawing her against him so he could reach past her for a spatula. She pointed at the napkins on too high a shelf for her to reach without climbing on the counter and Colin handed them to her. They needed to switch places and Colin grabbed her by the hand and twirled her, humming a tune under his breath, making her laugh when he dipped her low like they were on a dance floor instead of in her cramped kitchen, cheap linoleum under their bare feet.

"I like your apartment," he said later, when they'd carried their sandwiches into the living room on paper plates and after he'd pulled on his freshly laundered boxer briefs. He'd taken a seat in the middle of her couch and dragged her down onto his lap and now his chin was hooked over her shoulder. He smelled bright and clean like her laundry detergent and the citrus notes of what had to be his cologne and there was something intoxicating about the combination. She couldn't stop huffing in breaths through her nose, breathing him in between bites of the food he'd made for her.

As much as she got a thrill from playing verbal tug-of-war, there was an argument to be made for this tenderness, in laying down her sword and letting Colin hold her. No more keeping score, just the gentle sweep of his hand along her back and his warm, steady breaths whispering against her skin. As right as his lips had felt against hers, as right as his fingers felt sliding up her thigh, this? This was as good, if not better. Like finding a missing puzzle piece buried under a couch cushion. The satisfaction was dizzying, had her clasping his shirt between her fingers like if she let go, he might float away.

She laughed and his arm tightened around her waist. "Thanks, but I know the place is a mess, McCrory."

The living room was cluttered, brightly colored decorative pillows knocked on the floor, a knitted blanket strewn carelessly across the arm of the couch, sticky notes everywhere, half-dead Sharpies littering the coffee table. A few shriveled leaves lay in front of the window from the pothos plant Mom had given her, the poor thing barely clinging to life because Truly had overwatered it. Her bookshelves were in desperate need of reorganizing, her beloved Underwood typewriter desperately needed dusting, and why was she only now noticing her favorite family picture was hanging crooked on the wall?

"No." Colin's lashes fluttered against her throat when he pressed a kiss to her bare shoulder, his shirt sliding down her arm. A butterfly kiss, some candy-coated corner of her brain noted. "It's . . . happy."

"*Happy*?" That wasn't what she expected. Far from it.

He didn't elaborate, just *hmmed* and kissed her shoulder again, this time a little higher.

"What do you mean?" she pressed.

"I was trying to figure out how you organize your bookshelf," he said, voice quiet, lips brushing her throat with every word. "Because it's not alphabetical by title or author and it's not color coordinated. Honestly, it kind of seems like there isn't any rhyme or reason to it. But that doesn't make a lot of sense."

"No." She smiled. "I guess it doesn't."

"It took a bit for me to work it out," he said, "but the books whose spines are the most cracked are in the middle of the shelf. I think you put the books you've read the most, the ones you love best, front and center. Ease of access is a possibility, but I think you just want to look at the things you love."

She followed his gaze as it swept the room, dare she say lovingly, his eyes lingering on her knitted purple blanket with its lumpy edges and dropped stitches, and on the framed stick figure crayon drawings courtesy of Lulu's daughter. The clutter was still there, her painting still crooked, but in following Colin's gaze it was a little like seeing her living room through fresh eyes.

"It's like how I noticed inside your wallet, in the slot where most people keep their ID, you keep a picture of your parents instead. Because you like looking at it. Because it makes you happy."

"Don't most people like to look at the things that make them happy?" It hardly made her special. "Don't you?"

"Yeah." Colin gripped her chin between his fingers, gently forcing her eyes level with his. "I do."

She couldn't breathe, couldn't blink, was utterly ensnared in Colin's stare. She wasn't sure what it was about this moment that felt more special than any other, but if she could, she'd pause it, this snapshot in time, and she'd frame it, and she'd put it on her shelf, dead center.

"That was incredibly corny," she whispered.

Colin threw his head back and laughed, sharp and loud and bright and it put a funny lump in her throat, made it hard for her to swallow. With anyone else she might've considered the moment broken, but with him it just felt like turning to the next page in a book she'd never read. A book she'd left lingering on her nightstand for weeks, picking it up and putting it back down, her hopes for it so high she feared there was no earthly way the reality of it could live up to her expectations, too afraid she wouldn't like the ending.

She didn't know what would happen next, but for the first time, the thought didn't make her want to close the book and it didn't make her want to flip ahead.

Chapter Thirteen

Up against your front door?" Lulu shrieked. "*Truly!* You little hussy, you. When's the wedding?"

Truly fumbled her phone, nearly dropping it in her shopping cart. She pressed it against her ear and hissed, "Slow *way* down. There's not going to be a wedding."

"Uh-huh. *Sure.* I know you, Truly, and I might not know Colin well, but clearly the guy's obsessed with you. I give it six months before you're shacking up together and a year before one of you pops the question."

Truly tossed a bag of jumbo marshmallows into the cart with a little more force than necessary. "Would you chill?" She snagged six Hershey's bars off the shelf. The one on the bottom cracked in half and she cringed, loosening her grip. No need to take her frustration out on the chocolate. "Please. I don't want to think about weddings or—or anything like that right now, okay?"

"I'm just saying, you were with Justin for how long before you moved in together? How long before you proposed? You have a tendency to move hot and fast—"

"His lease was up, Lulu," she snapped. "Justin's lease was up, and he needed a place to stay and maybe your memory's foggy, but mine isn't. We were together for three years before I proposed, and I only did it then because I knew if I didn't it was never going to happen."

By the time she finished, she was breathing hard and—oh.

The writing had been on the wall, and she'd been so desperate for a happily ever after that she'd done everything she could to ignore it.

Nothing more than a careful intake of breath came over the line.

Truly sighed. "Sorry. I didn't mean to yell at you. I just . . . you're right, okay?" She hated writing middles, often found herself sprinting to the happy ending. Life was no different. With Justin, she'd been eager to flip to the next chapter in their relationship; it had been a race to the finish line. "But I don't want to get ahead of myself. Let me enjoy this. Please."

"No, I'm sorry. I shouldn't have been so pushy," Lulu said, sounding regretful. "I'm just happy for you. When are you seeing him next?"

Truly winced.

That was a great question.

If Saturday night had been a fairy tale, Colin had been the princess, dragging his feet as he left her apartment just before midnight so he wouldn't turn into a pumpkin. Or, you know, so his car wouldn't get impounded. Same thing.

He'd left her with a kiss and a promise to text that he'd made it home safely. And he had.

COLIN (12:34 A.M.): Made it home.

COLIN (12:35 A.M.): Next time, I'm letting them tow my car.

TRULY (12:36 A.M.): Bold of you to assume there's going to be a next time.

COLIN (12:39 A.M.): Nice try. I've got your number. You like me.

TRULY (12:42 A.M.): I like your mouth. Your fingers aren't so bad, either. Your ego, on the other hand . . .

COLIN (12:44 A.M.): ☺

COLIN (12:45 A.M.): Sweet dreams, Truly.

TRULY (12:46 A.M.): Good night, Colin.

TRULY (12:46 A.M.): And thank you. For tonight. I had a really wonderful time.

COLIN (9:18 A.M.): So. Next weekend. Ikea?

COLIN (9:19 A.M.): Or we could try going on an actual date, if you want.

And she just . . . hadn't responded.

Only a day had passed, but a pang of guilt still struck each time she opened her messages and saw that time stamp. Considering how prompt she usually was with her responses, Colin had to know she was avoiding him.

"I'm in Chelan, remember?" she said, sidestepping the question. "I've got Dad arriving tomorrow and Mom the day after that and— I've got my hands full. I spent all of yesterday airing the place out and changing linens and making sure everything's perfect. I need this to work, Lu."

Lulu snorted. "I knew you were gonna spritz the joint down with pheromones, you freak."

Hardly, but she did eye the strawberries and chocolate melts in her cart. Too much? "I'm buying groceries. There's nothing sexy about bran cereal."

"Hey, I personally find a partner who values regularity to be the *pinnacle* of sexiness."

"And you call *me* a freak?" She eyed the paper shopping list crumbled in her fist. She still needed to hit up the meat and sea-food sections, praying they had everything she needed to re-create the Sardinian-style paella her parents had eaten on their honey-moon and *still* raved about. "Hey, you think my parents would notice if I subbed razor clams for cockles?"

"I don't know what the hell a cockle is, but it sounds dirty."

Truly rolled her eyes. "Could you get your mind out of the gutter for a minute and—"

Another cart collided with the nose of hers as she turned the corner, the clang of metal on metal more jarring than the im-pact itself. She jumped, shopping list fluttering to the floor, nearly dropping her phone, too. Truly scowled and bent down to pick up her list.

"I am so sorry. I wasn't paying attention to where I was— *Truly?*"

No goddamn way.

She stood so fast her head spun. Or maybe it was because Colin McCrory was standing in the middle of her favorite mom-and-pop grocery, five hours outside of the city, wearing a pair of pink gingham shorts that showed off an indecent amount of thigh and knees that bore faint bruises that would've sparked her curiosity had she not known firsthand that he'd spent Saturday night kneeling on concrete, head buried between her thighs.

"Truly? Are you still there?"

Shit, Lulu was still on the line. "I'll call you back."

"What? No, you can't just—"

She ended the call and slipped her phone in the back pocket of her capris. "Hi."

Hi? *Hi?* That was what she chose to open with? *Hi?*

He scratched the side of his jaw, looking adorably out of his element, but pleased to see her. "Small world? Um, what are you doing here?"

She made a pointed show of looking down at where their carts still kissed. "Grocery shopping?"

"No wonder you let your fridge get lean if you do your shopping in Chelan." Colin smiled. "Seriously, what are you doing all the way out—"

"Colin? Did you grab the Marcona almonds I asked—oh, hello."

The woman who rounded the corner was pretty, hair bleached a crisp champagne blond, gray roots peeking through her perfectly teased coiffure. Her coloring was paler than Colin's, but the way her eyes crinkled was almost identical, as were the moles splattering her skin and the upturn of her delicate nose. "My apologies. I didn't mean to interrupt." She turned to Colin, brows rising expectantly. "Colin? Are you going to introduce us?"

"Sorry. Where are my manners. Mom, this is Truly. Truly, this is my mother. Truly's . . ." He looked at her, lips quirking in something too forlorn to be a smile. "A friend."

Truly averted her eyes, stomach sinking.

She offered his mother her hand. "It's a pleasure to meet you, Mrs. McCrory."

"Call me Muffy." Her grip was surprisingly firm. "You wouldn't happen to be Truly St. James, would you?"

Muffy. Thank God Lulu wasn't here; Truly could only imagine the jokes she'd make.

"That's me."

"Caitlin's told me so much about you." Muffy beamed. "She's so thrilled to have you on her little show."

Little show? Interesting way to describe 3.1 million subscribers and a Spotify exclusive contract.

Truly kept her smile pasted in place. "Oh, yeah? How sweet of her."

"That's our Caitlin," Muffy said. "A total doll."

Colin rolled his eyes.

"*Such* a doll," Truly said. "Anyway, I should probably—"

"Are you renting a place on the lake?" Muffy asked. "With all these Vrbo and Airbnb sites cropping up, it's hard to keep track of who owns around here and who doesn't. It's been a *real* point of contention with the HOA." She laughed. "I think there's been more noise complaints in the last year than ever before."

Truly glanced down at her outfit—a short-sleeve, lightweight cream-colored cowl-necked sweater, ironed khaki capris, and pale blue Sperry Top-Siders with clouds on them—and wondered what about her screamed noise complaint. "Oh, you're on the association?"

Her parents *disdained* the HOA. *Cop lite*, Dad called them. Mom just said they all suffered from inferiority complexes. Truly was pretty sure they were one and the same.

"I am. But you know, I like to think I'm a *cool* board member," Colin's mother said, shoulders shimmying. "So, are you? Renting?"

Colin pinched the bridge of his nose. "Ma—"

"It's fine," Truly said, reeling. She had no business finding it sweet that he called his mother *Ma*. "No, my parents own a house over on Foxglove Lane. It's the blue house with the dark green shutters and the mailbox shaped like a—"

"Shark!" Muffy clapped her hands. "The Livingstons! Your parents are Diane and Stanley? Well, golly. Why didn't you just *say*? I'd have spared you the interrogation. It's a close-knit community, but I'm sure you understand."

"Totally," she agreed, withering a little on the inside. *Writhing.* "Anyway, I should probably—"

"How *are* Stanley and Diane doing? It's been *ages* since we last caught up. Don't you dare spare a single detail." Muffy wagged a finger. "Tell me."

Colin tugged on her arm. "Ma, come on. Truly's busy."

"She's shopping, Colie-kins." *Colie-kins?* Yikes. "How busy could she be?"

"I mean, I should probably—"

"Are your parents in town?" Muffy asked, steamrolling her. "Or are you by yourself?"

"Uh—"

"You can't just ask someone that," Colin said. "It's creepy."

"It's fine. My parents are arriving tomorrow." It was easier to say that than explain to a stranger that her parents would be arriving separately and only because she'd tricked them into coming here. "I'm just stocking up on the essentials before they arrive."

Muffy frowned. "You're all by your lonesome tonight?"

Her eyes flashed to Colin, who was looking at her curiously. "I—yes?"

Muffy tutted. "Well, that just won't do. You'll have dinner with us."

She could scarcely think of anything more awkward than joining Colin and his parents for dinner after leaving him on read.

"That is *so* kind of you, but I'm sure you already have plans."

"Nonsense." Muffy McCrory batted at the air. "Tell her she's welcome, Colin."

"If she doesn't want to come, Ma—"

"It's not that I don't want to," she said, pleading with Colin with her eyes. "I just . . ." She didn't know how to finish that in a way that wouldn't be saying too much in front of his mother. "I wouldn't want to impose."

"You wouldn't be," Colin said. "Imposing."

She stared, studying the way he held himself, spine rigid, jaw clenched, eyes wide, lips pressed into a flat line. He barely blinked, almost like he was trying to impress some meaning upon her with his eyes. Communicate with her telepathically.

It was the second chance she hadn't realized how desperately she wanted until Colin was standing right there in front of her, staring at her.

Truly turned to Muffy and smiled. "What should I bring?"

Chapter Fourteen

The shadows had lengthened by the time Truly climbed the front porch stairs of the McCrory's lake house.

Granted, the place was less of a lake *house* and more of a lake mansion, taking up at least three lots' worth of well-manicured acreage with grass she'd bet her left tit was regulation length and not a centimeter longer. The siding looked perfectly pressure-washed, not a hint of moss growing on the foundation. *Better Homes and Gardens* could've given it a centerspread.

It couldn't have been more different from her parents' lived-in two-bedroom cottage with its faded green shutters, crooked door knocker, and chaotically gorgeous flower beds, well-tended but sprawling and wild, like something out of a storybook full of fairies and woodland sprites.

Here went nothing. She held her breath and rang the doorbell.

Of course it was Colin who answered, still wearing those gingham shorts.

"Hi." She nervously shoved the pie tin into his chest. "I made a pie."

His brows rocketed to his hairline. "You made this?"

"It's, like, fifty percent Cool Whip and the crust is store-bought, but yeah, I did." From her tote, she yanked out a bottle of pinot noir and a bottle of chardonnay, both nice vintages from a nearby vineyard. "I wasn't sure if your parents preferred white or red, let alone what would go best with dinner, so I brought both. And then I remembered some people don't drink, hence the pie."

Colin whistled when he saw the labels. "Ma's two juleps deep and Pops has been in his office since five, which means he's had at least one whiskey by now. You could serve 'em Carlo Rossi at this point and they'd smile and nod." He stepped aside. "Come on in."

She slipped the wine back inside the tote, bottles clanking. "You, uh, have a lovely home?"

Colin looked amused. "My grandfather built the place; wanted it to be a getaway for the whole family, hence the size. Grandpa McCrory, that is. Never met my mother's father, but according to Ma, he fancied himself too good for working with his hands."

She slipped out of her Sperrys, adjusting the heel of her right sock when it slipped down her foot, flushing hot because Colin had his eyes trained on her. "I take it you're not close to your mom's side of the family?"

Hard to forget how close the McCrory side of the family was after Caitlin's recount of how they'd all crowded around to watch Colin's solo *Sex Sent Me to the ER* horror show.

"Nah," he said, gesturing with a tilt of his head for her to follow him down the hall. "Mom's older sister married into some ultra-rich family that owns a bunch of newspapers around the world. I've only met my cousin on that side of the family once, but he was a real prick, so I figure I'm not missing much."

Like the hall, the kitchen was all off-white paint, stainless steel appliances providing the only color. The granite counters were spotless, not a crumb in sight, and the sink? The sink was undermounted and immaculate, the basin free from soap residue and water spots.

Colin set the pie inside the fridge and she placed both bottles of wine beside the sink, not knowing where else to put them.

"So, where's your mom?" she asked, folding the tote and setting that on the counter, too.

"Finishing touches on her hair, she said. You're early."

The clock above the mounted microwave read *7:03*. "Your mom said seven."

"Which everyone knows means seven thirty."

"Everyone who?" That was patently ridiculous. "Wine opener?" She could *really* go for a drink.

"On your right, top drawer. And I don't know. Probably the same white Anglo-Saxon Protestants who invented beach loafers and Cape Codders and decided names like Bitsie and Muffy were en vogue. Mom's got some weird holdovers from her life before she married Dad."

"Well, my parents always told me if you aren't early, you're late." He snorted. "Okay, Ricky Bobby."

"Okay, *Colie-kins*. It's a theater thing. Early is on time, on time is late, and late? That's unacceptable. How was I supposed to know your mom didn't plan on serving dinner promptly at seven? Speaking of"—she held both bottles—"what's on the menu?"

"Waldorf salad accompanied by Muffy McCrory née Fairchild's specialty."

"Which is?"

Colin grimaced. "Creamed chipped beef."

Ew. "Okay, um, I'm guessing that pairs best with . . ." She cringed. "Red?"

"The only thing creamed chipped beef pairs with is an industrial incinerator." Colin grabbed both bottles from her and made quick work of tearing the foil off the bottle of pinot, before doing the same with the bottle of chardonnay. "And if you can't get your hands on one of those—"

"Lemme guess—store-bought's fine?"

Colin chuckled softly and handed her a glass filled with white wine.

"I missed you."

She narrowly avoiding choking on a mouthful of wine. "You saw me on Saturday—"

"Yeah, and I missed you as soon as I walked out your front door." He crossed his arms. "What's your point?"

Her knees weakened and she slumped against the counter. "I—I ghosted you, I—"

"I don't think it counts as ghosting if it's been under forty-eight hours," he mused.

"Be serious, will you?"

She gasped softly when he set his hands down on the counter, boxing her in, the granite biting into her back. Her heart rabbited inside her chest, pulse skipping.

"Who says I'm not?"

She stared up at him through her lashes. "I figured you'd be upset."

She would be angry. Hell, she *was* angry. Angry at herself for acting like such a coward. Angry that a tiny part of her wished Colin would be angry with her, too. Not because she was trying to punish herself, but because if he were angry, maybe he'd stop treating her so softly. Maybe they'd argue and maybe he'd be the one who wouldn't answer her texts next time and she could tell Lulu and anyone else who asked that she'd tried.

If denying herself what she actually wanted counted as a form of self-flagellation, maybe she *was* trying to punish herself.

His expression softened. "You don't owe me anything, Truly."

Her eyes prickled and her sinuses burned. He wasn't supposed to be *nice*. "Don't I?"

The smile slid off his face. "*No.*" He sounded appalled. "Jesus, no. I figured after Saturday, you either needed space or had changed your mind. If you want me to back off all you have to do is—"

"No." She fisted her hand in his shirt, suddenly terrified by the prospect of him going anywhere. "I don't want that. I don't. I'm sorry, okay? I—" The lump in her throat swelled, making it difficult to swallow. "You're right. I do like you. I like your obscure facts and how your eyes light up when you talk about them, when you share them with me. I like it that you aren't afraid to call me out on my bullshit and that for some reason that's completely beyond me, you haven't given up on me even though I've given you a hundred opportunities and a thousand reasons why. For some reason you like me and most of the time I'm not even sure why, but you do and I like that, too. I pretty much *melt* when you say my name, it sounds better when you say it, and when I'm with you, it's easy to forget what I'm afraid of, but when I'm not, I guess I have a tendency to get in my head."

And in her own way.

His hands drifted from the counter to her hips. He leaned in, nose brushing hers for one breath, two, and her socked toes curled against the tile floor.

"You want me to tell you why I like you?" he whispered. "I can do that. Gladly."

She strained closer, wanting his lips against hers like she needed her next breath. "Colin, you don't actually have to—"

"You're the most stubborn person I've met in my entire life. You're stubborn and you're proud—"

"Those aren't compliments. Those are—"

"—and you're bossy," he continued as if she hadn't spoken. "You're also passionate and when you believe in something, you believe in it with your whole heart. And maybe"—the softest of shuddering sighs escaped him—"I've been looking for someone who believes in me like that."

Finally, *finally* his lips crashed against hers.

She reached up, burying her fingers in his thick hair, trying to drag him impossibly closer, would crawl inside him if she could. The drag of his lips against hers was slick and hot, the kiss wet and messy, the way she liked, the way a kiss was supposed to be, openmouthed desperation tinged with desire, raw and a little filthy, breathing another person's air into your lungs, swallowing their spit, tangling together until whose parts were whose became a mystery.

The doorbell rang and Truly jolted. "Is someone else joining us?"

He stepped back, his brows drawing down into a frown. "Not that I'm aware—"

Muffy McCrory breezed into the kitchen. "Truly, you're here! And good, you already have a drink. Colin, be a dear and set the table?"

"Are we expecting somebody?" he asked.

"Oh." Muffy paused halfway to the hall. "Did I forget to mention Caleb and Ali are joining us?"

"Did you forget—" A muscle in his jaw twitched, his nostrils flaring softly. "Really, Ma? Again?"

Muffy huffed, hands poised on her narrow hips. "Collie, it's been *years*."

"Holidays and special occasions," he spoke slowly, with obvious forced restraint. The words sounded practiced, like they'd been said before.

The doorbell rang once more.

"It would be rude to keep your brother waiting," Muffy said, already moving.

"And that would be tragic." Colin spent a moment glaring at the door through which his mother passed. Before Truly could even open her mouth to ask any of the dozen questions on the tip of her tongue, he turned and with the absolute flimsiest smile asked, "Help me set the table?"

EVERYONE WAS *PERFECTLY* polite.

"Dinner's delicious, Muffy," Ali—Caleb's wife, she'd discovered—said.

She was pretty and willowy, all peaches and cream skin, her heart-shaped face framed with a halo of springy blond curls. She sat across the table from Colin and to her left—Caleb.

Who Colin had forgotten to mention was his *identical* twin.

His hair was different, cropped short all over, which made him look older than thirty-two. Or maybe it was the tan that did it, his skin weathered in a way that Colin's wasn't. The sleeves of his plaid overshirt were rolled up to his elbows, revealing forearms smattered with small silvery scars. The hand holding his fork was rougher, knuckles thick and scarred, and his pinky had a Band-Aid wrapped around it. He wasn't as handsome as Colin, as far as she was concerned, but clearly his whole rugged lumberjack aesthetic did it for Ali, who sat so close to him she might as well have been in his lap. Atop the table, their free hands sat, fingers tangled together.

Muffy glowed at the praise. "Thank you, sweetheart." Her eyes dropped to Truly's plate and her smile dimmed. "Truly, dear, you've barely touched your chipped beef."

She froze with the tines of her fork buried in the mush Muffy called a meal. "It's, um, it's delicious. I'm just . . . savoring it."

Colin disguised his snort of laughter with a cough. "Pardon me." He reached for his water. "Tickle in my throat."

"You're not a vegan, are you?" Muffy asked. "Shoot, I didn't even ask about allergies."

"I'm not a vegan. And no allergies."

"Except to cow cod," Colin said, straight-faced. "Truly's allergic to cow cod."

Truly kicked him under the table, landing a glancing blow to his ankle that didn't do much more than make him grin.

Muffy frowned. "Is that a type of fish?"

"Ignore him. He's—he's mistaken." She pasted on a smile and scooped a disgusting heap of chipped beef into her mouth. "Mm, *mm*. So good."

"Truly, what is it you do?" Ali asked, big blue eyes wide with interest.

She washed the taste of processed meat and milk gravy from her mouth with a sip of crisp white wine. "I'm an author."

Ali gasped excitedly. "An author! Oh, fun! I've always wanted to write a book."

"You could write a book if you wanted to, honey," Caleb said, the most words he'd spoken in a row so far. Loquacious, he was not.

His wife pouted prettily. "If only I weren't so busy."

"I've been telling you, you should just go ahead and quit—"

Ali's lashes fluttered rapidly and the tines of her fork clanged noisily against the gold-rimmed charger beneath her plate. Caleb cut himself off with a cough.

Silence settled over the table. *Awkward.*

Ali recovered like a pro. "What kind of books do you write?"

She dabbed her mouth with her napkin. "Romance."

"Dreamy!" Ali beamed, all pretty, perfect white teeth. "Anything I might've heard of?"

By all accounts, Ali seemed perfectly nice, all bright smiles and big blinking eyes and endless enthusiasm. Which was why Truly couldn't put her finger on what exactly it was about Colin's sister-in-law that rubbed her the wrong way, only that something about her felt *off.* Like how Splenda tasted sweet, but wasn't actually sugar.

"I'm not sure." She smiled. "How familiar are you with queer historical romance?"

The rise of Ali's brows was far from subtle. "Not very. But I'd love some recommendations."

"Sure. After dinner, I'd be happy to give you a list."

The conversation petered off, replaced by the sound of cutlery scraping softly against bone china.

Ali cocked her head, a tiny furrow appearing between her brows as she stared contemplatively across the table. Truly smiled back benignly.

Ali's lips parted, then closed. She cleared her throat delicately.

"So." It was primal, the way that tiny word made the hair on the back of Truly's neck stand on end. "Are you a member of the community?"

"Jesus Christ," Colin mumbled just loud enough for her to hear and reached for his wine.

"Oh." Muffy fluttered her hands in the air. "Ali, dear, I don't know if that's an appropriate question to—"

"It's fine," Truly said, smiling tightly, insides writhing because it was *not* an appropriate question to ask, but she'd answer it gladly anyway. "I am."

The *is that gonna be a problem* was silent and implied.

"That's nice." Ali's eyes flitted between Truly and Colin. "Is that how you and Colin met? At a parade or something?"

Jesus.

"Oh, sure," Colin said, deadpan. "Our mutual friend Dorothy introduced us."

Truly swallowed her laugh and with it, another sip of wine.

"Who's Dorothy?" Muffy frowned. "I thought Caitlin introduced you."

"Oh, Caitie," Ali said, saving Truly from explaining the queer subtext of *The Wizard of Oz* and Judy Garland to the table. "Caleb and I had hoped she'd be here."

Muffy waved Ali off. "You know Caitlin. Hard to pin that girl down."

"Actually, she had a meeting with several execs at Spotify," Colin said, cutting his eyes at his mother. "Or did she forget to mention that?"

Muffy pursed her lips and stabbed at an apple on her salad plate.

"Mr. McCrory? Colin told me your father built this house.

I'm afraid I don't know much about architecture, but the place is beautiful," Truly said, trying to keep the conversation going. These weighted silences made her skin crawl.

"My father was a talented man. Built his business from the ground up." Cormac McCrory shoveled a forkful of chipped beef into his mouth. "How's work, Colin?"

Colin strangled the stem of his wineglass. "Great, Dad. Thanks for actually asking."

Not for the first time tonight, Truly felt more like she'd stepped into a minefield than a dining room.

"Truly—it is Truly, isn't it?" Cormac asked, lifting his glass of whiskey to his lips. "Interesting name."

"The Livingstons," Muffy said, as if that were an explanation.

"Ah," Cormac said, managing to pack an absurd amount of condescension into that tiny word. "Do you like jokes, Truly?"

Beside her, Colin stiffened.

She set her fork down carefully. "If they're funny."

"This one is," Cormac promised, taking a healthy swig of his drink. "Do you know the difference between a lawyer and a jellyfish?"

Across the table, Caleb chuckled under his breath.

Colin heaved a sigh.

Truly felt like she was going to be sick.

"What's the difference, Dad?" Colin asked. "I can't wait to hear this one."

"The difference"—Cormac rested his elbows on the table, eyes on Truly—"is that one is a spineless, gutless blob. The other is a form of sea life."

Colin shoved his plate away.

Truly looked around the table, waiting for someone, anyone, to speak up in his defense.

Everyone was studiously focused on their plates except Caleb, whose shoulders shook with silent laughter.

"Cormac," Muffy chided weakly. "Be nice."

Be nice? Fuck that and fuck everyone at this table.

"I'm sorry." She smiled benignly, reaching under the table and finding Colin's hand. She squeezed his fingers tight. "I don't get it."

Ali dropped her fork.

"Could you explain it to me?" Truly asked sweetly.

"Lawyers are—well they're—" Colin's father turned a shade of red that couldn't be healthy. "Never mind."

"Huh." She shrugged affably. "I guess it must not have been very funny."

Cormac scowled into his whiskey and Truly bit back a smile, a bitter part of her wanting to freeze *this* moment, frame it, and place it . . . not in the middle of her proverbial shelf, but somewhere just left of center.

She'd burn a hundred bridges if it meant erasing the frown from Colin's face. Beneath the table, he laced their fingers together and that alone made this moment worth remembering.

"So, Ali." Truly smiled. "What is it *you* do?"

"I'm a donor relations specialist. Which is fine, but you know." She smiled and shrugged and sipped her water. "It's not a forever thing."

A pointed glance passed between Ali and Caleb, his brows rising. She nodded.

Caleb set his napkin down beside his plate and cleared his

throat. "There's actually something Ali and I wanted to say. We're—do you want to say it, babe?"

Ali beamed at Colin and Caleb's parents across the table. "Muffy, Cormac, you're going to be grandparents."

"A baby?" Muffy screeched and stood so fast she knocked the table, her glass toppling over, blessedly empty. "Oh, I'm so *happy*." She sniffled, rounding the table and dragging Caleb and Ali into a hug.

Mr. McCrory held his nearly empty glass aloft. "Congrats, kid. Knew you had it in you."

The sound of wood screeching against wood made her shiver.

"Congratulations," Colin said, perfectly polite, congenial even, smile fixed. And if she weren't watching him so closely, he might've seemed okay. But she was watching him, was so attuned to Colin that he could've blinked wrong and her spidey-senses would've tingled. His eyes were focused an inch over everyone's heads, gaze distant and smile just this side of too wide to be real. A flimsy veneer. "Excuse me. I'd like to check on the dessert. Be back in a sec."

Bullshit, bullshit, *bullshit*. Truly had brought a cream pie and he knew it.

But she sat perfectly still, quietly seething with a smile pasted on her face as everyone took his excuse at face value, didn't even question as he strode from the room, shoulders unnaturally stiff.

When he hadn't returned after five minutes and the conversation about potential baby names grew grating, Truly asked after the restroom.

Muffy gave her vague directions to pass through the kitchen, hit the hall, and *you can't miss it*. Which didn't matter because

Truly didn't really need to pee. She was mostly looking for an excuse to find Colin.

. . . who wasn't in the kitchen. Big shocker there.

He wasn't in the bathroom, either. But she did find a window in the half bath overlooking the drive. It was foggy out for this time of year, but not so foggy she missed the gray-blue BMW backed into the drive, a rainbow sticker on the bumper.

Oh, she *knew* there was a reason she didn't like that bitch.

Truly tore out of the bathroom, a woman on a fucking mission, daring anyone to get in her way. God only knew what drew her to the French doors at the end of the hall, but she followed her intuition.

Moonlight glinted off Colin's hair, as glossy and dark as the lake. He was down on the dock, bare feet cutting waves in the still water.

Truly shut the door behind her softly and crept down the knoll leading to the dock, cool grass tickling her feet. It wasn't her goal to sneak up on him, but she wasn't exactly looking forward to announcing herself, either.

Until she glimpsed the cigarette between his fingers and saw fucking red.

Her feet slapped against the aged wooden boards of the dock. Colin craned his neck, looking over his shoulder, about a second too late to stop her from reaching down and plucking the cigarette from his hand. She didn't think, just tossed it in the lake with a noise she wasn't ashamed to call a growl.

"The *hell*?" Colin spun toward her, water rippling around his ankles.

She stomped her heel against the dock, wood trembling beneath her foot. "Those will *kill* you, you know that?"

"Something's gotta do it," he mumbled, and her blood reached boiling.

"Not on my watch," she spit out. "I swear, Colin—"

"It wasn't even lit. I didn't even bring a lighter."

With that dumb as shit confession hovering in the space between them, the fight drained from her. She sank down to her knees, rough wood biting into her skin as she swiveled, twisting to the side, letting her bare feet skim the surface of the water. "*God*, I hate you."

She didn't. Not even a little bit. Not at all.

Colin knocked his shoulder against hers. "I like you, too, Truly."

She laughed. "So what? Were you gonna, like, absorb the nicotine through your skin? Was that your security cigarette? Like a blanket but dumber and deadlier?"

He cringed. "I don't even smoke. Not anymore. I quit . . . God, I don't even remember. Two years ago? Yeah, two years ago." He looked at her, sly smile spreading across his face. "You realize you probably just gave some poor, unsuspecting fish cancer, right?"

"Shut up." She buried her face in her hands and groaned. "If you don't smoke anymore, where did you even get that?"

A moment passed and then another before it registered that her question might've been loaded.

"Ali. Her jacket, I mean. She smokes—smoked? I don't know now because of the . . ." Colin let out a loud, painful-sounding breath through his nose and gripped the side of the dock, his knuckles turning white. "I figured she'd have a pack on her."

She dragged in a breath and held it until her lungs burned. Here went nothing.

"I saw the rainbow bumper sticker on her car. 'Puts the *A* in ally'? You sort of failed to mention your ex-girlfriend is married to your brother. Not that you had to! I know it's not my business."

Colin gave a self-effacing laugh. "When your ex dumps you for a guy that has your same face you *know* it has everything to do with your personality. With who you are. I guess it's hard not to have a complex about it. I'm over her, I am, but I won't lie and say it's not difficult seeing her do all the things with my brother that we talked about doing one day—getting married, starting a family. And Mom and Dad want to sweep the whole thing under the rug. We were together for three years and they act like we never even dated."

"No offense?" But while they were being one hundred percent, no-holds-barred honest with each other? "Your family sucks."

"None taken," he said, lips twitching. "I went no-contact for a while, but then Mom had a cancer scare about a year ago and . . . there's a lot of hurt and I know it's not okay, how they act, blindsiding me, trying to force me to mend fences with Caleb. That wasn't the first time Mom's pulled that sort of stunt. My boundaries could admittedly be better." He smiled ruefully. "It's something I'm working on with my therapist."

"That's good," she said. "That you know it's not okay, I mean."

Colin reached down and plucked her hand off her thigh and brought it to his lips, laying a kiss against her knuckles. "Thanks for sticking up for me in there. You didn't have to, but it means a lot to me that you did."

Someone ought to. "Pretty sure your family hates me now."

"They started it." His thumb stroked over her palm, sending a shiver through her. He must've thought she was cold because he draped an arm around her and drew her snuggly against his side.

"Play stupid games, win stupid prizes. They don't like you? Their loss. I do. So. Screw 'em."

There wasn't exactly any love lost on her side, either. "If you say so."

He looked at her, then back at the house, an appraising glint in his eye. "I wonder . . ."

"Hm? You wonder what?"

"How long do you think it would take them to notice if we left?"

"Leave?" She laughed. "Really?"

"You can't tell me you seriously want to go back in there."

Her face must've spoken volumes because he stood and grinned down at her, dark eyes glimmering under the light of the moon.

"Come on." He held out his hand. "Let's get out of here."

Chapter Fifteen

M y turn." Colin dunked a particularly crisp fry into the dregs of Truly's strawberry milkshake. "Would you rather kiss your ex or your mortal enemy?"

"Hm." She leaned back against the hood of her car, admittedly too small for two grown adults to sit on comfortably without getting extra cozy. Then again, Truly wasn't complaining. "What if I don't have a mortal enemy?"

"Ah come on, everyone's got a mortal enemy." Colin turned and reached inside the grease-stained paper bag they'd set on the hood and grabbed out a napkin. "High school rival? Neighbor who constantly steals your favorite parking spot? Twitter nemesis?"

Truly took a swig from the bottle of pinot they'd pilfered from his parents' kitchen—the bottle she'd brought—and stared out at the lake. "I already kissed my high school rival, my parking spot is assigned, and I stay off Twitter for my own sanity."

If someone had asked her two months ago who her mortal enemy was, she'd have half-jokingly answered Colin McCrory.

But that was then, and this was now, and he was a lot of things with the potential to be more, but her mortal enemy wasn't one of them.

"You kissed your high school rival?" He took the bottle of wine from her when she held it out. "I feel like there's got to be a story there."

"It was a stupid game of truth or dare freshman year." She rolled her eyes at the thirteen-year-old memory. "She told everyone I drooled on her, and I got called *Drooly Truly* for two weeks before everyone moved on to the next equally dumb high school drama. Not much of a story, all things told."

"I, for one, happen to think you are an excellent kisser." He pressed his lips against her hairline, and like each time he did, she had to bury the urge to thrash her feet and squeal her excitement up at the stars, the piece of her heart that would always be a teenage girl shrieking *he likes me, he really likes me.* "Come on. You still have to answer the question."

She let her hands fall to her sides. The wind was cool against her skin, a gentle breeze blowing across the lake; it had rained earlier in the afternoon and the air smelled like ozone, pungent and sweet. "I don't have a mortal enemy, and the only person I've ever *really* been in competition with is myself. I don't want to tongue kiss my personal demons, but I *definitely* don't want to kiss my ex, so I'm sort of at a stalemate here."

Colin took a swig from the bottle. "You were with your ex for six years, right? Any big relationships before that?"

"It's been a while since I've been on a first date, but isn't discussing exes more of a third date topic?"

His jaw fell and she had to bite back a laugh at the wide-eyed look of shock splashed across his face. "First date?"

"You like me, I like you, we've got food and a pretty spectacular view." She shrugged. "Like I said, it's been a while for me, but I'm pretty sure we've got all the trappings of a date."

A slow smile spread across his face, bringing out the dimples in his cheeks and the creases at the corners of his eyes. "If that's your definition of a date, I'd argue this is our third."

"Are you seriously trying to—what, negotiate up our date count?" She laughed. "Wow, I really am on a date with a lawyer."

He set the bottle of wine on the roof and rolled onto his side the best he could on the hood of her tiny car, looming over her. Backlit by the canopy of stars in the sky, Colin's moles reminded her more of constellations than ever.

He raised his left hand and started ticking off these supposed dates on his fingers, beginning with his thumb. "We had coffee together."

"You mean the day we ran into each other? You're counting a total coincidence as a date?"

"I liked you then, you liked me, we had food and a view. Ergo, according to your definition, a date."

"We were sitting inside a coffee shop. There was no view."

"Sure there was." He grinned and she already knew what was coming. "I was looking at you."

Just because she was expecting the line, didn't lessen its impact. An answering smile took over her face, cheeks warming pleasantly. "Fine. I'll give you that one. What was our second date?"

"Saturday, obviously. The bar on Lenora."

Truly called foul. "That was *not* a date. Your sister was there."

"People used to go on dates with chaperones all the time."

Laughter sputtered from her. "A chaperone? Oh my God, I can't wait to see the look on Caitlin's face when I tell her that according to you, she chaperoned our second date."

"Considering she ditched us, she wasn't very good at it."

"Agreed. You did sort of ravish me against my front door that night."

A breathless laugh escaped his wine-stained lips. "Ravish? Wow, I really am on a date with a romance author. A third date at that."

"Oh my God, fine. You win. Third date."

Colin raised a fist in the air.

"Dork." She rolled her eyes fondly. "To answer your original question, considering I was twenty-one when I met Justin, not really. I had a boyfriend in high school, but we split up after graduation. It was amicable. He lives in New Mexico with his wife and their daughter, who just turned three. We send each other Christmas cards."

"That sounds nice." He squeezed her fingers. "I'm not in touch with any of my exes—aside from Ali and that's not as much my choice as it is a begrudging desire to keep some semblance of peace."

"Someone wise once told me peace isn't the absence of conflict. It's about being able to have disagreements without being contemptuous or defensive and I'm pretty sure that requires both parties be on board."

"Someone wise, huh?" He smirked. "Tell me more about this wise somebody. Is he cute? How's his ass? Come on, St. James. Curious minds want to know."

"He's all right," she teased, reaching over to pinch the soft skin of his arm. "Kind of cocky but sweet. He gives great head and makes a mean grilled cheese. Can't complain."

Colin grinned up at the sky, looking adorably pleased by the praise. "Any chance I could get that in writing or—"

She poked him in the stomach, muscle unyielding. "Was Ali your first serious relationship? Can I ask, or is that not—"

"You can ask." He draped an arm around her, dragging her close. "I dated around in my twenties, but either I wasn't looking for something serious at the time or they weren't, so all those relationships fizzled out pretty fast. And then I met Ali and I thought she was—she was *it*, you know? On paper, we wanted the same things. Marriage, kids . . . and she had all these plans. She was in an LPN to RN program when we met, talked about wanting to become a CNP one day, maybe a pediatric nurse. She talked about all these hopes and dreams and then about a year after we'd been dating, out of nowhere she dropped out of her nursing program and it—that was fine. I didn't *care*, I just . . . I wanted her to be happy, you know?"

Truly nodded.

"Only, it wasn't what I'd call reciprocal." He leaned back, pillowing his head against a folded arm. "We'd have dinner with my folks and Dad would start in on me and my job, just like he did tonight, and I used to take the bait. We'd have these—these all-out screaming matches. Dad would just tear into me, belittling all my choices. I'd yell, Mom would cry into her fucking napkin, and Ali . . . Ali would just sit there picking at her food, acting totally unfazed by it all. She'd sit there, perfectly polite, and later we'd leave and in the car I—I needed someone on my side. Someone to tell me my dad was wrong. That I wasn't a total fuckup for wanting to carve out my own path and follow my own dreams. And Ali, she'd play fucking devil's advocate. *Your parents just care about you, Colin. Is it really so bad that your dad's proud of his business?*" He scoffed. "It's funny. My parents loved—*love*—Ali. Dating her was probably the only thing I did that my parents were actually happy with."

"For whatever it's worth, I don't think you're a fuckup, Colin. You're far from it."

He cleared his throat once, twice, staring up at the sky, expression indecipherable. "It's worth a lot, actually." He found her hand and squeezed her fingers. "Sorry, that, uh, got heavy fast."

Heavy wasn't necessarily a bad thing in her book. "In case you forgot, I am the one who was trying to poke around and ask about your past after only having met you . . . what, twice?"

"Oh, right. How could I forget you telling me you were surprised I'd never been divorced?"

"In my defense, I didn't know you then."

"Okay, now that you know me, what's the verdict?" He grinned. "Still think I'm ex-husband material?"

"If I say no, does that imply I think you're husband material or just plain unmarriageable?"

"Do you? Think I'm husband material? Generally speaking."

"Hm." She schooled her expression. "How's your health insurance?"

"Oh, I see." He smirked. "Want me to talk about my PPO, baby? I could tell you about my deductible?"

She faked a moan. "Don't stop."

"You know, I'd have mentioned that I get dental insurance a lot sooner if I'd have known that did it for you."

She snorted. "Oh, did you think because I'm a romance author that I like candlelit dinners and grand gestures? We're experiencing late-stage capitalism, McCrory. Health care's hot."

He tugged her closer, tucking her head under his chin. "Joking aside, you realize I'm fishing to find out whether I'm going to get a fourth date, right?"

"Odds are looking decent," she teased. "I'd say . . . eighty–twenty."

He whistled. "Damn. Anything I can do to tip the scales a little further in my favor?"

She lifted her head and hummed, pretending to think. "I could possibly be swayed with a kiss."

"Possibly, huh?" He was already leaning in. "I'll take those chances."

His lips pillowed softly, sweetly against hers in the chastest of kisses. He drew back and smiled. "Odds?"

"Hm. Eighty-five to fifteen."

Colin buried a hand in her hair, tugging gently until she tipped her head back. He left a trail of kisses from her temple down to her jaw. "Now?"

"Eighty-six to fourteen," she said, grinning up at the sky.

Colin huffed, breath hot against her skin. "And now?" He punctuated the question with a hard nip against her jaw.

"Mm, eighty—" Her breath stuttered when his lips migrated south, sucking stinging kisses into the side of her throat that were sure to leave a mark. "Eighty-seven to—to thirteen."

He lifted his head, regarding her with low-lidded eyes. His gaze lingered on the side of her throat, almost appraising. He abandoned his grip on her hair and reached out, tracing the progression of his mouth with his thumb, pausing at the juncture where her neck met her collarbone, where he'd left a bruise in the shape of his mouth on Saturday. It had faded slightly, but a faint outline persisted against her best attempts to cover it with concealer.

He pressed his thumb against the bruise and even though it was mostly healed, Truly whimpered. His gaze snapped to hers and—

Colin looked like he wanted to devour her.

"I'll be so fucking good for you, Truly," he promised, thumb sweeping against the front of her throat. "You want me on my knees? Say the word and I'll eat you out until my jaw fucking locks. Tell me what you want, and I'll do it."

Jesus *Christ*. "You're unreal." She slipped her hands under his shirt, popped the button on his jeans, and lowered his zipper far enough to reach into his briefs.

"Truly," he warned.

"What?"

Colin dropped his forehead against hers. "Are you *trying* to make me come in my jeans this time?"

"Worked out okay for me last time."

"I'm not going to come in my jeans like a goddamn teenager," he promised. "The next time I come? It's going to be inside you." She gasped and he tilted his head to the side, heavy-lidded eyes considering. "*On* you, maybe, if you're into that."

She clamped her thighs together and swallowed a whine. "*Fuck.*"

"Please tell me I can put my mouth on you." His hips rocked against her hand. "I've been thinking about it all day. Want you to come on my tongue."

She nodded frantically. "Yes. Okay. Yeah."

Colin laughed breathlessly like he was relieved. Un-fucking-real.

"Get comfortable," he said, settling between her thighs and flipping up the skirt of her sundress. "I'm going to be down here a while."

God. "Overachiever."

Colin kissed the inside of her knee and dragged her underwear down her legs. "When it comes to making you feel good? No such thing as overachieving."

He took his time, peppering kisses along the inside of her thighs and the top of her mound, his hands sweeping over her hips and up her sides in a circuit that made her shiver. She grabbed him by the hair and tried to drag his mouth closer.

When he laughed, his breath ghosted over her clit. She shivered and huffed. *"Colin."*

"Shh, just lay back and relax." With his thumbs, he spread her apart. "Let me enjoy this."

"You're so—"

She broke off with a moan when Colin ran his tongue up her slit.

"Sorry, I'm what?" he asked, eyes wide and expression innocent, smiling like butter wouldn't melt in his perfect mouth.

"You're *going* to be a dead man if you don't put your mouth back on me."

He chuckled. "You say the sweetest things to me, baby."

She'd thought it couldn't get any better than the first time Colin went down on her against her front door, but each time he put his mouth on her, he redefined the word *mind-blowing*. He dropped a kiss to her clit before sucking it between his lips and flicking it with his tongue, pace fast and pressure firm, his grip on her bruising, fingers digging into her thighs.

She lifted a trembling hand and rested it against the back of his head. "Can you—can you—"

Colin hummed in question and her back arched off the hood.

"Can I what?" He licked her clit and she whimpered.

Her cheeks warmed. Why was it so much harder to ask for what she wanted than to tell him what to give her? "Can you put your fingers inside me?"

"You feeling empty, baby?"

She held her breath as his fingers slid between her folds and circled her entrance. "Uh-huh."

"I can fix that," he murmured, watching as he sank a finger inside her. He hissed under his breath, the sound devolving into a groan. "You're so goddamn hot on the inside."

She whimpered and clenched desperately around that one finger. "Don't tease me."

Another finger slipped inside her, and Colin crooked both, making her back arch. "I think you like it when I tease you. It sure seems to get you wet."

A moan tore itself up her throat. "Can I have another?"

Colin pressed a tender little kiss to her hip bone and added the third finger she'd asked for, stretching her sweetly, making her blood sing.

"See." The way he fucked her with his fingers was maddening, his pace slow, fingers dragging almost all the way out before sliding back in. "That wasn't so hard, was it?"

She whimpered when he curled his fingers, grazing a spot that made her thighs quake.

Colin dropped a kiss to her clit before lifting his head, tongue sweeping against his bottom lip. In the moonlight, his mouth looked bruised.

"You close?" The slick sound of his fingers pumping into her grew louder as she grew wetter. "Already?"

Her lips trembled, gasps spilling out from between them. "Uh-huh."

Instead of saying anything, Colin groaned against her and doubled down, fucking her harder. With the hand not buried between her legs, he reached up and pressed hard on her lower stomach, somehow making everything he was doing to her feel that much more intense until with the right curl of his fingers, he sent her flying.

Heat spread through her veins, her lungs aching, the muscles in her stomach burning as she curled forward, hand buried in Colin's hair. She couldn't make up her mind whether to hold him against her or shove him away, the pulsing pleasure sharp and good and too much.

Colin gave her clit one last lick that made her muscles jerk, then lifted his head and smiled up at her, looking pleased with himself.

She sighed, slumping against the hood of the car, boneless and spent, and tried to catch her breath. "Oh my God."

He eased his fingers from her, leaving her empty, her walls clenching down, wanting him back inside her, filling her up.

Colin prowled up her body. "Good?"

She couldn't make her mouth work.

"*That* good, huh?" He smirked.

Yes. Rather than answer, Truly slipped her hand inside his briefs and grazed his cock with her fingertips.

His breath stuttered from between his lips.

A ring pierced the air and Truly froze.

Colin groaned. "My phone."

"Ignore it," she said, wrapping her hand around him.

He nodded jerkily and rocked his hips.

His phone had only stopped ringing when it started up again.

Colin swore under his breath.

Her hand fell to her side. "Put it on silent?"

He nodded and stretched over her, grabbing his phone off the roof of the car. A scowl twisted his features. "It's my mom." With a sigh, he lifted the phone to his ear.

"Yeah?" he answered tersely.

Whatever his mother said caused his face to darken.

"Can't he just—" He pinched the bridge of his nose. "Yeah, okay. Fine. Bye."

He jammed his thumb against the screen, ending the call.

"I take it they noticed we were gone."

Colin let out a laugh that sounded far from amused. "Ali's car won't start, so Dad's letting them borrow his. They need me to move my car so they can get out of the garage."

She could do nothing to stifle her groan.

Not only did Muffy McCrory not understand the meaning of boundaries, but she was also a complete and total cockblock.

"Lyft exists for a reason," she grumbled, watching with a frown as Colin stood and tucked himself back inside his pants.

He leaned down and pressed a kiss to the corner of her mouth. "You're cute when you pout."

Whatever her face did then made him laugh.

"Fine. I'll drive you back." Truly stood and brushed off the back of her dress. "But that doesn't mean I have to like it."

Or his family.

Hands on his zipper, Colin paused. He chuckled under his breath and looked up at her with a wicked grin that had her insides fluttering wildly. "What do you say we take the long way back?"

THE McCRORY'S GARAGE was open when Truly pulled up, idling in front of the curb.

"Give your parents my best," she said, stone-faced.

Colin leaned across the console and with two fingers resting beneath her chin, leaned in, kissing her sweetly, *briefly*. Parting was such sweet sorrow and all that.

"Thank you," he said, thumb stroking her cheek. "For tonight."

"Shouldn't I be the one thanking you? For . . ." Her brows rose meaningfully. "You know."

He huffed softly. "You don't ever have to thank me for doing that."

"I'm going to return the favor one of these days," she promised.

Colin lingered, seat belt still fastened like he was as disinclined to leave as she was to let him. "I'm, uh, I wanted you to know. I'm not seeing anyone else. And I'm not planning on it, either. Just so you know."

He looked at her, eyes flitting across her face almost as if he was nervous.

"I'm not seeing anyone else, either." She didn't laugh, but it was a near thing. "Clearly."

Colin breathed a barely perceptible sigh of what could only be relief and this time, she couldn't help herself.

"Did you seriously think I'd be interested in dating anyone else when it took you how long to convince me to agree to go out with you?"

He grinned. "I'm a patient guy."

"What you are is a handful, McCrory."

His teeth sank into his bottom lip and his gaze dropped to his lap.

"Get out of my car."

Colin snickered. "But Truly—"

"Out. Go. Skedaddle."

"Ooh, I love it when you get bossy."

She smacked his arm, which only made him laugh harder.

"You're beginning to make me regret agreeing to go steady with you."

A slow, sly smile spread across his face. "*Steady?* Do I need to ask your dad for permission to pin you? Wanna wear my letter-man jacket?"

Thank God it was practically dark in the car, only a soft glow emanating from the dash, because she had no doubt her face was bright red. "I don't know what else to call it!"

Back when she'd started dating Justin, she'd sort of . . . assumed. One date had led to another and then he'd moved in and some-where along the way she'd just started introducing him to everyone as her boyfriend. And that was that.

"Exclusive?" Colin supplied, still grinning. "Or you could just call me your boyfriend."

She wrinkled her nose. "You aren't really much of a *boy* though."

He had too much chest hair to be called that.

Colin laughed. "How about your boo? Your bae? Your beau? Your manfriend?" He wiggled his brows. "Your *lover?*"

He let the *r* roll off his tongue, so exaggerated she couldn't help but laugh.

"On second thought, we can stick with boyfriend." It must've been her turn to be struck with a case of nerves, because her chest seized, her breathing suddenly shallow. "I mean, if that's what you want," she said, aiming for nonchalant and no doubt missing by a mile. "I don't want to assume—"

Colin gripped her by the chin and dragged her across the console, kissing her until she couldn't think, until it was just his lips against hers, his breath, her breath, *theirs*, her concerns melting away.

"Assume," he murmured against her lips. "*Please*, assume."

She grabbed him by the collar of his shirt. "When can I see you next?"

"Depends on when you're heading back to the city," he said. "I know you mentioned earlier that your parents are arriving to-morrow, but I wasn't sure if that was just to get my mom off your back, or—"

"Oh, no." Her grip loosened. "It's . . . it's kind of a funny story?"

He frowned. "Okay?"

"Do you remember that conversation we had where I said I wished I could lock my parents in a room together and then I joked about *Gerald's Game*, and we talked about *The Parent Trap*?"

Colin nodded along. "I remember."

"Well, I started thinking about what you said and about how if I could just get my parents to talk to each other, *really* talk, I think—no, I *know* they can fix whatever's wrong. But with them dead set on taking time apart, they're only ever together when I'm there, too. As soon as I leave, it's back to their metaphorical respective corners. It's too easy for them to hide in the city." Hide from each other, hide from their problems, hide those problems from her. "But the lake house is relatively remote and it's full of happy memories."

Happy memories that would hopefully remind them that the love they had was worth fighting for.

"That's really great, Truly." Colin sounded genuinely happy for her. "That's got to make you happy that they agreed to spend some time out here."

"I mean, yeah." She laughed. "If they actually knew what they were agreeing to, it would."

He laughed along with her, though his laughter was more of puzzled amusement than true mirth. "I'm lost."

She put the car in park so she could actually turn and fully face him without her seat belt biting into her neck. "I knew there was no way they'd agree to spending time together, so I kind of . . . conveniently left that part out. Dad thinks I invited him here to see a local production of his favorite show and spend some quality father-daughter time, and my mom thinks the same, except instead of a show it's antiquing and visiting wineries."

"I . . ." Colin blew out a breath. "Is that wise?"

Was it—she sat straighter. "It was your idea. You're the one who brought up *The Parent Trap.*"

"It was a joke. It was—I was kidding. You and I, we were messing around. I wasn't seriously suggesting you trick your parents into spending time together."

Yeah, well, true words were often spoken in jest. Didn't he want her to take him seriously?

"They're not exactly chomping at the bit to spend time together without me pulling strings."

Colin struggled for a second with his seat belt, the latch sticking. Finally, he managed to free himself and swiveled in his seat, facing her fully.

"And as much as it sucks, and I know it does, that's their choice," he said, voice infuriatingly even. "These are your parents, Truly. I know you love them—"

"I'm doing this *because* I love them."

So much. She loved them and she loved the love they shared, the love that she supposedly represented.

Was it so wrong that she wanted to do whatever she could to salvage it?

"Your heart"—Colin's hand drifted, fingers skimming the

swell of her breast, skin left bare, pressed up by the sweetheart neckline of her dress—"is in the right place. I'm not doubting that."

"You're doubting *something*."

He dropped his hand and even though she was miffed that he wasn't on board with her plan, the disappearance of his touch left her bereft. "This isn't something you can fix. Your parents, they have to want to fix their marriage. *Their* marriage."

"So I'm just supposed to sit back and watch them do nothing? Watch them throw thirty-three years away?"

She still wasn't entirely sure this wasn't all because of a midlife crisis, a seven-year itch multiplied by four and change.

"Not all relationships are built to last, Truly."

Hot, frustrated tears sprang to her eyes. She blinked fast to keep them from spilling over.

"Hell, McCrory." Hurt leeched out into her laugh, giving it a sharp edge she couldn't have blunted had she tried. "With an attitude like that, what's the point in trying at all?"

If some relationships were doomed from the start, why ever put your heart on the line? Why risk it?

"I don't want to fight with you," he said.

Neither did she. Arguing with Colin, *real* arguing, made her stomach ache.

She sucked in a slow, steady breath and counted to ten. When she spoke, she was careful to keep her tone even and her voice level. "Maybe you should just go."

Before she said something they'd both regret.

His face crumpled. "Truly—"

"You've got to move your car, right?" A flicker of movement caught her eye; the curtains in the window beside the front door had been drawn and someone was looking out. She jerked her chin toward the house. "Looks like someone's getting restless."

Colin scrubbed a hand over his face. "I don't like the idea of leaving like this. Can I text you later?"

She gave a jerky shrug, feeling disconnected from her body. Like there was too much happening inside her head to care about the rest of her. "If you want."

With a grimace, Colin opened the door. The breeze blew and even though it was a balmy night, she shivered.

"Drive safe?"

She nodded, hating the stiltedness, hating that Colin was only two feet from her but he felt miles away.

The opposite of being on the same page.

"I will. You, too. Drive safe, I mean."

Colin lingered, looking like there was more he wanted to say. He closed his eyes and shut the door and Truly—

She put on her seat belt, took two deep breaths, and shifted the car into drive.

Regardless of the time, she had a feeling she was going to be awake for a long, long time.

Chapter Sixteen

Well, excuse me for caring." Truly tossed the box of Cocoa Puffs back into the pantry. Chocolate equaled comfort and if anything called for comfort, it was Mom glaring daggers at her from across the kitchen island.

They'd been going round and round for the better part of a half hour, Mom tearing into her as soon as she stepped through the front door of the lake house, arriving just after four. Dad's Toyota in the driveway had been hard to miss and Mom . . . to say she was displeased by Truly's plot to get them both in the same place would be an understatement.

"Caring and meddling are two entirely different things, Truly." Mom set her hands on her hips and scowled across the kitchen island. "Two guesses which this is and the first doesn't count."

"Oh, what a puzzle." She scoffed, grabbing the oat milk from the fridge. "It's only meddling because you don't like it."

"Big shock that your father and I aren't happy about being lied to by our daughter."

Dad, who'd been mostly silent, turned on his barstool, glasses slipping down the bridge of his nose. "Your mother and I aren't keen on being manipulated, Buttercup."

Oh, that was rich. "Did either of you stop and think that maybe I'm not keen on being kept in the dark? You tell me, out of the blue no less, that you're separating, and then you act like everything is hunky-fucking-dory each week at brunch. What else was I supposed to do considering you two refuse to talk to each other if it's not in goddamn Sondheim lyrics?"

"Language," Mom chastised weakly, one hand held limply against her forehead like she was staving off a headache. A headache that was assuredly Truly's fault.

"You know what? No." Truly crossed her arms. "I am twenty-seven years old, I pay my own rent, and I'll say *fuck* if the occasion calls for it."

"Your *rah rah, I am an adult, hear me roar* manifesto would carry a lot more weight had you not tried to pull a Lindsay Lohan on your mother and me," Dad said.

"If I pulled something over on you, it's only because you weren't paying attention," she argued. "I invited you both here, but I never lied; not once did I say I was only inviting either one of you. It's not my fault you didn't ask questions. That you didn't talk to one another and compare notes."

"Duplicitous." Dad's mouth was still set in a stern line, but his tone was all fond exasperation. "We raised a hellion, didn't we, Diane?"

"Our daughter tricked us into a lakeside retreat and you're treating this like it's some big joke. Stop clowning around, Stanley."

The poorly disguised mirth in his eyes flickered and faded. "Clowning around? Gee, Diane, just call me Emmett Kelly because I'm—"

"Would you both cut it out?" Truly shoved her bowl of cereal aside. All this bickering had made her lose what little appetite she'd woken up with. "I overstepped? Fine. My bad. But are you even listening to yourselves? Mom, the words *lakeside retreat* literally just came out of your mouth. It's Chelan! We all love Chelan. We used to come here all the time. Do you know how many people would kill to have a lake house to retreat to?"

"That is entirely beside the point, and you know it. The location is far from what your father and I are taking umbrage with. Neither of us appreciate being tricked."

Truly slumped atop the counter, forehead pillowed against her folded arms. "And I admitted that I overstepped. What else do you want me to say?"

"An apology would be nice, and we have yet to hear one of those."

Maybe because she wasn't in the habit of apologizing for things she wasn't sorry for.

Truly lifted her head and let her gaze drift between Mom and Dad and the ocean of space between them. "Your daughter is standing here begging to spend time together as a family. Most parents would be overjoyed by that prospect."

"You know we adore you, Pumpkin," Dad said. "It's your methods we're upset about."

Mom pursed her lips and looked away and for the first time all morning Truly wondered whether she actually had fucked up. If she'd taken this whole plan a bridge too far.

"Is it so bad that I just want you two to talk?" That she just wanted them to care enough to fix this. "I'm just asking that you *try*."

Truly bit down on the inside of her cheek so she wouldn't cry. She clutched the edge of the counter until her knuckles turned to white to keep from clasping her hands together and literally begging them to give this a shot.

Dad's face softened. "Sweetheart—"

"This isn't about you, Truly." Mom's voice rose, a sure sign that she'd reached the end of her rope. "We love you. Always, but this?" She gestured across the room to Dad. "This is not your business."

"Not my business?" Her laugh came out sharp and wet. "You kind of made it my business when you told me you were separating."

There was no way they could've thought she wouldn't care. They knew her better than that; they'd raised her to be inquisitive and curious and to never give up, never back down. But yeah, go ahead and sue her for caring about the two most important people in her life.

"Maybe—" Dad coughed into his fist and stared out the window over the sink, looking for all the world like he'd throw himself out it if he could. Dad never handled it well when she and Mom fought, few and far between as their fights were. "Maybe your mother and I made a mistake."

"What? Are you . . . ?" She couldn't breathe let alone finish her sentence. It felt like someone had punched through her chest, squeezing her heart in one hand and reaching up with the other to seize her vocal cords in a viselike grip.

Dad rubbed his forehead. "Perhaps we shouldn't have told you about the trial separation."

The air left her lungs as if she'd been punched in the gut.

"Because keeping me in the dark would've been *so* much better." She bit down on the inside of her cheek so she wouldn't cry. "I don't know what went wrong between you and when it happened because apparently, it's *not my business*. But you two claim to love each other and people who love each other? They don't just give up. They don't run and they don't hide."

"Truly—"

She cut Dad off with a curt shake of her head. She didn't want to hear it. The excuses, the brush-offs, the handling her with kid gloves and treating her like she was incapable of handling the truth.

She dumped her cereal in the trash and made a beeline for the back door.

"Take your stupid time apart, but ignoring a problem won't make it go away. It'll just make it blow up in your faces later."

As soon as she hit the dock, Truly kicked off her flip-flops. She shoved her jean shorts, already unbuttoned, down her hips, not even pausing when a thread ripped. Clad in her bikini, she took a flying leap off the dock, plunging headfirst into the frigid water.

At some point, lulled by the softly lapping waves, her eyes slipped shut. She wasn't sleeping, just . . . drifting. Not really thinking about any one particular thing, because there wasn't any one particular thing that was safe to think about. The soft, sherbet-colored sun shined mutedly through her eyelids, and she focused on that, on the safe-simplicity of the sun rising and setting each day, inevitable.

"You might want to be careful swimming in that water. I heard some freak's running around tossing cigarettes in the lake."

Truly reared forward too fast, balance off-kilter, her head slipping beneath the water. She broke the surface with a gasp and glared. Colin stood on the dock holding a bright bouquet of flowers.

She skimmed her hand against the surface, sending a spray of water at him. "You couldn't say *hello* like a normal person?"

She could only imagine how she looked. Like a drowned rat, sputtering and spitting water.

Colin set the bouquet down on the dock and took a seat. He was wearing another pair of obscenely short shorts, this time pastel blue and checkered, thin fabric creeping higher up his thighs when he sat. His feet were bare, and he let them sink beneath the lake's surface.

Damn him for looking so good all the time. It would be infinitely easier to be upset with him if she didn't want to kiss his stupid mouth.

"Thought about it. Decided against it." He shrugged. "Nice bikini, by the way."

"I could've drowned, and you'd have been what? Busy staring at my tits?"

His gaze dipped, eyes unrepentantly focused on her chest. "To be fair, they are nice tits."

Truly sent another spray of water at him. "How'd you know where to find me?"

"'Dark green shutters, mailbox shaped like a shark,'" he recited. "It's not far from my folks' place." He gestured behind him to the private riverwalk all the houses on this stretch of the lake could access. "It's a nice day. I walked."

She treaded water. "And the flowers?"

Colin picked the bouquet up and if she wasn't mistaken, blushed. "The flowers are for you."

She swam a little closer and wiped the lake water from her eyes. An ivory-colored bow held together the bouquet of blush-pink camellias, lavender roses, and delicate lily of the valley, all soft, shaded petals set against a backdrop of lush green leaves.

I adore you, you enchant me, and *I wish you a return to happiness,* the arrangement said. Lovely and unassuming, giving and demanding nothing in return.

She didn't know if Colin meant it, if he even knew flowers could mean anything at all. Given his frequent research spirals, his late nights spent on Wikipedia, she wouldn't put it past him. Regardless, it warmed her all the way to her toes, frigid lake water forgotten.

"What's the occasion?" she asked.

"I'm sorry," he said without pretense or preamble.

"What for?" She kicked her legs harder, keeping her head above the water. "You didn't say anything you didn't mean."

He set the flowers aside. "I only said what I said the other night because I didn't want to see you get hurt. I still don't."

Her bottom lip wobbled. Too late for that. "Not that I don't appreciate the concern, but it's completely unnecessary. You don't need to worry about me."

"That doesn't mean I'm not going to."

"Why?"

"You're killing me." He turned his face up to the sky and shut his eyes, baring his throat and those two perfect moles on either side of his clavicle. "You worry about your parents, don't you?"

She frowned. What a bizarre question. "Of course I do. I care about them."

His brows crept up his forehead and—

"Oh."

"Yeah, Truly. *Oh.*" Colin laughed. "I care about you. Is that seriously a surprise? Because if it is, I've been doing a seriously shitty job of courting you."

"Courting—" Her head slipped under the water. She broke the surface of the lake and coughed. "Who says that?"

The nineteenth century called and asked for their verbiage back.

He snorted. "Says the girl who asked me to go steady. Glass houses, baby."

"Yeah, well, maybe I jumped the gun."

Colin looked like she'd punched him in the gut. "We had a fight. Fuck, not even. It was—it was a disagreement, Truly. I know I said some things—"

"It was far from our first disagreement." Maybe she should've taken their first fight as a sign, a portent of what was to come. "Look, Colin, I like you. I like you a lot." So much. Too much, probably. More than she had any business liking anyone when she was as messed up as she was. "But I told you I wasn't in the right headspace for a relationship. All things be told, my parents are likely on the brink of a divorce and my faith in love is . . ." Questionable at best. "My parents are the blueprint for me, okay? And if they can't make it work . . . if I can't believe in love, I . . ." What could she believe in? "I don't know what the point is, okay? You don't want to date me."

"And what if I do?" he demanded, obstinate as ever. "What then?"

"Are you not hearing me? I am—I am far, *far* from girlfriend material," she said—no, *warned.* "I'm a mess right now. I'm more trouble than I'm worth, okay?"

Colin was *sweet.* Against all odds, despite his WASPy mother and taciturn, judgmental father, his asshole of a brother, and his—his cow cod of an ex, he still tried.

He was putting in all of this effort and for what? A gun-shy girl who craved a forever love, but flinched in the face of affection?

"That should be for me to decide, shouldn't it? Not you. Me. Whether or not I want to be with you is my choice," he said. "You said it yourself; we've all got flaws. But the day I don't want you is the day the earth starts rotating backward, okay?"

"That's a hell of a bold statement from a guy who's known me two months."

"Remember this moment in twenty years. Can't wait to tell you I told you so."

Well, *shit*.

Truly ducked under the water, needing a second to gather herself before she did something ridiculous like burst into tears.

She surfaced to the sight of Colin scrubbing a hand against his jaw, stubble dark and thick. The late-afternoon sun bathed his face in sherbet shades of pink and orange, so handsome it made her breath catch.

"Are you gonna sit there and look pretty? Or are you gonna join me?" she asked, the muscles in her thighs starting to fatigue, her lungs heaving only partially from exertion.

Colin stood and stripped.

Clad in just his shorts, he executed a perfect swan dive into the water, surfacing a foot away, paddling the distance with ease. Droplets of lake water clung to his lashes and flattened his hair against his head. His tongue swept against his bottom lip, and she wished it was her that he was licking off his lips instead of lake water.

"I missed you," he whispered, hands finding her waist, dragging her against him. She locked her legs around his waist and—he was already half-hard against her.

Goose bumps broke out across her skin.

Colin dragged his lips across her cheek, stubble rough against her as he pressed openmouthed kisses along her jaw. He found the pulse pounding away in her throat and nipped, soothing the sting with a drag of his tongue. "Missed how you taste, missed how you sound, missed how good you feel in my arms."

She arched her neck, giving him more room to work with as he sucked stinging kisses along her throat. "It hasn't even been twenty-four hours. Eighteen, maybe."

He was making it hard for her to think.

"Eighteen too long." He stole her lips in another kiss, hips jerking, cock pressing against her exactly where she wanted, only two layers of soaked fabric separating them.

Water lapped at their chests, making it hard to get the friction she desperately craved as she rocked against him.

Colin tore his lips from hers. "Shit. Hold on. I've got you. Just lemme—" He shifted her in his arms, wedging a hand between their bodies. He tugged at the crotch of her swimsuit, dragging it aside, fingers sliding over her clit.

She dropped her head against his shoulder, teeth finding the thick tendon straining in his neck and biting hard.

She sucked lazily at the junction of skin where his throat met his shoulder, brain fuzzy, comforted by the feeling of his arms around her, keeping her afloat. Her back hit something sturdy and she lifted her head, opening her eyes.

He'd paddled them to the dock and pinned her up against the ladder.

Colin rested his forehead against hers. "Want me to make you feel good?"

"Uh-huh." She nodded and, trusting him to keep her from drowning, dragged the top of her swimsuit down.

Colin stared at her chest, looking like he'd seen God in the flesh. *"Fuck."* He managed to make that word sound like praise and condemnation all in one. "Knew you'd have perfect tits. *Christ.*" Two of his thick fingers slipped inside her, filling her up, water washing away most of her natural slick, friction flirting with the line of *too much*. His thumb found her clit and his fingers slid deeper, pressing against that place that made her see stars, that had made her gush all over his face and left his chin dripping. "Touch yourself, baby? Please? *Fuck*. Pretty please?"

Who was she to deny such a polite request? She reached down and plucked at her nipples the way she liked, pinching hard enough that her back arched, the pleasure sharp and bittersweet, just the right side of painful.

"You like that, don't you?" He crooked his fingers forward against that sensitive bundle of nerves, making her whimper. "You're strangling my fingers."

She panted up at the darkening sky, water lapping at her chest, tension coiling in her belly. "Imagine what I'm gonna feel like around your cock."

Colin jerked against her and swore. "Fuck. I want that so bad. You have no idea."

If she didn't get her hands on him, she was pretty sure she'd die. "Can I touch you? Say yes."

He bobbed his head. "Yeah. *Yes*. Anything you want." His hips jerked against her, clothed cock sliding against the crease of her thigh.

It was enough to make her dizzy, being granted permission to reach between them and slide her fingers beneath his waistband, to slip her hand inside his shorts and fist his cock, to feel the slide of silky soft skin over his rigid length.

His thumb sped against her clit and her own rhythm faltered.

"Go on," he said. "Whatever you need." His fingers curled harder, the pressure inside her coiling tighter. "I'm yours, Truly."

One of her legs spasmed, her heel kicking the back of his thigh as she fractured, feeling like her soul was being ripped from her body. Her hand gripped his neck, nails biting into the skin of his shoulder, mole-splattered perfection. If it weren't for his hand cradling the back of her head, she might've knocked herself unconscious against the pile at her back, her neck arching and her whole body jerking.

"That's it," Colin murmured, voice reaching her ears over—oh, she was the one making those noises, soft mewls and pitiful whines as she squirmed against him, the pleasure so good, *too* good, it was like she couldn't handle it. Like her body didn't know how to process this much pleasure. "Shhh. That's it. I've got you."

Tears dripped freely down her face, mingling with the lake water trickling from her bangs. Colin kissed her cheek, tongue darting out, tasting her tears. Her cunt clenched around his fingers and he kept going, curling his fingers inside her with even more determination.

"I can't," she muttered, head thrashing.

Colin scoffed, almost mean, the sound softened by the gentle press of his lips against her temple. "That's a lie. You and I both know you can."

She gripped his cock and tugged, swiped her thumb over the head where, if it weren't for the lake water, she knew without a fraction of a doubt he'd be weeping for her. Colin hissed and shifted, pinning her against the ladder, knees keeping her thighs spread so his right hand could reach up and grip the dock.

Truly buried her face against him. "Want you to come. Want to *make* you come."

Colin choked on his next breath, cock jerking in her fist as he managed to thumb her oversensitive clit with just the right pressure to send her careening over the edge for the second time.

Distantly, over the rush of blood inside her head and the high-pitched whines escaping her throat, she heard him swear. His fingers spasmed inside her, his thighs shaking and neck straining, a silent shout trapped in his throat.

"Ah, shit," he slurred, after only a handful of heartbeats. "I think you killed me. I think I'm dead. Is this heaven?"

She giggled and slapped his arm weakly, her limbs limp as noodles. "You're still alive, you cornball."

"I don't know." He grinned at her, lids low and eyes hazy. Pride swelled inside her because she'd done that. "Sure you aren't an angel?"

She scoffed and ran her fingers through the water between them, wisps of his come clinging to her fingers. "Considering what we just did? I think not."

Colin slipped his fingers from her and popped them right in his mouth, sucking them clean, lapping at the space between them like he didn't want to miss a drop. "*Definitely* considering what we just did."

A rush of aroused embarrassment washed over her and she tucked her head under his chin. "Hush."

"Don't get shy on me now, St. James," he teased. "Pretty sure we've got a few kinks we need to share with each other before you clam up."

"You got a pen?" she joked. "Might need to write these down."

Colin snorted. His cock was softening inside her fist, and she didn't want to let go. "Like I'm not going to remember?"

"I'm not underestimating your memory, but I think you might be underestimating my imagination."

He laughed, strangled. "Okay, fair."

She shut her eyes and sucked in a deep breath, drawing the

light lemony-sage scent of Colin's shampoo into her lungs. "This is nice."

Almost nice enough to make her forget the reason she'd retreated to the lake in the first place. *Almost*.

"You were right, you know," she said. "This plan was a mistake."

He shifted, lips pressing against the crown of her head. "Do you want to talk about it?"

What she wanted was to close her eyes and go to sleep and pray that when she woke up this whole thing would be a nightmare.

"They're pissed off at me for tricking them into coming here under false pretenses, which I probably should've seen coming." She'd known it was a possibility, but she hadn't cared enough to let it stop her. "Mom told me to mind my own business and Dad said he regrets telling me about the separation in the first place and . . . I didn't think it was possible, but I'm worried I might've made everything worse."

Colin stroked his hands up and down her waist. Or, more accurately, *hand*. The other was still holding on to the dock, which couldn't have been comfortable, but he had yet to complain.

"I don't even have a clue what I'm going to be walking back into," she said.

In the time since Truly had stormed off, Mom and Dad had probably had plenty of time to come up with a litany of new and inventive ways to berate her for meddling. That was assuming they hadn't retreated to their separate bedrooms to stew in their self-inflicted misery.

"Feel free to tell me if I'm overstepping," Colin began, "but do you want backup?"

"Backup?"

"Yeah, you know, a buffer?" He adjusted his grip on the dock, choking up on the ladder. "Might take the heat off you if they have something else to focus on."

"You would—you'd really do that? For me?"

Colin rolled his eyes. "Do you even need to ask?"

Her heart swelled. "I—my parents are kind of . . . eccentric on a good day. And I can't promise they'll be—"

"*Truly.*" He smiled at her, exasperated and oh so fond that she was weak to do anything but smile back.

"Okay." She pressed a kiss to the corner of his mouth. "Let's go introduce you to my parents."

Chapter Seventeen

"When I suggested meeting your parents, I didn't think I was going to have to do it with the word *Juicy* stamped across my ass." Colin tossed the pair of hot-pink terry-cloth pants back at her. "Absolutely not."

She caught them with a laugh. "You have a problem with my choice of loungewear?"

"On you? Those are probably cute as hell. On me?" He huffed. "I've got seven inches on you. They won't even fit."

"Six inches, *maybe*," she said patiently. "And so what? These are a little long on me. On you they'll be . . . capris."

She bit down hard on the side of her cheek so she wouldn't crack up.

"Maybe I should just wait in here until my shorts finish drying."

The lake house had been suspiciously quiet when she'd led Colin in through the back. A note left on the island addressed to Truly clued her in—Dad had gone for a drive to give everyone a little space to cool off. Mom was out front, ripping weeds from the flower bed.

"That's going to take at least twenty minutes." She held the pants out to him. "It's either these or my sweats that have *Baby Girl* written on the ass. Your choice."

"Jesus Christ," Colin muttered, ears flushed the same color as the pants he snatched from her. "Look, I'm not opposed to experimenting with a little light humiliation if you are. But I'm just saying, maybe we should keep it relegated to the bedroom."

As expected, the pants hit him about mid-calf. He set his hands on his hips and heaved a beleaguered sigh. "All right. Lay it on me. How ridiculous do I look?"

Not that ridiculous, actually. If it weren't for the word *Juicy* printed on his butt—which, hello, where had he been hiding that peach of an ass? *God*, she wanted to sink her teeth into it, which was probably weird, but whatever—she'd tell him to keep them. They looked better on him than they'd ever looked on her.

"Take a look for yourself." She swept a hand out at the mirror hanging over the back of her door. "I think that might be your color."

He adjusted himself, dragging down the crotch of the pants so he could walk more comfortably, and headed for the mirror. He frowned at his reflection, turning to the side. "Huh. My ass doesn't look half bad."

That startled a laugh from her, not at all the reaction she'd been expecting. "You got dumps like a truck, McCrory." She reached for his hand and led him back out into the living room.

Mom was seated at the table, straw sun hat discarded beside her and a glass of lemonade in her hand. She looked up when they entered, expression frosty, leaving no doubt that she was still upset. She looked away, then did a double take, eyes widening as she spotted Colin over Truly's shoulder. "Truly. Who is this?"

Her brow furrowed. "And why in God's name is he wearing your pants?"

Colin groaned under his breath.

"Mom, this is Colin McCrory. Colin, this is my mother, Diane. And he's wearing my pants because his were wet from swimming."

"The boy you said you hated?" she stage-whispered, a gleam in her eye. "Your father owes me twenty dollars."

Colin's cough did *nothing* to disguise his laugh.

"I never said I hated Colin. And what about twenty dollars?"

Mom was an actress, a great one. But Truly could see right through her façade of faux confusion, all big eyes and frowning lips. "I could've sworn I remember you saying you hated him and then I told you *hate* was a strong word and you told me that's why you used it."

Mom smirked and Truly was no mind reader, but she was willing to bet Mom was thinking something along the lines of: *payback's a bitch.*

Truly had to hand it to her—death by mortification was a fine punishment indeed.

Colin reached around her, holding out his hand. "It's a pleasure to meet you, Mrs. Livingston. Truly's told me so much about you."

"Please, call me Diane." Mom shook his hand. "I'm glad my daughter doesn't actually hate you. You're *very* handsome."

He looked inordinately pleased. "I can certainly see where Truly gets her beauty from."

Mom blushed. "You're a real charmer, aren't you?"

"I prefer to think of myself as honest." He grinned and Mom all but swooned.

Truly couldn't help but beam. A real charmer, indeed. Maybe, just maybe, this day wasn't going to be a total bust after all.

The front door opened, and Dad stepped inside. "Truly! I was worried you'd walk in here looking like a prune, but—oh. Hello, stranger." His eyes dropped. "Stranger who is wearing my daughter's pants."

"Dad, this is Colin McCrory. He's going to be joining us for dinner."

Dad turned and walked out of the room without so much as a word.

She looked at Mom for help. "What's he doing?"

Mom shrugged. "How should I know?"

Dad came stalking back into the room from the hall, walked right up to the kitchen table, and slapped a twenty-dollar bill down in front of Mom.

She pocketed the cash with a small smile.

"Did you—did you bet on my *love life*?" she asked, mildly horrified.

"What else are we supposed to bet on, Pumpkin?" Dad buffed a kiss against her cheek. "Sports?"

"*Ha*. That was a good one, Stanley."

Dad preened. "I thought so."

On the bright side, her parents were getting along, even if it was courtesy of conspiring against her.

"And you wonder where I get my boundary issues from." Hypocrites, the both of them. "So, what? You just walk in the door, take one look at us, and *assume* we're together because what? We're not at each other's throats?"

"No," Dad said calmly, crossing his arms. "I took one look at the boy wearing your pants and then on my second look I spotted the sizeable love bite you've got"—he pointed at his own neck—"right about there, and well." Dad razzle-dazzled his fingers. "Clearly *someone* was at your throat, Pumpkin Butt."

Colin wheezed, the sound of a dying man. A death rattle.

She wrapped her fingers around his wrist and dragged him toward the kitchen. "Colin and I are going to take turns trying to fit ourselves down the garbage disposal. 'Kay? Bye."

"Now, wait just a gosh darn minute, young lady. I'd like to talk to this young man."

She slowed reluctantly.

Dad drummed his fingers against his arm. "Tell me, *Colin McCrory*—how well do you know musical theater composers?"

"Dad, no. Colin doesn't want to play."

"Colin doesn't want to play what exactly?" Colin asked.

She sighed. "My parents have this rule—"

"Tradition," Dad corrected. "It is a family tradition."

"*Tradition*, where when you're in a room you have to use a song title or lyrics by the composer the room is named for in every sentence. We've got the Sondheim sunroom, the Irving Berlin half bath, etcetera, etcetera. It's a pain in the ass."

"It's inspiring," Dad argued, hands on his hips. His offended stance. "Gets the creative juices flowing." He shimmied his shoulders in a way she'd pay to never again witness.

"It's a little like a puzzle," Mom conceded. "Keeps you sharp."

Dad crossed the room and threw an arm around Colin's shoulders. "We do things a little differently at the lake house. You see, the lake house is a wild card. Sondheim, Rodgers, Hammerstein, Bart, Bernstein, Tesori . . . strictly mealtimes and any composer goes."

She tugged on Colin's sleeve, dragging him away from Dad and dropping her voice. "We can go out for dinner. You do *not* have to do this."

Colin rubbed his fingers against his lips, brow furrowed. "It's okay."

"I mean it." She wouldn't think any less of him if he wanted to ditch. Her family could be a lot. "There's this restaurant not far from here at Vin du Lac Winery. If I call now, I bet I can get a late reservation for four. Or you and I can just—"

He leaned in, lips pillowing against hers in a chaste kiss, shutting her up and stealing her breath in one go. He leaned back, a smile playing at the edges of his lips. Lips she wouldn't mind kissing a few thousand times more. *"And I'm Telling You I'm Not Going."*

The quiet conversation her parents had been having on the other side of the room died swiftly.

Dad straightened, pointing at Colin across the room, a smile spreading across his face. *"Dreamgirls*, 1981. Tom Eyen. You familiar with any of his earlier work?"

"Like *The Dirtiest Show in Town*?" Colin shrugged. "I only saw the film version on Showtime, but yeah, I know it."

Dad slapped both hands over his chest and fell to his knees. "Be still my heart. Truly?" He looked at her, eyes wide, expression solemn. "Either you marry this boy, or I adopt him. Do you hear me, young lady?"

"Dad," she hissed, face hot and ears burning. "Can we try *not* to scare him off?"

For all the push and pull she'd done, the mixed signals she'd sent, she was kind of attached to the idea of Colin sticking around.

Colin chuckled, seemingly unbothered by her father's gun jumping. "Gonna take a lot more than that to scare me off," he whispered. He turned back to her father. "I'm guessing you know the show?"

"Know it?" Dad scoffed as he stood, wincing when his knee crunched. "I caught my older sister sneaking out and demanded she take me with her otherwise I'd tattle to Mommy and Daddy. I was *nine* when I first stepped inside Astor Place Theatre, fingers clutching her coattails, drinking it all in." Dad sighed dreamily. "I didn't understand half of what was happening on that stage, but God if I didn't love every goddamn second of it."

Earnest enthusiasm lit up Colin's whole face, making his eyes sparkle. "The original 1975 production? You saw it?"

"Hell yes, I did. That night was revolutionary for me." Dad grinned. "I'll tell you all about it over dinner. You drink wine, Colin?"

"I do, sir."

"White or red?"

"Whatever you think will go best with dinner."

"That's a good boy." Dad nodded. "We'll open a bottle of Chianti Classico. You sit, assuming you can in those pants."

"*Dad.*"

"I've got eyes," he said, defensive. "Your boy's got junk in his trunk."

Colin's face went neon. "Um, thank you?"

"Polite. I like that, too. You two sit. Take a load off. Google some songs, if you need a refresher, kid. Because when we sit down to eat?" Dad grinned. "Let the games begin."

"BULLSHIT."

Truly glanced between Colin and the cards she'd discarded in the center of the table. She arched a single brow. "You sure about that?"

Colin narrowed his eyes. "You heard me. *Bullshit.*"

"Oh ho!" Dad laughed. "You heard him. He called bullshit."

Truly smirked. "Go on. Flip 'em over."

A flicker of doubt crossed his face, his brow creasing as he reached for the cards she'd tossed down. He flipped them over, revealing one, two, three jacks.

Colin dropped his head back and groaned.

"Read 'em and weep, McCrory, read 'em and weep." She shoved the discard pile toward him.

"Yeah, yeah." He gathered the cards up and added them to the half a deck he already held in his hands, unable to bullshit to save his life. "Two queens."

"Bullshit." Dad grinned.

Colin laughed and took the cards he'd only just discarded back. His inability to lie was almost as endearing as his willingness to lose graciously.

After dinner, during which Colin had managed to hold his own—his musical knowledge was only slightly better than average, but what he lacked in skill, he more than made up for in enthusiasm; even when his phone battery ran low, he borrowed a charger and took a seat on the floor beside the outlet, plate balanced on his knees so he could keep googling lyrics—they'd adjourned to the back patio with a deck of cards.

An hour and three games of Bullshit later and Truly felt hopeful in a way she hadn't in weeks.

"You're a terrible liar, Stan." Mom flung a card at Dad, giggling when it smacked him in the face.

"Some would consider that a virtue." Dad added the card to his hand and topped off Mom's glass of wine. "Not all of us are gifted thespians, dear. Even fewer of us are Tony award–winning actresses."

"Tony award–winning?" Colin rested his elbows on the table. "And I'm only now hearing about this? You've been holding out on me, Diane."

Mom blushed prettily.

"Best Performance by a Leading Actress in a Musical," Dad said.

"It's not a big deal," Mom demurred.

"Not a big deal?" Dad scoffed. "Now to *that*, I call bullshit. Truly and I couldn't be prouder, could we, honey?"

Mom rested her chin on her hands. "Remember when you installed a spotlight over the mantel just for the award?"

"Well, it deserved to be admired. It's only a shame I nearly burned down the house." He cringed at Colin. "An electrician, I am not."

"It was only a small fire." Mom giggled into her glass. "I thought it was sweet."

"Maybe I should start house fires more often."

Truly held her breath as Mom's gaze locked with Dad's and maybe she was wrong, maybe she was only seeing what she wanted, but this didn't seem like regular looking; from the outside looking in, it seemed as if they were actually seeing each other, the two of them lost in their own world in a way she hadn't witnessed in—too long.

Beneath the table, Colin squeezed her knee as if asking, *are you seeing this?*

She rested a trembling hand atop his and squeezed back.

Mom cleared her throat and dropped her eyes, the moment over, but not forgotten. Dad's face had gone pink and Mom reached for her wine, draining half the glass with one deep swallow.

Truly hid her grin behind her cards. "My turn?"

Three rounds later and Colin's hand continued to grow.

Truly wasn't faring much better.

"Shame!" Dad tutted. "Diane, our daughter has no poker face."

"Oh, that's just what she wants you to think." Mom's tongue pressed against the side of her cheek. "Truly's quite the little liar."

The scoff escaped before she could swallow it. "Gee, Mom, tell me how you *really* feel."

Mom scowled down into her glass, swirling the wine with a little more gusto than strictly necessary, considering she was knocking it back far quicker than she could let it breathe. "Now's not the time, Truly."

Truly gritted her teeth, just barely soothed by the circle Colin's thumb was making against her knee.

"Not so fast," Dad said, either oblivious to the tension or uncaring. Either way, Truly braced herself. "Colin, sate my curiosity, would you? Were you aware of your girlfriend's—Truly *is* your girlfriend, no?"

Truly groaned. "Dad, I love you, but really?"

"Hey, I'm on TikTok. I'm hip with the lingo. Simping and smashing, sneaky links and situationships. Are you two still in the talking phase or have you DT'd the R?"

"DT'd the—" Christ on a cracker. Truly groaned. "Jesus, Dad, please do me a favor and never, *ever* say that again."

"Come on, I'm cool! I'm hip!"

"More like you ought to be careful you don't break a hip," Mom teased. "Don't act like I didn't catch you doing one of those Tik-Tok dances."

Truly clapped a hand over her mouth. "*No*. When was this?"

Mom waved her hand. "It was . . ." She looked at Dad and frowned. "Weeks ago, I guess."

Right. Because Dad had moved out.

"All I'm saying," Dad continued, "is that I was a child of the sixties. I'm all about the free love and rock 'n' roll if that's what this is. Can't a father be curious about whether it's serious between his daughter and the"—Dad gestured at Colin—"zaddy defiling her?"

Colin choked on his wine and Truly set her own glass aside so she could pat him on the back.

"Dad, I will literally pay you to never say that word again," she pleaded. "Name your price. I'm serious."

Colin cleared his throat, face still a worrying shade of purple, but he looked a little more with it, less in danger of passing out. "For the record, if anyone's defiling anyone, it's definitely Truly."

A laugh erupted from Dad. "You're honest, kid. Got to give you that." He took a hearty sip from his glass. "Speaking of honesty and since you and Truly are so close"—in his continuing effort to embarrass the hell out of her, Dad waggled his brows—"*were* you aware of our darling daughter's devious ploy to get her mother and me together?"

"Stanley—"

"It's not much of a secret, Diane." Dad polished off his cordial glass of nocino and Truly's gut clenched. Dad wasn't a big drinker; not quite a teetotaler, but he was usually a *one glass of wine and call it quits* guy. This stuff was strong. Forty percent ABV strong. And Dad was on his second pour. "Colin, in case you weren't aware, Diane and I are separated."

Mom's expression went pinched as she stared out at the lake. "Do you really think this is appropriate, Stanley?"

"He's a divorce attorney. I'd say he's qualified to hear this." He looked at Colin. "You are, right?"

"Family lawyer, technically, but yes, sir."

"*Sir.*" Dad snorted. "I think considering the number of love bites on my daughter's neck, you can call me Stan, kid."

"Got it." The sweetest blush crept up Colin's neck. "*Stan.*"

"So were you? Aware of Truly's mad scheme?"

Colin looked at her and all she could do was shrug. No point in lying now.

"I, uh, Truly cares about you both," he said, his careful diplomacy reminding her that his job required he be just as gifted with words as she was. "Anyone who knows her knows she would do anything if it meant making you happy."

"That is a generous interpretation of our daughter's motivations," Mom murmured.

Truly scowled down at the table, too tired to argue, far from in the mood to defend herself to someone who seemed hell-bent on reading the worst into her actions.

Colin leaned his forearms against the table. "Diane, I think you raised a brilliant daughter who sticks by her principles, principles I'd be willing to bet every cent I have that you instilled in her. Is she stubborn? Yeah. She's headstrong and it's a little infuriating, yeah?"

Mom chuckled a little less darkly. "That's one word for it."

Colin grinned. "You raised a real firecracker. Hell, Truly doesn't let me get away with shit, you know? Sorry," he said, sounding less than remorseful. "I shouldn't swear."

Mom threw her head back and laughed. "Truly's first curse word was—*God*, I shouldn't say. It's embarrassing."

"It was *fuck*," Dad said in a faux whisper. "Two guesses who she learned it from and it wasn't me."

Mom smacked his shoulder. "*Stan.*"

"*Fuck, fuck, fuck*," Dad recited, laughing. "Said in the most adorable little voice from her car seat."

Mom buried her face in her hands. "That asshole wouldn't let me merge!"

"Sure, honey." Dad laughed. "You tell yourself that."

Mom harrumphed.

Colin chuckled. "Then you know that when Truly makes her mind up about something . . . Godspeed if you disagree."

Dad laughed. "Godspeed, indeed."

Mom cracked a smile and Truly couldn't find it in her to be sore when Colin reached across the table and grabbed her hand, lacing their fingers together.

"Maybe you disagree with her methods, and you know what? That's fair," he said, gripping her hand. "But Truly loves you. Truly . . . *God*, she admires you. It's not my business; I don't know you and I know you don't know me. But I care about your daughter, and it's so obvious she cares about you. Your daughter, she has one of the biggest hearts of anyone I've ever had the pleasure of knowing. And I think anyone would be lucky to be loved by her."

Truly's heart beat loud inside her head, a near violent *lubdub*

lubdub that drowned out everything else. All her fears, her *what ifs* silenced by the surety of Colin's words.

"Well, shit, son," Dad said, smile watery. "You're a walking green flag. Truly, honey, this one's got some real *rizz*."

Colin threw his head back and laughed.

Truly grinned.

Chapter Eighteen

"Thank you. For tonight." Truly paused outside the gate leading to the McCrory's backyard.

After the three glasses of nocino Colin had had, she'd insisted she walk him home; she liked him too much to let him walk home alone, lest he trip and fall into the lake.

That, and she kind of was loath to end the night and say goodbye.

"For what?" he asked. "Your parents are awesome. They're passionate people." His thumb swept across her knuckles. "I can see where you get it from."

Her face warmed. Her chest, too. "That's a nice way of looking at it. Thank you."

"I just call it like I see it." Colin squeezed her fingers. "They, uh, they seemed to be getting along?"

A welcome, if not bizarre turn. "I think it helped that they had a common goal of giving me as much grief as possible. It doesn't hurt that they were on their best behavior because you were there. I think they really liked you."

Colin cringed. "I still think I made a shitty first impression. *Hey, I just got carnal with your only child, nice to meet you.* Not the way I wanted that introduction to go down."

"Your willingness to play along with our bizarro family tradition definitely won them over."

Justin had been to her parents' house how many times? A dozen? Two dozen times over the years? Not once had he genuinely played along with Mom and Dad's theater games. He'd treated it like a joke, throwing out quotes at random that made no sense in a conversation. His favorite thing to shout was *five hundred, twenty-five thousand, six hundred minutes* without rhyme or reason or even very much knowledge of *Rent*. She'd pulled him aside once and asked what the hell he was on about. He laughed and told her that's how long it felt like these theater games of her parents dragged on for. Jerk.

Why she'd ignored the writing on the wall for so long was honestly horrifying in hindsight.

"I had fun. Your parents are great." He chuckled. "If it wouldn't make dating you weird, I might be tempted to take your dad up on that adoption offer."

"Too kinky for you?" she teased.

He sighed dramatically. "Didn't think it was possible, but alas, we all have our limits."

"For what it's worth, I think they want to keep you. Which is, you know . . ." She ducked her chin, hiding her smile. "Handy."

"Handy, huh?" He squeezed her fingers. "Why's that?"

She stared at their clasped hands, at the veins crisscrossing the back of his, blue where hers were green, his fingers longer, her cuticles more ragged. She liked the way her hand looked in his, liked the way it felt even better. Colin didn't squeeze too hard, but his grip was firm, reassuring, his thumb sweeping a constant arc against her wrist or knuckles depending on how he held her. Justin's grip—if she could even call it that—had been limp, like he'd forgotten he was even holding her hand.

"Because I'd like to keep you, too," she confessed, heart in her throat.

No, heart in her *hand*, which was conveniently nestled inside Colin's.

He cupped her face, his little finger pressing just beneath her jaw where her pulse pounded. His touch was solid and sure, and so unlike her skipping heart, racing over one beat and stuttering on the next. No one had ever made her heart skip a beat like he did.

"Jokes aside," he said, "I'm pretty keen on being kept by you."

She swallowed hard, heart thundering, reveling in the firm press of his fingers against her throat, the place where she was most vulnerable, all thin skin covering squishy veins pulsing with hot blood. Anytime Justin had touched her throat some primal part of her had flinched and she had wriggled away. Yet here she was, tilting her neck up, bearing her throat to Colin and leaning into his palm, silently begging him to keep touching her.

The blunt edge of his nail raked gently against her skin, sparking a shiver. Colin cast a glance at the back of the house. He arched a brow and the left corner of his mouth rose. "You know, I've, uh, I've never snuck a girl over before."

A laugh escaped her. "Colin McCrory, you sly dog. You want to fuck me down the hall from where your parents are probably sleeping?"

He pressed his palm to his chest, eyes wide with mock affront. "Good to know where your brain is at, St. James. *I* wanted to cuddle. It was kind of hard to do that in the fucking lake."

"Oh, ho, *sure*. And if cuddling happens to lead to a little touching . . ."

He held up his hands. "I'm a go-with-the-flow kind of guy."

"You're full of shit is what you are."

"That wasn't a *no*."

"Your parents are going to be *right* down the hall."

His teeth scraped against his bottom lip, almost taunting. Biting that lip was her job, from now on. "You afraid you can't stay quiet?"

"I thought you wanted to cuddle."

"Maybe I'm a vigorous cuddler, huh? You consider that?"

"I'm going to amend my previous statement and upgrade you to *so* full of shit."

Colin cracked the gate leading up to the walk that wound its way through the backyard and up to the set of French double doors. "Sounds to me like someone's chicken."

"Take that back."

He slipped through the gate, then turned and met her eyes. *"Bok, bok."*

Oh, it was on. "I'm expecting some *vigorous* fucking cuddling from you, McCrory."

She followed, hand in his, as he led the way through the back door. When she paused to take off her shoes, Colin steadied her, hands on her hips.

He ducked down, lips skimming her forehead, lingering at her temple. His hand slipped lower, gripping her ass, squeezing.

She arched her back, encouraging. "Where's your room?"

Colin laughed against her skin. "Those Juicy pants really did it for you, huh?"

"*You* really do it for me. Now shut up and take me to bed."

He rocked against her, his shorts doing nothing to hide how hard his cock was. "You mean you don't want to fuck in my parents' kitchen?"

Next time. "I'm pretty attached to the idea of having you in an actual bed."

He backed slowly down the hall. "*Having* me, huh? You got plans for me, baby?"

"A few. If you play your cards right, I might even tell you what they are first."

A floorboard squeaked beneath her foot and they both froze, Colin's eyes deer-in-the-headlights wide and her lips parted on an interrupted inhale. Her heart raced. She was twenty-seven, had been living on her own and paying all her bills by herself for five years, and yet something about this felt illicit.

A laugh escaped the tight press of her lips. "This is ridiculous," she whispered.

Colin pressed a finger to his lips, shushing her. "Shh. You're going to get us caught."

"Then *go*. Walk faster."

"You're bossy tonight."

Another squeak erupted under her foot. Damn it. "Why am I the one stepping on all the loose floorboards?"

"Bad luck," he said. "Hold still."

"What are you—*oh*."

Palms cupping her ass, Colin hoisted up her body with surprising ease. "Legs around my waist."

"Ask me nicely," she teased, locking her ankles behind his back.

"It's gonna be like that, huh?"

"Your fault for telling me you didn't want to play nice." With Colin carrying her, Truly's mouth was free to roam and roam it did. She ghosted her lips across his cheek and down to his jaw, stubble tickling her. She paused there and sucked what she hoped would bloom into a bruise against the tender skin just beneath his ear, smiling when Colin shivered and stumbled, footsteps weaving at the base of the stairs.

"Brat." He shifted her weight, one hand disappearing, returning a split second later, palm cracking against her ass, tearing a gasp from her lips. The sting followed a moment later, impact barely blunted by the light cotton of her sundress.

Her breath went ragged, and she could feel the wetness gathering between her thighs.

No one had ever spanked her before.

"Too far?" Colin sounded unsure.

"No." A breathless laugh bubbled up and burst free. "But I'd expect payback if I were you."

"You're not going to hear me complaining about you putting your hands on my ass."

"Is that what you like?"

The tips of his ears turned that endearing shade of pink she adored. "Truly, baby, you could spit on me, and I'd say thank you."

Her brain did the equivalent of a keyboard smash, and she let out an undignified little "Hngh?"

He chuckled under his breath. "Did I break you? Already?"

"Not broken," she muttered, face burning. "I just . . . I just want to make you feel good."

He stopped a handful of stairs from the landing, expression incredulous. "I shot off like a fucking bottle rocket in my jeans just from eating you out. Making me feel good should be the least of your worries."

If he thought she was going to let him off the hook just like that, he had another think coming.

At the top of the stairs, Colin made a left, passing several rooms, some shut and others not. He slipped inside the last room at the end of the hall, sparing a second to kick the door shut. Enough ambient light spilled into the room through the window and from the hall that they weren't totally in the dark.

She bit down on his bottom lip, earning a groan. That was what *she* wanted. More of those noises spilling so sweetly from his lips.

Colin broke away with a gasp. "You're killing me."

She stepped back to strip her dress over her head and—Colin's mouth was streaked with scarlet, his bottom lip bleeding.

Her stomach clenched, confused. That was *not* supposed to be hot . . . was it? "I'm so sorry."

He frowned. "For?"

"I bit you." She reached out to thumb away his blood, only managing to streak it against his cheek and make more of a mess. "You're bleeding."

Colin chased her hand with his mouth, his tongue wrapping around her finger and lapping the rust away from her thumb. "I'm not mad about it."

Truly whimpered.

His grin was wicked. "That turn you on?"

"Shut up." She slipped her fingers inside the waist of his shorts and tugged. "Take these off."

He shoved them down his thighs without taking his eyes off her. "You're so fucking cute when you blush."

She pressed her hands against her cheeks, face on fire. "Stop."

"I'm not making fun of you. I just think it's sweet that you're getting all shy on me."

"It's *weird*, that's why."

Colin cupped her jaw, cradling her face in his hands, giving her little choice but to look at him. Gone was the teasing glint in his eyes, replaced with absolute sincerity. "It's not weird if we both like it."

She swallowed hard, heart hammering. "Yeah?"

He leaned in, nose brushing hers sweetly. "Yeah, baby."

When he kissed her, there were faint traces of copper still on his lip, his tongue when he swept it inside her mouth. She didn't let herself think; she fisted her hands in his shirt, sucked his lower lip into her mouth, and worried it between her teeth.

His hips jerked. Heat unspooled inside her belly, and she pressed against him, trapping his cock between their bodies. Close wasn't close enough; she wanted to climb inside him.

He tore his mouth from hers and groaned. "Fucking hell, Truly."

"Take this off." She tugged on his shirt, then stepped back to strip her dress over her head.

Wearing just his briefs—light gray except for where the fabric had darkened over the head of his cock—Colin pressed her down against the bed.

His hand dove beneath the lace waistband of her underwear, his fingers finding her sopping. "Christ. How'd I get this lucky?"

"If memory serves"—her breath stuttered when he circled her clit—"you insulted me and then begged for my forgiveness."

Colin chuckled. "That's how, huh? I think you might be forgetting several keys steps along the way."

"Yeah, yeah, we were both there." She reached for the band of his briefs. "Now stop teasing me and take these off."

He slapped her hand aside. "It's called foreplay."

"Don't need it," she argued, bucking her hips. "I'm ready. I'm ready, just—"

She palmed his cock through his briefs, making him swear.

"Okay, shit. Hold on." He hooked his fingers in the waist of his briefs, shucking them and tossing them across the room.

Taking advantage of his momentary distraction, she pressed against the sun-warmed skin of his shoulder and knocked him off-balance. He landed on his back with a surprised laugh.

Moonlight streamed through the open blinds, casting slanted shadows across his face. He was so pretty it hurt, a physical ache blooming inside her chest and in the spaces between her ribs. Splayed out on his dark green duvet, his mole-splattered skin looked paler than it was, his mussed hair fanned against his pillow.

He wrapped a hand around his cock, stroking it twice, staring up at her with dark eyes. "Get up here."

She grabbed his wrists and pressed them against the duvet, earning an incredulous look. "Not until you tell me what it is you like. Don't think I didn't notice you avoiding the question."

A scarlet flush stained his cheeks. *"Truly."*

"It can't be *that* bad."

"It's not bad." He chuckled and she didn't fail to notice that he hadn't tried to move his hands. "I already told you." He cleared his throat. "I don't want to play nice with you."

Her heart crashed against her sternum. "Do you want me to be . . . mean?"

His lips quirked. "Little bit. If you want."

Uncertainty gnawed at her, warring with the heat from the memory of his lip streaked with scarlet. "What does that even mean?"

"Just be you. I'm sure it'll come naturally."

"Jerk," she said, without any heat.

"See, you're a natural."

Ha fucking ha. "You want me to boss you around? Tell you what to do?"

Colin laughed, bold, bright, and infectious. "You do it outside of bed. I don't see why our sex life should be any different."

She let go of his wrists and walked her fingers down his stomach, toying with the trail of downy hair beneath his belly button. Colin shivered and she suppressed a smile at how easy it was to get a reaction out of him. "What if I told you that you couldn't come until I said?"

"Bold of you to assume I'd listen."

"You saying you've got a hair trigger, McCrory?" She slipped her underwear down her legs.

"No, I'm saying I could choose to ignore you, St. James."

"Now who's acting like a brat?"

"Just stating the facts," he said, awfully smug and sounding like he needed to be knocked down a peg or three. "Give me an incentive and maybe I'll consider your proposition."

"You'll listen to me because I told you to." She knee-walked higher up the bed and threw a leg over his, settling in and sitting atop his thighs. "And because you want to be good for me, don't you?"

His breath caught then went ragged. "Truly, I swear to God, if you don't get up here, I'll—"

"You'll what? Bat your lashes at me and pout?" she taunted. "I asked you a question and I'd appreciate an answer."

His nostrils flared. "At the moment, no, I don't particularly feel like being *good* for you." His lips twitched upward. "You're kind of getting on my last nerve."

"If that's your last nerve . . ." She whistled quietly. "But that's fine. I know how to get off perfectly fine on my own."

"*Perfectly fine?* A ringing endorsement," he snarked.

Her heart raced and she could feel her thighs getting sticky damp. "You think you can do it better than me?"

His tongue swept out against his bottom lip. "I know I can."

"Say *please* and I'll let you try to prove it."

He nibbled on his lip, looking contemplative. "Truly, will you *please* get your ass up here and sit on my cock?"

She rolled her eyes. "Since you asked so nicely."

He reached inside his nightstand and grabbed a condom, tearing it open—without his teeth, thank God; Justin had tried that one time and one time only—and rolling it down over his cock. "You just gonna sit there and look pretty or are you going to get up here and fuck me? I'm starting to think you're all talk."

She flipped him off and rose onto her knees, inching closer, delighting in the way Colin's breath stuttered when she took his cock in hand and ran it down her slit. Wasting zero time, she notched him against her entrance and sank down slowly.

He hissed and so did she, her eyes fluttering shut, lip stinging as she bit down hard. Colin was thick, the stretch of him inside her delicious, straddling that fine line between pain and pleasure. For a split second she rethought the lack of foreplay—in the strictest sense of the word—but then he slid a little deeper, hit a place she didn't even know existed, and everything inside her went buttery and lax. A moan escaped her lips that she couldn't have stopped for anything in this world.

Her lashes fluttered, eyes opening. Colin's gaze flickered between the place where they were joined and her face, finally settling on the latter, a dopey little grin stretching his lips wide and sending her heart aflutter. His thumbs pressed against the space just above her hip bones, dragging another moan from her lips. *Fuck*. She didn't even know that could be an erogenous zone, let alone that it was one for her.

"You okay there, princess?" he asked, awfully arrogant considering his hands were shaking, tone mismatched against the sincerity shining in his eyes.

Two could play that game. She clenched around him purposefully, quivering with satisfaction when Colin arched, spine bowing, a pretty moan rolling off his tongue. "Are *you*?"

He choked out a laugh and swept his hands over her hips, settling them against her thighs. "Honestly? You're driving me crazy."

"Me?" She widened her eyes, playing innocent, and clenched around him one more time. "I'm not doing anything."

Colin's neck arched, his head digging into his pillow. "Then fucking *do* something." His hips bucked, driving him deeper, making her gasp. "It's not a chair, you know." He reached up, hand cupping the back of her neck, and dragged her down until their foreheads touched, until his breath ghosted across her lips, their noses brushing. "Come on, wreck me. I dare you."

Well, if he *dared* her . . .

With her palms planted against his chest, she rose up onto her knees, the drag of his length inside her exquisite. Chasing that feeling, she let herself fall back down and—

Squeak. Squeak.

Stupid fucking bed frame.

She huffed in annoyance, breath ruffling her bangs. First the floorboards and now the bed? Had no one in this house heard of WD-40?

Colin's fingers bit into her thighs. "It's fine." He shifted, wiggling against the sheets, maneuvering them both closer to the center of the bed. "Keep going."

She nodded, rose onto her knees, and—

Squeak. Squeak. SQUEAK.

"This is ridiculous." She smacked a hand down against the bedspread and groaned. Here she was with Colin's cock inside her, all delicious pressure but none of the friction she needed to actually get off.

Colin looked as desperate as she felt, heels of his hands dug into his eyes. His arms flopped against the bed, earning another, albeit softer yet no less ominous, squeak. "Fuck it. Floor?"

Yes, *the floor.* Brilliant.

Truly scrambled off his lap, careful not to knee him anywhere vital. He followed, letting out a gentle *oomph* when she shoved him down on the carpet, flat on his back.

"My ass is gonna get rug burn," he joked, scrambling blindly above them for a pillow, which he snatched off the bed and shoved under his head.

"You asked me to wreck you, remember?"

"I *dared* you to wreck me." He took himself in hand and ran the head of his cock through her folds, teasing her clit. "If it were a request, I'd have said *please.*"

She sank down quickly this time, grinding against him once they were flush. Colin's brow furrowed and his teeth sank into his bottom lip, trapping a groan she could feel rumble against the palm pressed to his chest.

"Jesus, baby, you feel so good," he said, breathy and awed and she couldn't help but feel a little smug.

Before the night was over, Colin McCrory would be *begging*

her to wreck him just a little harder, to fuck him just a little faster.

She set the pace, rising, falling, ending with a hip swivel that gave her the friction she desperately craved. Each time she dropped down, Colin's cock bottoming out inside her, his grip on her thighs would turn bruising and a breathy punched-out moan would escape his lips. The sounds he made drove her almost as crazy as the way the coarse hair at the base of his cock rubbed perfectly against her clit each time she ground against him.

Disappointingly soon, her knees started to ache from the floor, her thighs burning. Her rhythm faltered and she huffed, frustrated.

"Getting tired?" Colin teased, hands gliding up her sides to cup her breasts, thumbs sweeping over her nipples.

She covered his hands with hers, urging him to be less gentle with her. She wasn't going to break. "No."

"I don't know. Looks to me like you need a break." He took the hint and pinched until her face screwed up and her hips bucked, rolling rather than rising and—*oh*, that was good. "Need me to take over?"

"Shut up." She leaned back, hips tilting, then rocked forward and *that* was even better. It probably wasn't doing much for him, but for her it was fantastic.

"You gonna use me, baby? What am I, a toy to you?" Her breasts felt heavy in his hands, and this time when he pinched, a little cry fell off her tongue at the sting that shot from her chest to her cunt.

"Maybe you are." She slapped at his hands. "And I thought I told you to shut up?"

He chuckled under his breath, hands returning to her hips, helping to drag her forward. "Make me."

His lips were parted, his tongue curled against the back of his teeth. She'd never wanted to stick her fingers in someone's mouth so badly.

Before she realized what she was doing, her fingers were resting against his bottom lip.

"Open," she demanded, giving him the chance to tell her no if he wasn't into it.

Without hesitating, Colin dropped his jaw, hot tongue swirling around the tips of her fingers, practically beckoning her inside. She held her breath and pressed past his lips, watching his face for a single sign of distress, finding none. His pupils were blown, swallowing up the chocolate brown of his irises the same way he swallowed her fingers, causing her to slip deeper, hitting the back of his throat. His hands trembled against her thighs, his lashes fluttering as his eyes rolled back, his hips bucking, moan muffled by her fingers in his mouth.

Her chest heaved and her thighs quivered and she could feel herself dripping, probably forming a wet spot on the rug beneath them. Two weeks ago, she'd have sworn nothing could top the sight of Colin McCrory on his knees. But now? This took the cake, Colin holding so still he shook, abs flexing and relaxing, a blotchy red blush mottling his skin all the way down to his belly button.

If she didn't move soon, she was going to combust. Truly slipped her fingers from his lips only to gasp, Colin's teeth scraping her knuckles as he chased after her, arching forward and swallowing her back down.

Scratch that, *this* was the hottest thing she'd ever seen; she couldn't fucking take it. With the hand not currently being fellated, Truly reached out and grabbed his face, pinching his cheeks. "Stop it."

Colin listened, jaw dropping. Her fingers slipped free and

she wasn't sure what possessed her to do it, but she wiped them against his lips and over his chin, against his throat and down his chest, finally bringing them to where they were joined and circling her clit.

"Fuck me," he swore, not bothering to wipe his face, leaning up on his elbows instead, watching as she got herself off on his cock. "Make yourself feel good, baby. Use me."

She whimpered and rocked against him, tension coiling in her gut, fingers speeding. She was so close she could taste it, everything inside her drawing up tight. Colin bucked beneath her, tipping her over the edge, her rhythm faltering as she fractured, shaking atop him, lips pinching to hold in the scream that wanted to escape.

"Holy fuck." Colin reared forward, hands gripping her waist, working her harder against him, his hips rocking up. His forehead pressed against her shoulder, his panting breaths hot against her breast, making her shiver.

With shaking hands, she shoved at his chest, knocking him back, a little huff of surprise escaping him as he hit the floor.

"You didn't think it was gonna be that easy, did you?" she asked, tucking sweaty strands of hair behind her ears. Her heart had yet to slow, tiny aftershocks racking her when she pressed her thighs together. "That I'd let you come after you were such a brat?"

He flopped back against the carpet with a groan. "You're fucking cruel."

The insult, if she could even call it that, bounced right off her. She huffed a breathless little laugh and wiggled down his body, nudging his legs apart and making a space for herself between his thighs. "You should be nicer to me, you know."

"Why's that?" he demanded, eyes glued to her as she reached out, stripping the condom off his cock.

"Because." She tossed the condom into the wastebasket tucked beneath the desk in the corner of the room with shaking hands. "I could decide you don't deserve to come at all."

"I got you off," he argued. "I deserve it."

"*I* got myself off," she corrected, taking his cock in hand and just holding it, getting a thrill from reminding him who was in charge here. "You didn't really do much, did you?"

Colin glared at her, expression verging on petulant, his bottom lip swollen from where she'd nipped at it. So fucking pretty it pissed her off, indeed.

She tightened her grip until he whimpered, music to her ears. "I asked you a question."

It was heady, having Colin under her, at her mercy.

Knowing he wanted to be there, that he wanted her and all her sharp edges, was half the thrill.

"*Fuck*. No. I didn't do much." His head dug into the carpet, back arching, hips rising off the floor. "You didn't let me."

She pumped her fist up his length, slow, avoiding the head of his cock, teasing. "But you want to be good for me, don't you?"

"What I want is for you to make me come," he bit out, the tendons in his neck standing out in stark relief when he threw his head back.

Such a brat.

She got comfortable, giving herself a second to let spit pool under her tongue, and once she had, ran her tongue up the length of his cock, smiling when he swore.

"Christ, Truly." His fingers clutched at the rug, hips bucking when she leaned back and spit, letting it dribble down his cock, getting him wet and messy. *"Fuck."*

Slowly, so as not to gag, she took him into her mouth, tongue working along the underside of his cock. Colin made the sweetest, breathiest sound, half whimper, half moan, one hundred percent desperate as his knuckles turned white, gripping the rug.

The leftover taste of latex and lube was far from appealing, but she worked her mouth a little faster, chasing the flavor of his skin and the slightly bitter pre-come weeping steadily from his slit. A chorus of stifled moans and desperate sighs spilled from his plush, parted lips, encouraging her to take him just a little deeper, to pump him a little faster.

"'m close," he warned, and wasn't that something?

A string of spit connected her lips to his cock when she pulled off, teeth sinking into the meat of his left thigh. She dragged her nails down his stomach, pretty pink welts rising in their wake.

This time, Colin didn't complain; he just panted, staring up at the ceiling with unseeing eyes, mouth lax, chest heaving. A tiny whimper clawed its way up his throat and one of his legs kicked out, straightening against the rug.

She waited a moment before sliding the ring her fingers made down his cock, earning another desperate whimper. "You want to come?"

Colin nodded eagerly. "Uh-huh."

The bruise blooming so stark against the skin of his inner thigh made something possessive stir in her gut. "Then ask me nicely."

His throat worked, Adam's apple bobbing, staring down at her with hazy eyes. "Truly—I—*fuck*."

She chuckled, leaning in and lapping at the head of his cock, where he was steadily weeping. Colin groaned. "Part of being good for me is being quiet. You don't want to wake your parents up, do you? You don't want them hearing what a desperate slut their son is for me, do you?"

His thighs twitched and his cock jerked in her fist. "Whatever you want, just tell me what you want and I'll do it," he babbled. "I'll do it. Please. Just—" He sobbed. "Want to be good for you."

The air whooshed from her lungs like she'd been punched in the gut.

"You are," she promised, feeling oddly choked up. "You've been so good for me. You can come whenever you want, okay?"

She didn't give him a chance to answer, didn't need one, just swallowed him down and doubled her efforts, using every trick and tool in her arsenal to send him over the edge.

In no time, Colin was tapping her on the shoulder. *"Truly."*

She closed her eyes and breathed in through her nose, sinking down and swallowing around him. Colin came a moment later with a gasp, leg twitching against her side and even though she'd been waiting, ready and eager, that first pulse of come against the back of her throat still took her by surprise. She drew back, managing not to cough, but instead she made an even bigger mess, come and spit dribbling past her lips and down her chin, tears stinging her eyes and spilling down her cheeks.

She kept his cock in her mouth until he twitched, oversensitive, then stroked him twice more, having to clench her thighs together at the whine he made, squirming against the carpet. His cock had softened, slipping from her lips as soon as she parted them. Her mouth was puffy, lips tender and swollen, a small puddle of come still pooled under her tongue. Oddly, she wasn't eager to rid herself of the evidence that she had made him come so hard tears leaked from the corners of his eyes, matching the salty tracks striping her cheeks.

"You're so far away." Colin sniffed hard and gestured toward her with a limp hand. "Get up here."

She laughed, come dribbling free. Colin reached out and with his thumb, pushed it back inside her mouth, stroking over her tongue as she swallowed, crawling toward him on her hands and knees.

He cupped her face in his hands and grinned. "You're so fucking pretty."

He sounded awed and that made her laugh harder, more tears spilling from her eyes as her chest squeezed. He was unreal and he was all hers.

She laughed. "I'm a mess."

"Nah, you're beautiful," he said, looking at her all dopey even though there wasn't a doubt in her mind that she looked utterly debauched. "Kiss me? Please?"

Who was she to deny such a polite request?

Truly bent down, cupping his cheek sweetly, kissing him thoroughly. Colin parted for her eagerly, sweeping his tongue against hers like he was searching out the taste of himself inside her mouth.

The thought alone made her whimper.

Colin drew back, hand still cupped around the back of her neck. Keeping her forehead pressed against his, he breathed against her lips. "Can I touch you? Say yes."

Truly laughed at how it wasn't really a question, but half a plea, half a demand. "I already came, remember?"

"Yeah," he agreed, fingers sliding through the damp curls between her thighs, parting her folds. "But I didn't *make* you."

She shivered at the way his voice dropped and the way his thumb found her swollen clit with ease. "You don't have to."

He scoffed against her lips.

"*You don't have to*," he mocked, chuckling, thumb circling her clit like it was the easiest thing in the world. "In case I haven't made it crystal clear, I kind of live to get you off. It's like my . . . my modus operandi."

"Fancy words for a guy who just came so hard he cried."

"*Please*, Truly?"

Those little *please*s were going to short-circuit her brain one day. "Okay."

He laughed. "Once more with feeling."

"Touch me," she said, trying her damndest not to turn it into a question.

Two of his fingers slipped inside her with ease. He hummed under his breath and added a third, filling her up, still no replacement for his cock but close. He crooked all three inside her, smiling against her lips when she gasped. "You good?"

"Uh-huh." She nodded, fingers clutching his hair as she rocked against him. "So good. *You're* so good."

Colin made a choked noise and curled his fingers a little harder, the sound loud and lewd, making her flush.

She was close. Her heart beat fast and furious against her sternum, pulse thundering in her head, as her toes curled in the plush pile of the rug beside Colin's knees.

He panted against her mouth, sharing her air, making her dizzy as she strained against him. His teeth closed around her bottom lip, biting hard enough to sting, fingers curling incessantly inside her. He didn't slow, even when she cried out, voice muffled against his lips, clenching around him, vision spotting until it went black. The slick squelch of her around his fingers filled her ears, as humiliating as it was hot.

Colin's kiss lost its fervor, but not its intensity as he slipped his hand from between her legs. His mouth brushed hers, once, twice, pressing chaste little kisses against her tingling lips, her cheeks, her jaw, anywhere he could reach, as he coaxed her back to him.

"One of these days," she said, catching her breath, "we're going to have sex in an actual bed."

Colin tangled his fingers in her hair and dragged her down, laughing against her lips. "Next time."

Chapter Nineteen

Truly sneezed herself awake.

Colin was already propped up against the pillows, awake and staring down at her, an amused smile on his face. "Bless you."

She buried her face in his pillow with a groan. Feather pillows, no wonder she'd sneezed. "What time is it?"

"Just after seven."

"In the *morning*?"

Colin chuckled at her obvious disgust. "Nah, you slept for eighteen hours. Welcome back to the land of the living."

It was too early for sarcasm. "Don't tell me you're a morning person. I don't know if I can date a morning person."

"Alas, I am one of those people. The pitfalls of holding down a nine-to-five."

Funny. "You aren't working today." She smothered a yawn. "Go back to bed, you weirdo."

"Can't," he said, sounding downright chipper. *Annoyingly* chipper. If she weren't so stupidly fond of him, she'd push him onto the floor.

She was a brunch person at best, a happy-hour person, a stay-up-until-three-in-the-morning-finishing-this-chapter person, a just-one-more-page person. She was not built to watch the sun rise.

"What do you mean you can't?" This was already more words strung together consecutively than she'd spoken in years before at least nine in the morning. "Just close your eyes. Sleep."

Colin laughed and she really was gone on him because the sound didn't make her want to hit him with a pillow, but it *did* make her feel warm. She burrowed deeper beneath his duvet, tugging it up over her chin.

"Sleep," she repeated, shutting her eyes. "'s easy."

Something warm and soft landed against the tip of her nose. She screwed up her face, opening her eyes as Colin sat back, laughing at her.

"Did you just kiss my nose?"

"You happen to have a very kissable nose, St. James."

How was she supposed to stay grouchy when he was being so sweet? "You better make this early wake-up call worth my while, McCrory."

"Or else?"

She snagged a spare pillow and whacked him with it, missing his head, but hitting his arm.

Colin laughed. "You're a violent little thing before you've had your coffee, aren't you? Good to know."

"'m not little," she said, not bothering to refute the violent part.

He threw her weapon of choice down to the floor and slipped beneath the sheets until they were eye to eye. "Littler than me, shrimp."

"I like you, McCrory, but you're hardly Shaquille O'Neal."

"Ouch, you really are grouchy before you've had your coffee." He grinned. "And I am a perfectly average five foot nine."

"You're five eight," she argued. "I saw it on your driver's license when the bartender carded you that night we went out with your sister."

That startled a laugh from him. "Snoop."

"It was right in front of me."

"Uh-huh." He kissed her nose again, earning a giggle this time. "I see, caffeine and kisses are the way to your heart in the morning. Good to know."

"Caffeine's better."

He flopped onto his back and mimed shoving a dagger into his heart, really hamming it up, tongue lolling from the corner of his mouth and everything. She giggled harder.

"You're lethal to a man's ego." He rolled back over and grinned, the epitome of a morning person. Either that, or he was just like this after he got laid. She required more evidence, a larger sample of mornings spent with him to draw a conclusion. "If kisses won't do the trick, what do you say to coffee and pancakes?"

She'd never say no to coffee and pancakes. If she were one day to be held hostage and could only tweet in code for help, she'd definitely say something like *I hate pancakes and coffee and kisses from Colin McCrory.*

"With maple syrup?"

"Obviously."

"Well, if there's maple syrup, I suppose I could be convinced." She kicked off the covers.

"Hold on." He rested a hand on her now bare hip—she'd borrowed a shirt to sleep in, but pants weren't something she ever wore to bed—keeping her from sitting. "Don't I at least get a good morning kiss?"

She screwed up her face. "I have morning breath."

"So do I. Besides"—his hand drifted, cupping her ass and dragging her closer until they were chest to chest and she was tucked against him—"you kissed me with a mouthful of my come last night. I think we're past the point of being worried about morning breath."

She buried her face against his shoulder, hiding her blush. *"Colin."*

"Grumpy *and* bashful in the mornings?" He laughed. "Any other personalities I need to know about?" He laughed harder. "Hey, you've got Sleepy and Sneezy covered, too, don't you?"

She burrowed deeper into his shoulder. "Careful, Snow White, or I'll be the one calling you princess from now on."

"Nah, obviously I'm Happy." Colin tapped her on the ass. "Let's go get some coffee in you, hm, Grumpy?"

"Wait." She grabbed his arm before he could roll out of bed. "If you really don't have a problem with morning breath . . ."

He rolled his eyes and reached for her chin, tipping her face up so he could press a soft, sweet kiss against her mouth.

"Good morning." He smiled against her lips. "You sleep well?"

"The sleep I got was great."

"Note to self." Colin threw his legs over the side of the bed. "Don't wake Truly up before . . ."

"Ten?"

"That's half the day," he argued, making his way across the room dressed in only his briefs. He opened the top drawer of his dresser and pulled out a pair of sweats.

"What time do you wake up?"

He slipped the sweats over his ass. "Five, most days."

She tripped. *"Five?* Every day?"

Colin crossed the room and kissed the space between her

brows. "Look at it this way, by the time you wake up, I'll already have breakfast made."

Now *that* sounded like a match made in heaven.

Dressed and looking as presentable as she could after a night of debauchery, Truly followed Colin down the stairs. Colin paused to quietly point out with his finger pressed against his lips the room at the top of the stairs that was his parents', the door still closed.

They didn't speak until they were in the kitchen.

"Are you sure it's okay we eat here? I don't want your parents to—"

"It's fine." Colin hit the *start* button on the coffeepot, then opened the fridge and began setting ingredients on the counter. Eggs, milk, butter. "They're not exactly early risers. And besides, we're having breakfast. I'm hardly fucking you on the counter."

"Don't give me ideas." She braced her palms against said counter and took a seat on the granite.

"Keep it in your pants, St. James." He pressed the carton of eggs into her hands along with a mixing bowl. "Do me a favor and crack eight of these."

The smell of melting butter and freshly brewed coffee filled the kitchen and not long after, Colin approached holding a plate stacked with more pancakes than she could possibly eat.

"Say when." He upended a bottle of maple syrup over the plate.

"That's . . . more . . . okay, that's good."

Colin grabbed a fork from the counter and cut off a wedge of thick, fluffy pancake swimming in syrup. "Open."

Her face went hot, flashing back to saying the same thing to him last night in a very different context.

She set her mug aside. "You're going to feed me?"

He lifted the fork to her lips. "You got a problem with that?"

She opened and let Colin feed her little bite-size forkfuls of syrup-drenched pancake. She chewed and swallowed, wiggling against the counter.

"Good?" he asked, eyes creased with silent laughter.

"*So* good," she praised, mouth watering.

He speared another forkful of pancake. "Bite?"

She opened, accepting the offering.

For every two bites he fed her, Colin took one, until she'd eaten her fill, after which he polished off the enormous stack. He was rinsing the dishes and she was loading them into the dishwasher when his mother stepped into the kitchen.

"Good morning, Colin. You didn't tell me you were back. And Truly." She smiled. "You're here early." Her smile faltered, taking in Colin's sweats and her borrowed shirt, undoubtedly. "Or was it a late night?"

Truly's cheeks burned, and she looked to Colin for guidance.

"Truly stayed over," he said, rinsing the spatula before handing it to her to set inside the washer. "That a problem?"

"Of course not." Muffy McCrory smoothed the skirt of her sundress. "I only wish I'd have known we were having company. I'd have set out fresh towels in the guest bath for Truly."

"Oh, that's—"

"Unnecessary," he said, closing the dishwasher with his hip. "Truly stayed in my room."

Muffy cleared her throat. "Do you think I could steal you for a moment, Colin?"

"For?"

Muffy's gaze darted to and away from Truly. "There was just something I wanted to discuss. Privately."

Truly inched in the direction of the door. "I'm happy to step out—"

"No, stay." He held out a hand.

Muffy sighed. "You're making your guest uncomfortable."

"He's not making me uncomfortable. I just don't want to intrude—"

"You're not," Colin assured her. "And she's not a guest, Ma. She's Truly. And we have plans today."

An embellishment. At some point, Colin had to drive back to the city; until then the vague plan was, since last night had gone so well, they'd spend the day at hers.

Muffy's brows rose. "Is your phone working?"

He crossed his arms and leaned against the counter. "As far as I know."

"Then why haven't you returned my calls? I left you a voicemail and so did your father." Muffy reached inside the refrigerator and withdrew a pitcher of green juice. "You left the other night before we could talk."

"I didn't have anything to say that I haven't said a dozen times already."

Muffy huffed. "Colin, what is it going to take for you to let bygones be bygones?"

He straightened. "Maybe I don't want to let *bygones be bygones*. You ever think about that? And if I did? If I was open to it? It wouldn't hurt if you and Dad and everyone else in the family acknowledged that what Caleb did is shitty."

"Your brother and Ali are perfect for each other," Muffy said. "Are you really going to begrudge him his happiness?"

It was like watching Colin talk to a brick wall and it pissed her off like no other. If it weren't for the fact that he was speaking to his mother, she'd have stepped in. But since it was his mother, she scooted closer and rested her hand on his arm instead. Reminding him that she was there and on his side.

"No, I'm not begrudging my brother his happiness, and the fact that you'd even ask me that proves my point." Colin ran his fingers through his hair and Truly gripped his arm a little tighter. "Three years, Ma. I dated Ali for three years, and five days after she breaks up with me, I walk into her place to pick up a box of my stuff and I find my brother in her kitchen, in nothing but his boxers, drinking coffee out of the mug that used to be mine. It's not just what he did, it's how he did it and the fact that he refuses to acknowledge it was an asshole move. No one except Caitie wants to acknowledge it was low, okay?"

"You were broken up," Muffy had the gall to argue. "And you and Ali weren't right for each other, but she and Caleb—"

"I think Colin just wants you to acknowledge that his feelings are valid," Truly said, pulse racing, the hand not wrapped around Colin's biceps fisted at her side. "And if he doesn't want to talk to or about his brother, I think that's his prerogative."

Muffy straightened, lips pursing. "No offense, Truly, you seem like a nice girl, but this is a family matter. It's really not your business."

Gee, if Truly had a quarter for every time she'd heard that in the last two days, she'd . . . well, she'd only have two quarters. But it was still weird and it would probably be a long time before she could hear the words *not your business* without the phrase putting a terrible taste in her mouth.

"No, Truly's right," he said, resting his chin atop the crown of her head. "I told you I was willing to play nice on holidays and special occasions."

Which was generous, as far as she was concerned. But again, not her business.

"And does *this* not count as a special occasion? Your only brother is having a baby, your first niece or nephew. Do you really want to look back in twenty years and regret the fact that you missed out on so many family memories because of a silly grudge?"

A silly grudge? Un-fucking-believable.

"Truly and I've got places to be, Ma." He grabbed her hand, tangling her fingers with his. "I'm happy to talk to you some other time, provided it's not about Caleb."

"ARE YOU SURE you're okay?"

"Truly. Baby? That's the fifth time you've asked me since we left." He laughed. "I'm good. Promise."

It was only four times, but who was counting?

"It was shitty, okay? What she said. If she weren't your mother I'd have—"

She sighed, biting back words better left unsaid.

"You'd have what?"

She shook her head. "You don't talk about someone's mother unless you're ready to throw hands."

"Throw hands?" Colin laughed. "Things get real nasty over in Laurelhurst?"

Truly fished her keys from her back pocket, not sure if Mom and Dad had locked the back door. "That's, like, a universal cross-class truism and you know it."

No sooner had she stepped inside, did she trip over a—a suitcase? What the hell was that doing there?

She sidestepped the luggage, leaving the door open for Colin. "Mom? Dad?"

"Buttercup, hi." Dad poked his head out of the kitchen. "And Colin, too." He grinned and stepped around the island. "It's good to see you again, kid. And look! In your own pants this time."

Colin gripped the back of his neck and smiled sheepishly. "Good to see you, too."

"Dad, what's your suitcase doing out here? I almost took myself out on it."

He winced. "Sorry. I wasn't expecting you home for at least another hour."

"Colin's one of those gross morning people."

Colin laughed. "Guilty."

"The suitcase, Dad?" she prompted.

Dad hesitated and her stomach plummeted.

Colin cleared his throat. "I'm going to step out for a minute and check in with Caitie. I think I might've missed a call from her."

Bullshit, she wanted to call, just like she wanted to reach for his hand and ask him to stay.

She held her tongue and stayed her hand, staring at Dad, who watched them with a soft, nearly forlorn expression.

Colin's hand ghosted over her back and his lips pressed a kiss atop her head.

With that, he slipped out the back door.

"I like him," Dad mused. "He seems like a good kid. And he makes you smile. You were so serious when you were dating Justin."

"I like him, too. A lot." She crossed her arms. "But that doesn't mean you get to change the subject."

Dad rubbed his brow. "Truly, your mother decided to cut the trip short. She's already on her way back home."

Those fluffy, *perfect* pancakes Colin had made for her turned to lead in her gut.

"What? No. I know she was upset, but—but last night was good. You two were getting along. We had fun."

"It was a great night," Dad agreed, and if she wasn't totally mistaken, he sounded wistful.

"But?"

"But you tricked us, Truly. And while I can see the humor in it all and even appreciate your . . . ingenuity, your mother's a bit of a tougher sell. You didn't get your stubbornness from me, after all."

"Pride goeth before the fall," she muttered. "So, that's it? You're going to go back to the city and go back to not talking? Taking time apart?"

"Pumpkin—"

"You know, I always thought you and Mom had the perfect relationship, the kind I dreamed of having one day. I mean, *God*, you never even fought." Her laugh verged on hysterical.

Dad's face fell.

"No relationship is perfect," he said.

She scoffed. Tell her something she didn't know. "I kind of cottoned on to that." It had only taken her twenty-seven years and change. "Maybe you thought you were protecting me, keeping whatever problems have become oh so insurmountable behind closed doors. Maybe I only saw what you wanted me to see. I don't know. Maybe I only saw what I wanted." The specifics were neither here nor there. "But I know you, Dad. And I know you love Mom." She paused. She'd made a lot of assumptions about her parents, about their relationship. "Don't you?"

Dad couldn't have looked more winded than if she'd punched him in the gut. "Truly, I . . . whether I love your mother has never, *ever* been a question."

"Then what?" She crossed her arms, fists pressed snug against her ribs like a hug. "What could be so wrong that you can't fix it? Please, Dad. Just—just be honest with me."

Dad, always loud and larger than life, was disquietingly still. He looked small as he slumped against the island, small in a way Truly could never remember him looking before.

"Maybe . . ." he said. "Maybe love isn't enough, my dear."

A scoff bubbled up past her lips. "Bullshit."

Dad's eyes widened. "Truly—"

"No." She shook her head, vehement.

She'd be the first to admit that she'd had her fair share of misconceptions about love.

Her parents' marriage wasn't all sunshine and rainbows like she'd once thought.

And perfect relationships? Like unicorns, those didn't exist.

But love?

Love launched ships and started wars and inspired sonnets and drove people to madness. Love was heaven and hell, sin and redemption. It was as real to her as any other force of nature, hurricanes and earthquakes and lightning storms and meteor strikes. It fascinated her as much as it terrified her as much as it humbled her and—

She'd spent her whole life trying to put it into words, eighty thousand of them at a time.

Love had to be enough.

There was no point if it wasn't.

"Truly, *sweetheart*," Dad implored. "I do believe your heart was—*is* in the right place. And I think, deep down, your mother knows it, too. And that boy of yours? He's right. You, my lion-hearted daughter, are brilliant and bold and have the biggest heart of anyone I've ever had the pleasure of knowing. And if I had even the smallest hand in that? My life's work is done."

Truly blinked back tears.

Dad reached out and set his hand on her shoulder. Truly let him. "That boy outside, he's a bright fellow. And it's plain to see he loves you. I don't know how anyone who knows you couldn't."

Her scoff came out wet and weak. She dragged her wrist under her eyes, mopping up stubborn tears that clung to her lashes and had yet to fall. "Don't be ridiculous. We've known each other a couple months. He doesn't love me."

"Sometimes that's all it takes," he said. "And before you ask me how I know . . . that boy outside?" Dad exhaled shakily and tilted his head back, staring up at the ceiling and blinking hard. "He looks at you the way I look at your mother. It takes a sap to know one, Truly. And Colin? Maybe he doesn't even know it yet, but he is gone on you. Hook, line, and sinker. Call it a father's intuition, but I bet my bottom dollar he tells you inside a month. And Truly, my dearest, darlingest daughter? I look forward to the day I get to tell you I told you so."

Truly pinched her eyes shut and pressed her wrist against her lips, stifling a sob. She sucked in a greedy breath, air rasping past her lips. "So what? Say he does. What's the point? If you and Mom can't make it work . . ."

Her bottom lip wobbled. She bit down hard, staying it and the tears that threatened to spill over.

"You shine so bright, Broadway Baby," he said, and she had to stifle a sob at his use of her childhood nickname. "Your mother and I . . . I don't know when, but somewhere along the way, the two of us . . . we lost the plot. But don't let anyone, least of all us, dim your light."

"You lost the plot, Daddy?" She glared at him through a haze of tears. "Go find it."

Truly turned away, picking a spot on the floor to stare at, a dark knot in the hardwood, a blemish in an otherwise smooth board.

A few breaths later the front door shut with a soft click.

She pinched her eyes shut and pressed her wrist against her lips, stifling a sob, so, *so* tired of crying.

Several careful box breaths later, the back door opened, and Colin stepped inside.

"I heard your dad's car start. Is everything okay?"

She shook her head, too choked up to speak.

"Hey." Colin crossed the room, stopping in front of her and placing two fingers under her chin, tipping it up so she'd look at him. "Are *you* okay?"

In all of this, not once had Mom and Dad asked her how she felt. Whether she was all right. How she was coping with her world being rocked, with her cornerstone being cracked.

But Colin had.

How are you coping?

Do you have someone to talk to?

Seriously—do you want to talk about it?

From the very beginning, long before they'd so much as kissed, from his words to his actions, Colin had let her know he cared. Even when he'd questioned her methods, he'd never once cut her down or called her motivations into question. He'd only ever expressed that he didn't want to see her hurt.

His hands swept up and down her back, shushing her softly

because—*God*, she was crying, the tears she'd tried so hard to choke down spilling down her cheeks and soaking into his shirt.

"You're going to be okay," he murmured, and she clung to him a little tighter, fisting his shirt in her fingers. He sounded so sure. She wished she could say the same.

Chapter Twenty

Every summer, like clockwork, Truly got a damn summer cold. Fever? Check.

Headache? Yup.

Congestion? *Ugh.*

On top of the sniffling and sneezing and general malaise, she'd woken up to an email from her editor, edit letter on her latest book attached.

The book, the one she'd spent the better part of four months writing, was shit.

Okay, her editor had put it more delicately, but the second half of the book needed a complete overhaul, was going to require Truly to scrap thirty-thousand-some-odd words and rewrite the ending.

Apparently, the book lacked her signature *Truly St. James* spark. It was too heavy, light on the swoons, the dénouement lackluster, and the kicker?

Her editor found the romance unbelievable.

I'm just not sure I believe these two characters will be together past the final page, her editor wrote.

The most important element of the book and Truly had come up short. *Way* short.

The fact that she'd done this a dozen times didn't matter—Truly St. James had forgotten how to write a book.

She washed three ibuprofens down with a sip of peppermint tea—the only drink that didn't make her feel like she was gargling razor blades courtesy of her oh so lovely back-drip—rested her fingers on the keyboard, and stared blearily at the blinking cursor on her screen.

And stared.

And stared.

And stared.

Screw it. She slammed her laptop shut in disgust and shoved it away with a whimper, muscles aching worse than they had that time Lulu roped her into taking a pole fitness class. And all Truly had done today was move from her bedroom to her couch to her bathroom and back in the world's saddest, smallest circuit.

She sniffled, feeling completely pitiful, only the sound that escaped was more of a bleat, the dying honk of a goose, maybe. Everything hurt and Truly—

Truly really, *really* wanted her mom.

She pinched her eyes shut against a fresh onslaught of tears, tears that would do nothing but make her more miserable, her stash of Kleenex already worryingly low.

In the two weeks that had passed since Mom had left the lake house without so much as a goodbye, Truly had yet to hear from her. Mom hadn't texted and neither had Truly because if Dad was right about one thing it was that she had definitely gotten her stubbornness from Mom.

Mom was mad? So was Truly. But it didn't change the fact

that nothing, *nothing* sounded better than Mom's chicken noodle soup, a secret recipe she kept closely guarded. It was magic in a bowl, transcendent and comforting and it was the only food Truly craved when she was sick, the only food she could stomach.

Across the couch, her phone vibrated.

She studied the distance between her hand and her cell and did the complicated mental math on the effort it would take to reach across the space and grab it, factoring in that it was after six, *further* factoring that just thinking about moving even her pinky choked her up. Whoever it was could wait until her ibuprofens kicked in or her bladder forced her up from the couch. Whichever happened first.

Her phone rang and she groaned, forced to bite the bullet and grab it.

Colin.

Despite the crushing headache and soreness in her muscles, she cracked a smile.

"Hello?" she croaked.

"Hey, are you—are you okay, baby?"

"'m fine." She covered the receiver, muffling her cough.

"You don't sound fine," he said, concern obvious in his voice. "What's wrong? Where are you?"

"Home. 's just a cold." She sniffled. "Allergies, maybe."

"I just got out of the office and thought I'd see if you wanted to grab a bite. But now I'm more concerned about this cold. Are you running a fever? What are your symptoms?"

"I'm fine, Dr. McCrory." She laughed, which would've been reassuring had it not led to a coughing fit, all her hacking undermining her attempt at brushing off his concern.

"Truly." The way he said her name, all stern, sent a shiver down her spine. Either that, or it was the fever. It was probably the fever. Not that she'd tell him that. "What do you need? Talk to me."

"N-nothing." Her voice cracked and her bottom lip wobbled, the tears she'd resolutely kept at bay finally spilling over, the day finally taking its toll. "You can't. You're sweet, but you can't."

"Try me."

Tears sluiced down her cheeks and dripped off her jaw. The effort it would've taken to dry her face was too great. "My—my mom, when I was sick, she made me soup."

"What kind of soup?" he asked. "Chicken noodle? Tomato? Beef and barley?"

"Chicken noodle, but it was—" She pinched her eyes shut, not sure how to tell him it tasted better because it was Mom who made it. How she wasn't so much craving the soup as much as she was the comfort it provided. "You know, I don't have much of an appetite. Rain check on dinner?"

"Of course. Do you want me to come over?"

She cringed. "I'm all snotty and gross."

"That's not an answer."

"You don't need to see this."

Not the snot, not the phlegmy cough, and definitely not how being sick turned her into an emotionally fragile mess liable to burst into tears at any moment and for any reason.

"Truly, baby, the only thing I care about right now is making sure you're okay. A little snot isn't going to send me running for the hills."

She stared at the mountain of used tissues on the coffee table. This was more than a little snot. "I don't want to get you sick."

"I can afford to take a few sick days."

Her throat clicked painfully when she swallowed. "I think I

just . . . I think I just need sleep. I'm sure I'll feel better in the morning."

He sighed over the line. "If you're sure."

She managed to choke out a goodbye before a fresh wave of tears brought on by Colin's concern and exhaustion hit.

Eventually the tears subsided, and she managed to shut her eyes, but not before putting in an order of pho from the Vietnamese place down the block. It wasn't Mom's chicken noodle soup, but it would have to do.

She wasn't sure how long she drifted in the space between sleep and waking, but eventually the pressure in her sinuses abated. Maybe she'd be able to get some sleep tonight after all.

Against her hip, her phone buzzed.

Truly keyed in her password and stared blearily at the screen.

As if she'd manifested it through sheer will, a message from Mom sat at the top of her inbox. Truly's heart rose into her throat. She couldn't click the text fast enough.

> **MOM (7:32 P.M.):** Your father and I would love it if you'd join us for brunch on Sunday. We need to talk to you.

Truly's fragile heart plummeted into a pool of extra-corrosive stomach acid.

This was it. The moment she'd been dreading since that awful Sunday months ago when Mom and Dad first told her they were separating. Nothing good ever came from *we need to talk*. Those words could mean one thing and one thing only.

Mom and Dad had signed the DNR on their relationship and there wasn't a damn thing she could do about it.

Truly dragged herself into the bathroom, head pounding. She flipped on the overhead light and cringed. Her face was puffy, her eyes fever bright and her lids swollen, tear tracks dried on her blotchy cheeks. She reached for the mouthwash, desperately needing to erase the stale taste from her mouth, her hand bumping her toothbrush.

Not her toothbrush.

Colin's, blue where hers was purple, both set in the holder by the sink, the bristles of their brushes kissing. Across the city, in his apartment, two almost identical toothbrushes sat in the cup beside his bathroom sink.

His comb had found a home beside her brush and beside that was his pomade and her flat iron, the cord wrapped around his cologne and—

Truly's knuckles went white around the edge of the sink.

A knock sounded against the front door, jolting her from the panic creeping up her throat.

A dizzy spell hit her in the middle of the foyer, and she braced her hand against the wall. Food. She *definitely* needed to choke something down.

A second knock followed.

"Just a second!"

She stole in a deep breath and opened the door.

Colin stood on her doormat juggling several paper grocery bags, a plastic bag of takeout dangling precariously from one finger, which was turning white, handle cutting off his circulation.

"You're not my Doordash."

He chuckled and the sound warmed her all the way to her slipper-clad toes.

"I'm not." He buffed a kiss against her forehead, her skin undoubtedly clammy and gross, and slid around her and into her apartment. "But I did catch the delivery driver on the way into the courtyard. I figured I'd save 'em a trip to your door."

She shut the door and followed Colin into the kitchen, where he was already in the process of unloading the groceries onto her counter.

"You weren't exactly forthcoming with your symptoms, so I sort of bought out the pharmacy. Let's see . . . we've got Day-Quil, NyQuil, Robitussin Nighttime Cough, Claritin on the off chance it's allergies, which"—he shot her a look that was all fond exasperation—"clearly, it's not."

She jammed the heel of her hand against her breastbone, trying to quell the ache inside her that no amount of cough syrup or fever reliever could fix.

"Colin . . . what is all of this?"

"This?" He held up a bottle of Emergen-C. "Vitamin C. Good for your immune system."

"But—"

"I didn't have your mom's number," he said, and her protests died on her tongue. "So I texted Lulu."

He set several cans of Campbell's chicken noodle soup on the counter.

"Lulu, fortunately, did have your mom's number, so I gave her a call. Not to completely ruin your childhood, but it turns out her secret recipe is Campbell's with a liberal dash of"—he grabbed a bottle of Tabasco from the bag—"hot sauce. She swears by it."

She put a hand out, steadying herself against the fridge. "You . . . you talked to my *mom*? When?"

He looked up from the bag he was unpacking. "After you and I got off the phone. I called to ask for the recipe of the soup she used to make you." He ducked his chin and laughed. "She thought it was sweet that you actually believed she made it from scratch."

Colin reached inside the drawer beside the stove and pulled out a can opener she couldn't remember buying. A can opener he didn't have to hunt for, a can opener he just knew was there.

Just like Mom was the only one who could find Dad's glasses when he misplaced them and Dad always knew exactly where Mom had left her keys.

No amount of uncoupling, conscious or otherwise, could untangle thirty-three years. Not without leaving scars behind.

"I can't do this."

Colin paused with the opener poised over a can of Campbell's chicken noodle soup. "I've got this. Go sit. Have you taken your temperature lately or—"

She cut him off with a quick jerk of her chin, biting down hard on her lip so it wouldn't wobble.

"I mean"—she gestured between them—"this. I can't do this."

"Okay." He set the can opener down carefully and braced his hands against the counter. "Let's talk."

She shook her head and that—that was a bad idea. Her head swam and she gripped the back of the closest barstool.

Colin practically threw himself across the counter in his haste to reach her. "Truly—"

She stole a step back, out of arm's reach. If she let Colin touch her, she'd fold, and right now she needed to be strong and get this out.

That didn't stop the stab of remorse from striking her sharply in the chest as soon as his face fell. "I'm fine. I'm . . . there's nothing to talk about." Nothing to say she hadn't already said before. "I told you. I told you I'm not in the right headspace for—"

"And I distinctly remember telling you that whether or not I want to be with you is my choice."

"So, I don't get any say in the matter? I just have to go along with it because it's what you want?" She scoffed. "That sounds healthy."

He scrubbed a hand over his face. "Your mom warned me you were a terrible patient, but—"

She thrust a finger at him, poking him in the chest. "Do *not* talk to me about my mother."

Colin held up his hands, a *mea culpa* if ever there was one. "Forget I said that. Let me just make you this soup and—"

"God, would you *quit*?" she begged. Quit being so sweet, quit being so kind. "I—I am a mess, okay? A *mess*."

"So we'll get some soup and a nasal decongestant in you, and you'll be good as new."

This wasn't something soup could fix, *Chicken Soup for the* whatever soul be damned. "I'm serious, Colin. This isn't the time for jokes."

"Considering you're being ridiculous? I'd argue now is absolutely the perfect time for jokes."

"I am trying to break up with you, God damn it!"

He turned his head to the side and stole a shallow breath in through his parted lips, jaw clenched so tight the tendons in his neck stood out, corded beneath his golden, mole-splattered skin. So gorgeous she ached.

"You want to break up with me?" He crossed the kitchen, stopping in front of her. "Okay."

An awful sick feeling took up residence in the pit of her stomach, like she'd missed several steps walking downstairs.

Colin gripped her chin and tipped her head back, forcing her to look up at him. "But I need you to look me in the eye and tell me that's what you really want."

What she wanted didn't matter. Wanting was easy. Having was so much more complicated.

She opened her mouth and—a dam within her broke, a noisy sob bursting from between her lips.

Colin swore softly under his breath and drew her close, crushing her against his chest.

"It's okay," he said, rubbing her back. "You're okay."

"It's *not* okay." She lifted her head, leaning back far enough to drag her fingertips beneath her eyes. Colin's words, the way he looked at her, achingly earnest, cracked her open, all the feelings she'd tried to bury bubbling up and with them more tears. "I love you. Okay? I love you and I didn't mean for it to happen, but it did, and I do and—and I don't know what I'm doing, but I'm scared. I am *scared*, okay? Is that what you want to hear? I am *so* scared and I—"

Colin pressed a finger to her lips. "I need you to stop talking."

Her heart shrank inside her chest. She'd really messed up this time. "Colin, I—"

"You are *the* most infuriating woman I have ever met." His mouth came crashing down on hers, swallowing the desperate, needy sound that clawed its way up her throat.

"I'm sorry," she breathed against his lips. "Please don't go."

"I'm not going anywhere," he promised, thumbs resting on the crests of her cheeks, hands cradling her face, holding her like he always did. Like she was precious. "You're scared? We can be scared together."

She sniffled. "Colin—"

"No, listen to me. You think I'm not scared? Jesus, Truly,

I'm terrified. I swear to God, it was like I walked into the studio that first day and I saw you and I just . . . I know love at first sight is bullshit, but I saw you and I didn't know what was going to happen, but I had this feeling that nothing was ever going to be the same. My life was going to be divided into *Before Truly* and *After Truly* and the thought of there being an *after* still scares me. I'm terrified that one day you're going to tell me to go and you're actually going to mean it. But I'd rather be with you, try with you, than walk away on the off chance that calling it quits now might hurt less than some hypothetical hurt down the road."

She took Colin's hands in hers, clutching them so tight she was surprised his bones, hers, didn't creak. His skin against hers, his palms dry and warm, hands soft save for the rough callus on the side of his left middle finger, grounded her. "My parents—"

"We're not your parents." His eyes swept over her face like he was drinking the sight of her in. "We're going to make mistakes and we're going to have disagreements and sometimes we're even going argue. What we're not going to do is give up. I know you're way too stubborn for that."

Her heart fluttered inside her chest, hummingbird fast. "*I'm* stubborn? What about you?"

Colin McCrory was, without a shadow of a doubt, one of *the* most stubborn individuals she had the pleasure of knowing, and she loved, loved, loved him for it.

"Me?" He tucked a strand of hair behind her ear. "I happen to be wildly in love with you. Isn't it obvious? You fucking own me, Truly," he said, voice raw, rough with emotion.

Fresh tears sprang to her eyes. Blinking hard, she fisted both hands in the collar of his shirt and dragged his mouth down to hers in a kiss that curled her toes inside her slippers and made Colin shiver against her.

She drew back just far enough so that she could whisper against his lips. "Say it again? Please."

"I love you." Colin brushed the tip of his nose against hers. "I'm yours, Truly."

She grinned.

Yeah, he was.

Chapter Twenty-One

Truly idled in front of her parents' house, working up the nerve to go inside. Colin had offered to come with her, but this was something she needed to do on her own. The curtains in the front window fluttered as Mom looked out onto the drive and waved. Truly sighed and yanked her keys out of the ignition. Time to face the music.

"Sweetheart." Mom wrapped her up in a hug that took Truly a minute to return. "Are you feeling better?"

"Yeah," she said, praying Mom couldn't feel her heart thundering against her ribs. "Colin took good care of me. Made me rest and drink lots of fluids and all that. Made me soup, too."

Mom drew back, tucking Truly's hair behind her ear. "Good. Your father and I were so worried when he called."

Truly frowned. "You were with Dad when Colin called you?"

"Diane!" Dad yelled from down the hall. "Is that Truly? *Lovely Ladies!* The polenta is getting cold!"

"*The Natives Are Restless,*" Mom muttered, turning before Truly could glean anything from her expression. "Hold your horses, Stanley! *I'm On My Way!*"

Mom stepped over the threshold, but Truly lingered outside the door.

"Truly!" Dad called. *"Tick Tock!"*

Here went nothing.

She drew up short, feet faltering. Mom and Dad were seated on the couch, side by side, space between them, but not enough that she could squeeze in, leaving her the loveseat.

Dad beamed and swept out a hand, gesturing for her to sit. *"List a While, Lady."*

He passed Mom a plate from the coffee table and began dishing up another from the veritable breakfast buffet he'd prepared.

She sat stiffly on the loveseat, waving off the plate Dad tried to hand her. "I'm not very hungry. *Later*, maybe." She took a deep, bracing breath. "Could you please just put me out of my misery and give it to me straight? Are you getting a divorce or not?"

A look passed between them that she couldn't quite parse before they wordlessly set their plates aside.

"Pumpkin," Dad started, and she pressed both hands against her stomach as if that could quell the churning in her gut. "Your mother and I agree that we were too hasty in telling you about our separation. We know what's done can't be undone, but we're both so sorry for putting you in the middle of this, and for even a single second making you feel like our problems were something you could fix."

The words were meant to soothe her, but all they did was put a bitter taste in her mouth and a lump in her throat.

"I know this has been hard on you, but *We're Gonna Be All Right."*

Uh-huh. Any second now, the other shoe was going to drop. They'd tell her something like, just because they were no longer *in* love, didn't mean they didn't still care about each other, didn't still love *her*.

"*Our Time* apart helped us realize that"—Dad turned and rested his hand on Mom's thigh—"while we have our fair share of issues to work through, we're both dedicated to putting in the work."

A familiar fluttering filled her belly, the kind that could be perilous if left unchecked. Too good to be true. "What?"

"Truly, I shouldn't have been so hard on you." Mom frowned. "I was just . . . not in a good headspace, and while I still can't say I agree with your methods, I know your heart was in the right place. You made a good point."

"Several of them," Dad said.

"Several of them," she agreed. "Ignoring a problem won't make it go away. Little frustrations built up and somewhere along the way our communication suffered. We forgot to fight for each other."

"Which is why we've scheduled an appointment with a marriage counselor who comes highly recommended."

Truly's breath hitched. "Are you saying you're—you mean you're—you're not getting a divorce?"

"No, Truly." Mom set her hand on top of Dad's, their fingers slotting together with an unthinking sort of ease, like magnets snapping together. "We're not."

Before she could stop it, a shuddering sob burst from between her lips, the first of—*shit*, several gasping sobs. She ducked her head, hiding her face in her hands as weeks, *months*, of pent-up fear and anxiety poured out of her, eyes leaking and nose dripping.

"Truly, honey?" She jerked as Mom rested a hand on her shoulder. She hadn't even heard her get up. "Aren't you—aren't you happy?"

She scoffed, or tried to, but all that came out was another weak sob that had her pressing the heels of her hands harder against her leaking eyes.

What a silly question.

This was everything she'd wanted and exactly what she'd been too terrified to let herself hope for these last few weeks. Worried that, like a birthday wish spoken, it might not come true. That if she so much as breathed wrong, this fragile little flame might snuff out.

"Of course I'm happy," she said, once she could open her mouth without blubbering. "I'm . . ." She grappled for the right words to do her elation justice. "This is *The Best Thing That Has Ever Happened.*"

Sondheim was good for something after all.

Dad passed her a tissue, which she quickly used to blot her tears and blow her nose.

"I really am *So Happy.*"

She couldn't wait to tell Colin.

Mom looked at Dad, all soft eyes and warm smile, and said, "*A Love Like Ours* is worth fighting for."

"We should celebrate. With champagne or something."

"One step ahead of you, kiddo." Dad ducked out of the room, returning a moment later with a chilled bottle of brut that he popped open right in the doorway, spilling champagne all over the hardwood. *"Bang!"*

Mom shrieked with laughter. "Stanley! You're making a mess."

Dad smiled, downright roguish. "Didn't complain about that last night, sweetheart."

Truly choked on her spit. *"Dad!"*

Mom giggled—*giggled*—and kissed the corner of Dad's mouth. "Turnabout's fair play, Truly."

"Ah, that's right." Dad snapped his fingers. "What was that you told us? Something, something, no shame in intimacy issues?"

"I never asked for details." She snatched the champagne from Dad's hand and brought it to her lips, sipping straight from the bottle, bubbles burning all the way down her throat. She took a good look at the bottle, noting the vintage. *This Is Nice, Isn't It?*

"And not cheap, you menace." Dad bopped her nose and stole the bottle back. "Now, I'd like to make a toast." He drew Mom against his side. "To Diane—with you, *Life Is Happiness Indeed.*" He kissed her temple. "To *Happily Ever After.*"

Truly blinked back happy tears. "To *Happily Ever After.*"

Epilogue

COLIN

Colin rapped his knuckles against the bridal suite's door.

"Just a second!"

A promised moment later, the door opened, a sliver of sunlight spilling out into the hall. His breath caught, trapped in his throat.

She was breathtaking.

Backlit with the early-afternoon sun, bathed in shades of burnished copper and rusty red, dark chocolate hair falling down to her shoulders, tiny pearl bobby pins pinning back her unruliest strands, Truly looked like the subject of a Renaissance painting, down to the halo of light behind her.

"You can't be here," she hissed, drawing the door shut, only her eyes, the tip of her cute-as-a-button nose, and the purse of her red lips visible. "It's bad luck."

"Come on," he implored. "It's a vow renewal, baby. Stan just wants to see Diane for a second."

"The same rules still apply." She looked past Colin to where her father stood, fussing with his little sapphire pocket square. Her smile softened and he felt his heart thud, extra hard. Enough that he pressed the heel of his hand against his chest, suddenly breathless. "Dad, you can't wait five more minutes?"

"I don't need to see her," Stan said. "I'd just like to give her a note." He withdrew a small, perfectly folded rectangle from the pocket of his pressed suit pants. "Pass it along, won't you?"

"You're a sap." She took the note from him and turned as someone hollered something unintelligible within the confines of the bedroom. Whatever it was made her roll her eyes. "We'll see you outside, okay?"

"Wait." Colin pressed his palm flat against the door, earning a raised brow. "I love you."

The bridge of her freckled nose scrunched with the smile that lit up her face and the whole goddamn room. "I love you, too. Now, shoo. Places. We'll be out in five."

"Thank you. Five." Stan saluted.

Truly shut the door and Colin immediately missed her face, pout and all.

"You heard the lady." Stan clapped him on the arm. "We've got places to be, kid."

Colin followed him down the hall, past the vestibule (the living room of Truly's parents' lake house), and through the back doors out onto the lawn where the two-dozen-some-odd attendees had congregated.

"What did your note say? If you don't mind me asking."

Stanley laughed. *"There once was a man from Nantucket . . ."*

He groaned. "Come on. If you don't want to tell me—"

"I'm serious," Stan said, hand pressed over his heart. *"If my ear was a c—"*

"Okay!" He laughed. "Forget I asked."

"I'm pulling your leg, son," Stan said. "It was nothing special.

Just a letter letting Diane know that loving her is a privilege I'll never take for granted and that even though marriage, like any worthwhile thing, takes work, it's a labor of love and the most rewarding work I've ever had the honor of doing."

Nothing special, his ass. "I bet she loved it."

Stan chuckled.

"What?"

"Oh, nothing. Only that I typed the letter in Comic Sans." Stan wiped his eyes. "Diane *abhors* Comic Sans. Hates it with a burning passion."

"Why would you do that?"

Stan smiled and sighed dreamily, staring at the back doors of the house where, through the gauzy curtains, Colin could just barely make out movement. "Because marriage is work, but it's also play." He turned and winked. "Got to keep the spark alive somehow, right?"

The back doors opened, curtains dancing in the breeze. Truly stepped out onto the grass, feet bare, the skirt of her pale blue sundress fluttering around her knees. The intro to "With So Little to Be Sure Of" from *Anyone Can Whistle* filled the air and Truly lifted her head, glancing up from the small bouquet of daffodils and honeysuckle in her hands. Her eyes landed on him at the end of the makeshift aisle, their gazes locking.

He couldn't blink, couldn't *breathe*, couldn't help but imagine that she was walking down this aisle to meet him.

Sunlight glinted off the delicate platinum band on Truly's finger, the radiant cut diamond throwing fiery sparkles against her skin.

One hundred fifty-four days until forever.

Their story?

Was just beginning.

About the Author

ALEXANDRIA BELLEFLEUR is a bestselling and award-winning author of swoony contemporary romance often featuring loveable grumps and the sunshine characters who bring them to their knees. A Pacific Northwesterner at heart, Alexandria now lives in New York City, but still has a weakness for good coffee, Pike IPA, and Voodoo Doughnuts. Her special skills include finding the best pad thai in every city she visits, remembering faces but not names, falling asleep in movie theaters, and keeping cool while reading smutty books in public. Her debut novel, *Written in the Stars*, was a 2021 Lambda Literary Award winner and a 2020 winner of the Ripped Bodice Awards for Excellence in Romantic Fiction.

More from
Alexandria Bellefleur

THE FIANCÉE FARCE
"Bellefleur powers this fake dating masterpiece with boatloads of
heart and the result is perhaps her most divine tale yet."
—*Buzzfeed*

Lambda Literary Award winner and national bestselling author Alexandria
Bellefleur returns with a steamy sapphic rom-com about a quiet bookseller
and a romance novel cover model who agree to a modern-day marriage of
convenience...

COUNT YOUR LUCKY STARS
"Bellefleur has a droll, distinct voice, and her one-liners zing
off the page, striking both the heart and funny bone . . . Bellefleur writes
as if she's captured fairy lights in a mason jar,
twinkly and lovely within something solid yet fragile."
—*Entertainment Weekly*

Following *Written in the Stars* and *Hang the Moon*, Lambda Literary Award
winner and national bestselling author Alexandria Bellefleur pens another
steamy queer rom-com about former best friends who might be each other's
second chance at love...

HANG THE MOON
"Smart, sexy, and sweet. Readers will be
over the moon for this rom-com."
—*Kirkus Reviews* (starred review)

WRITTEN IN THE STARS
"I was hooked from the very first page!"
—Christina Lauren,
New York Times bestselling author of
In a Holidaze

DISCOVER GREAT AUTHORS, EXCLUSIVE OFFERS, AND MORE AT HC.COM.